A Flute in
Mayferry Street

To Richard Dunlop

A Flute in
Mayferry Street

Eileen Dunlop

CANONGATE KELPIES

First published 1976 by Oxford University Press
First published in Kelpies 1994

Copyright © Eileen Dunlop 1976
Cover illustration by Rob Fairley

British Library Cataloguing-in-Publication Data
A catalogue record for this book is available
on request from the British Library.

ISBN 0 86241 466 0

Printed and bound in Denmark by Nørhaven A/S

CANONGATE PRESS LTD, 14 FREDERICK STREET,
EDINBURGH EH2 2HB

1

A House in Mayferry Street

It was half-past four on an afternoon in late October, on the kind of day that stands on a knife-edge between autumn and winter; the sun and the shine and the bright stains of autumn were still unfaded, but the warmth had gone with the house martins, and the air was as sharp and as brittle as the leaves. Any day now, the first grey breathing of the northern winter would unhook the remaining leaves from the trees, and send them scattering among wild flurries of icy rain into the streets below. Then the city would sigh, and resign itself to the dark. So such a last, golden day was precious, and in the leafy streets of the New Town of Edinburgh, long, mellow stone houses were lying peacefully in the sunshine, undisturbed by the traffic which rumbled past them, and looking as if they were somehow quite aware that they at least were going to be just as beautiful when the sun and the leaves were gone, and the January wind whipped sleet across their faces.

For the New Town, which was really new two hundred years ago, but is still so called to distinguish it from the Old Town, which was old centuries before the new was built, is beautiful in every season. Street upon street, it stretches back from the familiar Edinburgh of the picture postcards, with its sculptured green terraces in Princes Street Gardens, and great black upheaving of castle and rock, an elegantly woven web of straight, wide roads and rising, moon-shaped crescents; slate-roofed terraces of greying stone with rows of long sash-windows, spiky iron railings, wide flights of steps and shiny, important front doors. There are gardens too, set among hedges of box and hawthorn, country hedges trimmed for town, full of lime and elm and flowering currant; here and there is a house wrapped in a cloak of dusty black ivy, or a shawl of cobwebby virginia creeper, and through gaps between the houses unexpected, plunging vistas of cobbled street lead the eye far across the dark, piled-up roofs of the city and the silver line of the river Forth, to a hazy patchwork of farmland along the shores of Fife. Always beautiful, but never more so than on an October afternoon, with the red leaves and the black shadows and the sunshine.

Colin Ramsay had lived in the New Town for as long as he could remember, and he knew that it was special, not because anyone had told him so, but because he was the kind of person who noticed such things, and not of the kind who stop noticing everything they happen to look at every day. Colin was always noticing something new, and he thought often how strange it was that you could look at something every day with your outer eye, without ever really seeing it at all, and then all of a sudden there it was, new and fresh and printing itself on your inner eye as if you had never looked at it at all until this minute. That was how it was today; as he clattered along with his duffel bag and his music case, he found that he was not looking at the autumn leaves, scarlet and coral and acid yellow and brown, nor at the dappled darkness of dusty windows liquid with the moving reflections of trees in the gardens opposite. He was looking at the pavements. Colin always came home from school by the same route, down Wemyss Place and along Heriot Row, with its graceful iron lamp-standards and polished brass name-plates announcing proudly, 'The Hon. Douglas Kinghorne', or, 'Mr. Brodie, Advocate', but he had never really looked at the pavements before. Yet here they were, all in an instant chequered pink and cream and rather beautiful, and next morning he would notice that they were more beautiful still when the overnight rain had washed and put a shine on them.

They were very different from the pavements in the street where Colin lived with his mother and sister, but by the time he arrived there, about five minutes later, Colin had forgotten all about pavements and was wondering what he was going to have for tea. His street was in the New Town too, but further back from the main thoroughfares than Moray Place and Heriot Row, with their grand houses and rather self-conscious, well-groomed air. For the further the streets retired towards the north of the city, the less magnificent they became, and by the time one got to Mayferry Street, where the Ramsays lived, the houses had acquired the tired look of having fallen upon hard times, and, in most cases, of not knowing what to do about it. They were a little blacker, a little dustier, a little less in their Sunday best. There the pavements were made of plain grey concrete, gaining their only colour from the small tussocks of grass and groundsel which pushed up to the light at the angle where the paving stones met the low wall which supported the basement railings. The cobbles, which once had diced the roadway, had long been smothered in tar, although sometimes they made a brief reappearance in patches, when the inferior modern surface was broken up by heavy traffic. No one, it seemed, bothered about 'preserving the character' of Mayferry Street. Not, as Colin's mother remarked, that that was necessarily a bad thing, since at least it left the street free to develop a more interesting character of its own.

And Mayferry Street did have a character of its own, in a way that no 'preserved' street could possibly have; it was like a running stream, compared with a still pool. The houses faced each other in two long terraces of late Georgian design, and were basically identical. There was a window on either side of the front door, above a basement, two upper storeys with three windows each, slate-hatted attic windows sprouting from the roof, and on top of all that, tall chimney stacks holding up television aerials that swayed and bounced in the wind from the east. Here and there, dreadful attempts had been made to brighten up the shabby façades with indigo-painted doors, and chrome yellow window frames; on the opposite side of the road from the Ramsays' house, a red-bearded man whom the children loved had spent several weekends busily erecting an orange rustic fence and gate, in place of railings which had been lifted out of a crumbling parapet as easily as candles from a birthday cake. Then, just when his neighbours had got themselves to the point of believing their astonished eyes, he had further confounded them by painting his basement steps blue, and putting plastic gnomes and potted geraniums on alternate steps. So much for the character of the street, said Mrs. Ramsay, who was never able to decide whether she thought it was funny or not. But most people had sensibly left their houses alone, if they could not afford to restore them properly, and even if the front doors were kicked and scraped a bit — there were lots of children and animals in Mayferry Street — and badly in need of paint, they were still numbered with delicate brass numerals in the Roman style, and had the same plain, elongated brass letter-boxes which had been swallowing the mail and the evening paper ever since the reign of George the Fourth.

Colin's house was number seventeen, and there was nothing about it, outwardly or inwardly, so far as he knew at that time, to set it apart from the rest. It had a battered black front door with a brass *XVII* on it, and railings along the front which had not had a coat of paint for the last twenty years. There were unmatched, sun-faded curtains at its windows, and the usual drift of withered leaves and grime in the paved area at the foot of the worn basement steps. No purple paintwork, no gnomes, drew the attention of the passer-by to number seventeen. Nor would he have been more impressed by the shabby, darkly varnished hallway which presently received Colin through the front door, his nose twitching hopefully for the scent of food.

It was a rich, satisfying smell, at once identifiable as his favourite ham and egg pie, which floated out to him through the crack-opening of the kitchen door, as he laid his bag and his music case on the chair which stood at the bottom of the dark, silent stair. He took off his brown blazer, and because he was rather small for his age, stood up on the tips of his toes to hang it on one of the hooks behind the door, between his mother's old blue waterproof and Marion's tweed overcoat, which was as good as new because she hardly ever wore it. Then he removed his shoes, stood with his back against the umbrella stand, took a short, vigorous run, and slid the length of the hall over the polished brown linoleum. There was no carpet in the Ramsay's hall: that was one of the things Mrs. Ramsay had been saving for when she discovered that she was going to need what money she had for more urgent purposes, and now, having got into the habit of being philosophical, she said that it was just as well, since she didn't have to worry about children and tenants walking about on it with unwiped feet. She was not so philosophical about Colin's sliding activities, which wore out socks, and opening the kitchen door suddenly, just as he was about to coast into it, she made an irritated, tutting noise, and said, 'I'm sure I've told you a thousand times to stop doing that. Why won't you?'

It was not what she had intended. She was for ever resolving to be a calm, gentle mother, of the kind she supposed were remembered by their children in after years for their serenity and charm. But she was tired, and somehow he had caught her unawares.

'Well, I'm sorry,' Colin said, also for the thousandth time. 'I keep forgetting. What's for tea?'

'Ham and egg pie. Can't you smell it?'

'I'm just checking. Don't be cross, Mother.'

Mrs. Ramsay pushed back the uneven strands of her dark, greying hair, which grew like a chrysanthemum and kept flopping into her eyes, and smiled at him.

'I'm not,' she said.

'How long till tea?'

'Ten minutes. The pie is nearly ready. Go and talk to Marion while I get it on the table. She's in the sitting-room.'

It was her customary remark, made to Colin almost every evening when he came home from school, and sometimes he could not help wondering whether she ever noticed that it was unnecessary. It would have been remarkable if Marion had not been in the sitting-room, because unless she was in bed, in the room she shared with her mother across the hall, she was never anywhere else. The sliding spirit went out of Colin. He found his slippers and put them on, and went in to join his sister by the fire.

Many years later, when he was grown up, it would seem to Colin that there was something to be said for getting the worst year of your life over before you were nine, because then at least, whatever did happen to you in the future, you knew that nothing could ever be quite so terrible again. But at the time, when his father went out one morning as usual, and never came home again because he died of a heart attack at the office in the afternoon, and two months later his sister Marion was knocked down by a motor cycle in the street and badly injured, it was not surprising that he did not see it in that light at all. Even now, three years later, when he was already half-way to forgetting what his father looked like, and the ache of his loss had become less one of longing for a person than one of longing for a relationship which all his friends enjoyed and he did not, he still had fits of anger and despair over the unfairness of a world where everything seemed to go well for everybody else, and badly for him and the people he cared about. It made no difference, his mother's remarking, as she did often, that nine-tenths of the people in the world were worse off than they were; at these moments a kind of blackness came down over him, and he wanted to kick somebody, or smash something, because he thought that that would make him feel better. But of course he never did, and after a while his mother would tell him a funny story, or Thomas from next door would come knocking, wanting him to play football, and he would cheer up again in a moment. But Colin could see, more clearly as he got older, that no amount of joking was going to laugh the anxiety out of his mother's eyes, and as for Marion — it was not difficult for anyone who knew her as well as Colin did to see that something very terrible was happening to Marion, who had never walked since a winter afternoon three years ago when, crying for her father, she had stepped out heedlessly from behind a bus to meet a roaring horror of steel and cruel light.

There was nothing more they could do, the doctors had said at the hospital, after they had mended her broken bones and stitched up the cuts on her arms and forehead; Marion must rest, and wait, and the damage to her spine would be repaired by nature in the course of time. They had seen lots of cases like hers before, they said encouragingly, and in ninety-nine point nine per cent of them, the patient made a perfect recovery. Mrs. Ramsay accepted this, glad as she was that her daughter was still alive, and Marion, after some natural distress, had accepted it too. Neither of them worried terribly, probably because the fate of the other point one per cent was too appalling even to be contemplated. Arrangements were made for a bright lady called Miss Parkinson to come to the house three days a week, to teach Marion things she did not want to know, like Geography and Mathematics, so that when she got back to school she would not find herself too far behind with her work, and in the afternoons she had gone out in a wheelchair with her mother to the gardens, and sometimes even to the shops. Mrs. Ramsay and Miss Parkinson brought her books from the library, she played dominoes and draughts with Colin in the evenings, and made beautiful copies of wild-flower drawings from books on botany which had belonged to her father, while everyone waited hopefully for the day when her still feet would move again for the first time.

In a way, perhaps, Marion's preoccupation with her own misfortune had helped her to recover more quickly from the shock of her father's death than might otherwise have been the case. That event, along with all the other things that had ever happened to her, was on the far side of the sword-stroke of her accident, which had severed, apparently for ever, her self in the past from her self in the present. The future seemed suspended, indefinitely delayed. She had been just thirteen at the time, and through all the long months that followed, spinning themselves eventually into years, she had gone on being eager and friendly and hopeful that some day, perhaps today, the miracle would happen, and her arrested life begin to flow again. She never complained about the aching tiredness of doing nothing, or the irritation of somebody else's choice of library books, or the misery of needing her mother's help in every single thing she did, every day. She was a favourite with everyone, with the people from next door, and the doctors who came to see how she was getting along, and the physiotherapist who came to help her exercise her legs and feet, so that she would be able to stand on them later on, whenever that might be. Only lately, when she was almost seventeen, had Colin noticed a change in her, and although he did not mention it to his mother, or she to him, he knew too that it was the reason for the deepening of the lines between her eyebrows, the reason why she smiled at him with eyes that held no interior gladness. It was perfectly obvious to everyone who looked at her, that Marion had given up hope. It had begun when she started refusing to go out in her wheelchair because she said that people were staring at her, and Colin realized that if you had started noticing that, it was better for you to stay at home. Then, by degrees, she stopped knitting, and reading, and drawing her flowers, and seemed to spend whole days staring at the television set, with her mind on something else. And Colin, who was really fond of her, though he would never have dreamed of telling her so, was very anxious and unhappy. He would have done anything in the world to help her, but the terrible thing was that as her dejection deepened, Marion seemed to shrink more and more from accepting the sympathy of anyone else. She became remote, even from Colin, whom she loved the more because she had no friends at all of her own age, so that where before there had been teasing and laughter and friendly rudeness between them, now there was mostly awkwardness, and silence.

So it was without much pleasure that Colin crossed the sitting-room carpet, and sat down on the rug in front of the fire. Marion was sitting there in an armchair, with her long, unnaturally thin legs stretched out in front of her. She was a pretty girl, very like her mother in appearance, although less dramatically dark. She had the same kind of floppy hair, but hers was of a lighter brown, her eyes were of a flecked, rusty colour, and her skin, even under normal circumstances, would have been much fairer. Now it was intensely white, as was to be expected in a person who never went out in the fresh air, and this made her eyes extraordinarily large and bright. She was wearing a tweed skirt, and a brown jersey which she had knitted herself, last year, when she could still be bothered with such things.

'Hello,' Colin said to her, wriggling round to feel the blaze of the fire on his back.

'Hello,' said Marion absently. She looked down at him for a moment, then, in the tone of someone weary of such questions, but feeling obliged to ask, she added, 'Have you had a nice day?'

'All right,' replied Colin briefly. He too was weary of such questions.

'What did you do?'

'The usual things, Latin, and double Maths. Science in the afternoon. I had my flute lesson.'

The questioning continued, mechanically.

'What did you have for lunch?'

'Sausage stew. Prunes and custard, with lumps.'

Marion repressed a shudder. She had no appetite. She paused again, then she asked a question of a different kind.

'Colin, what did you see?'

And without thinking, Colin said, 'Some funny women in Binn's, trying on tartan hats.'

No sooner were the words out of his mouth than the expression on Marion's face told him that he had made a mistake. Of course this was not what she wanted to hear. He should have told her about the rough white terrier puppy he had seen, with a laughing face, rolling in ecstasy on the grass in Queen Street Gardens, or the pink and cream pavements, or the blackbird, singing high and clear above the noise of the traffic in Charlotte Square. These were the things she might have cared to know, but now it was too late to start again.

'Oh, yes,' said Marion listlessly, and silence again slid down the gap between them. Then Colin felt angry and helpless, and afraid of what he could only partly understand. He got up quickly, and went to turn on the television set.

2

A Letter from Alan Farquhar

Of the three Ramsays, Colin and his mother were certainly not the kind of people who readily believe in ghosts. If they had been, then probably they would have found their house haunted enough, for most of it was a deserted warren of dark stairways and draughty, uninhabited rooms, where everything one looked at had once belonged to another Ramsay, who was now dead. Marion was different; long ago, in her childhood, she had seemed to sense an alert, listening quality about the empty rooms of her home, confused music with the wind in the eaves, heard the rustle of skirts in the movement of dusty curtains when her mother had opened the windows to air the rooms. Sometimes then she had made excuses so that she did not have to go up-stairs alone, especially after dark, but now she had lived so long in the warm, prosaic security of two shabby, comfortable rooms that she no longer had anything in common with the child who had climbed the long stair with a stiff back and a prickling neck, afraid to look round, and afraid not to. She never thought any more about the mystery of the shadowy rooms above her; as her world had shrunk, so sadly had her perception shrunk to fit it.

When Mrs. Ramsay's husband had died, quite unexpectedly, before he was forty, leaving her with very little money, it had been her plan to sell the house in Mayferry Street, which Mr. Ramsay had inherited a few years previously in a very run-down condition. It was not that she did not like Mayferry Street well enough, but she was the sort of person who thought that a house should have no more than the number of rooms its occupants needed, and that, in the case of her own family, she now reck-oned as five. Number seventeen Mayferry Street had eighteen, including the attics. It did not have for Mrs. Ramsay, who came from Suffolk, any of the associations which made it important for her husband, and so she wanted to be rid of it, and to move with her children to another, more convenient house in the suburbs. But when she had gone to put her plan to her lawyer, he had told her that unfortunately this was not possible. Under the terms of her husband's will, the contents of the house were hers to dispose of in any way she liked, but the house itself was to be put in trust for Colin, until he was grown up, and she was not allowed to sell it. Colin, who had been looking forward to a new house, had been very cross when this was explained to him; he said that he certainly did not want the house, even if Ramsays had lived in it for more than a hundred years. He was one Ramsay who was not going to live in it, because he was going to go to sea, and when he retired he was going to live in an upturned boat on the sands at Gullane, with a parrot and an Afghan hound for company. But apparently none of this planning for the future made any difference, and number seventeen was to be his, whether he wanted it or not. And Mrs. Ramsay had to make the best of it, because there was nothing else she could do. She sold the best of the furniture, and some paintings, which was why there were now rectangular dark patches all over the faded sitting-room walls, and that brought in a little money, then she decided that the house, which divided into flats very conveniently for the purpose, might be let, partly furnished, perhaps to students from the University. She advertised in the newspaper, and had a number of encouraging replies, but when the prospective tenants came, through the murk of a February evening, and saw their breath vaporising in the bare, gloomy hall, and felt the cold, which bit more deeply the higher one climbed through bleak, half-furnished bedrooms, and thought of the fuel bills, their hearts failed them, and they left in a hurry, promising to let Mrs. Ramsay know. Which some did, and some did not, but in any case she never saw them again — all except Jen and Jake Taylor, who fell in love with Mayferry Street, and the view of gnomes and rustic folly from the front windows of number seventeen. They took over the first floor entirely, and had lived there very happily for the last three years, in an up-to-date style of the do-it-yourself variety which left the Ramsays, in their old-fashioned, cramped quarters downstairs, speechless with admiration. There was nothing, it seemed, that Jen and Jake could not construct between them, given some wood, some cloth, an old sewing machine, a hammer and a box of nails. They were not people who would trouble about ghosts either, and that was just as well, since above them ghostliness prevailed.

So, between the rent, and her small pension, and some extra money which she was able to earn by typing manuscripts at home for people who needed this sort of work done in a hurry, Mrs. Ramsay contrived to make ends meet. Her main problem was that she never seemed to have enough time to do everything, dusty corners became dustier, and one October morning, when prying sunbeams were sliding in at every window, pointing bright fingers at unswept places in every room, she realized with a mixture of shame and exasperation that she had not dusted the sitting-room for nearly a fortnight. It was fortunate for Colin that his mother was of the breed who consider the making of ham and egg pies to please their sons more important than the dusting of sitting-rooms to impress unexpected callers. Still, as she put her pie in the oven, and did the washing-up, Mrs. Ramsay told herself firmly that something would have to be done, and then told herself even more firmly that this time she really meant it. Before New Year, she said, setting a deadline within the bounds of possibility. So later that evening, when they were having their meal in the comfortable, untidy room which served them as sitting-room, dining-room, work-room and study, she said across the table to Colin, 'I was wondering — do you have a lot of homework tonight?'

'I don't have any,' said Colin, who was eating as if he did not know when he would eat again, 'I did my French on the bus. Why?'

'Would you do something to help me?'

'Yes, all right,' agreed Colin, readily enough. He was conscious that he was now the man of the house. 'What do you want me to do?'

'Well, you know how ever since the spring cleaning I've been saying that we would have to tidy up the bookcase? I was looking for a knitting pattern in it this morning, and really I don't think we can leave it any longer. It's a disgrace. The books are all higgledy-piggledy, and covered with dust, and there are all sorts of things in it that have no business to be there at all.'

'Like knitting patterns,' teased Colin.

'Exactly. I thought you might make a start on it. Even if you only managed a couple of shelves tonight, it would help. Marion will give you a hand.'

Marion, who was eating indifferently from a tray on her knee looked up in alarm and at once began to protest rather querulously, 'But Mother, I'd rather —'

Kindly, but decisively, Mrs. Ramsay cut her short.

'No, Marion. There's no reason why you shouldn't help. Colin can't do it all on his own. If he hands the books down to you, and you dust them, he can wash the shelves and put them back. You could do that easily, now couldn't you?'

'Oh, I suppose so,' said Marion unenthusiastically, looking

11

with disfavour at the vast, glass-fronted bookcase which ran the whole length of the sitting-room wall, and reached almost to the ceiling. She would really have preferred to stay quietly where she was, and wait for it to be time to go to bed.

'That's my good girl,' said her mother. 'Colin, you had better finish the pie, then go up and ask Jen to lend me her kitchen step-ladder. You'll need it to get up to the high shelves. I'm going into the kitchen this evening to finish typing Dr. Woolf's thesis. I'll be glad when it's finished — it gets so boring typing something you can't understand a word of.'

Jen was pleased to lend her step-ladder — she was always lending things to Mrs. Ramsay — and after the table was cleared, Colin helped his mother to draw Marion's chair across the floor to the bookcase, fetched a bucket of hot water and a sponge, and a duster for Marion, and opened the first of several finger-printed glass doors. The bitter, sneezy smell of dusty paper wafted into the sitting-room. An old theatre programme, which had been leaning against the glass, fell outwards and down, toppling with it a dead wasp, an Elastoplast tin containing lead shot, an egg cup with tiddly-winks and a plastic glue bottle, empty.

'This is going to be awful,' said Marion.

'Well, we'll just have to do our best,' said Colin soothingly, as he bent down to scoop up the assorted junk from the carpet. 'We'll put everything which shouldn't be in here on the table, then it can be sorted out later.'

'The table isn't big enough,' said Marion gloomily, looking down its incredible length.

The Ramsays' books, like their table, their chairs, their wardrobes, their umbrella stand, their linen and their china, had belonged to other Ramsays before they belonged to them. The bookcase had been in the house when they moved in, and since Marion's and Colin's great-grandfather, grandfather and father had all been compulsive buyers of books, it was stuffed, shelf upon shelf, row upon row, with volumes of every size and description. Leather-bound sets of the *Complete Works* of Sir Walter Scott and Charles Dickens had whole shelves to themselves, but other equally famous authors, such as Jane Austen, W. M. Thackeray and the Brontës, had to pay the penalty of having written less by having their works squashed in unceremoniously, cheek by jowl with cheap encyclopedias, dictionaries, medical books, books on nature, old school prizes, cookery books, railway timetables and optimistic titles from the *Teach Yourself* series. Colin had often diverted himself with the question of whether any one person had ever wanted to learn Swedish, Judo, Fortune-telling, New Testament Greek, Touch-typing, Wine-making and Afrikaans — and if so, how he had fared with his studies. Many of the titles in the bookcase he would remember all his life, without having ever had the least curiosity about the contents of the covers they adorned, while others he already looked on with the affection one feels for old and trusted friends. But the cleaning of such a bookcase was a daunting task, especially since it had always been too the family's repository for all the other things which had no special home of their own. Already he could see knitting needles and sewing reels, bottles of indigestion tablets, unanswered letters, pencils and paper, wallets of old photographs, and he knew only too well that what he could see would be barely a twentieth part of what was actually there. He put in his hand, removed some drawing pins and a packet of paper handkerchiefs, and heaved out four volumes of the *Waverley Novels*. All too obviously they had not been opened for many a long day.

'We had better start with these,' he said to Marion. 'No point in beginning with anything we might be tempted to read as we go along.'

They worked in silence for a while. The assortment of rubbish on the table accumulated, the books were carefully dusted and replaced on clean shelves. They had finished tidying one complete section of the bookcase, and were half-way through the second, when Colin realized that Marion had stopped dusting. He looked down from his perch on top of the step-ladder, and saw that she was sitting with Shakespeare and the *Modern Encyclopaedia*, 1907 edition, piled up at her feet, and a large, leather-covered book in her lap. He could tell from the yellow crackliness of the pages that it was very old, and for a moment he thought that the sheet of paper which Marion was holding in her hands was a page of the book which had come loose.

'Hey, you,' said Colin teasingly, 'we can't have this you know. It isn't time for a tea-break yet.' Then, as Marion did not reply, he added, 'Is it something interesting?' and climbed down from the steps.

'I don't know,' Marion said, 'whether it's interesting or not. It fell out of this book, *Flora and Fauna of the Hebrides*, by Oliver MacDougall. It's a letter — I think it's quite old.'

'Yes, it is, isn't it?' Colin came and sat on the arm of Marion's

13

chair, resting his pointed chin on her shoulder as he peered at the paper in her hands. 'But I don't think it's as old as the book,' he said.

His reason for saying this was that although the letter, and its envelope which Marion had laid down beside her, were yellowish and spotted slightly with brown, they did not have the parched, dried-leaf frailty of the pages of some of the books they had been handling. Old and worthless, Mrs. Ramsay said; she had had the books valued, so she knew. The old Ramsays had not been discriminating collectors.

'That's true,' Marion agreed, 'and it's very clean — that's because it has been protected inside the book. It hasn't faded at all.'

Perhaps it was this freshness which gave the letter its quality of immediacy, which Marion sensed so strongly; the curly handwriting stood out blackly from the page, and slowly, tracing the lines with her forefinger, as if somehow the words had a special importance, she began to read.

'"Edinburgh,
24th January, 1914.

My dear Charles,

It is a matter of regret to me that after all I must leave Edinburgh without seeing you and thanking you in person for the kind hospitality I have enjoyed in your house over the past months. It will, I think, please you to know that the work I have had in hand is now completed, and that without your encouragement and interest it could never have been accomplished at all. If and when I return, I shall be happy to hear your opinion of it, and if it pleases you, shall think that all my labour has been worthwhile. If I do not, I leave it to you with my most affectionate remembrances.

One more favour I have to ask. As you know, my plans are as ever undecided, although I fear they may be decided for me ere long. I hope to spend a few weeks in London, and then perhaps to go to Paris, where I have acquaintances who may assist me in bringing my work to the attention of the public. Whatever befalls, I shall have no settled home in the foreseeable future, and therefore if you will undertake to keep for me until I require it the small trunk which I have today put into your servant's hands, I shall be yet further in your debt. I enclose the key to same under this cover, lest at any time you should require to open it — this you have my full permission to do, for in the event of my not

14

requiring them, the contents fall to you. Let me hear from you soon. Letters can reach me at my sister's house in London — her address you know. Again my heartfelt thanks for all your goodness to me.

> Yours ever in friendship,
> Alan A. B. Farquhar."'

'Did people really talk like that in 1914?' asked Colin dubiously.

'I don't know. I don't suppose so,' said Marion. 'People don't always talk as they write in their letters.' She looked at the writing, which covered one side of the paper completely, and added thoughtfully, 'There isn't any address. Only, "Edinburgh".'

'Does it have anything written on the back?'

Marion turned the paper over and looked at the six blank rectangles defined by its folds.

'Nothing at all.'

'What about the envelope? Is there a stamp?'

There was no stamp. There was no address either. Written across it, in large, bold letters, were six words, 'For Charles Ramsay, Esquire, by hand'.

'What does that mean?' Colin wanted to know.

Marion wished he would be quiet, and let her think. However, she answered patiently, 'I suppose it means it wouldn't be put in the post — just handed over, you know.'

Colin lost interest, and slid off the arm of the chair. 'Well, I expect we should be getting on,' he said. 'It isn't a very interesting letter, is it? I mean, there's nothing exciting about it — just a man going away, and asking his friend to keep his suitcase. There's not much to that, you must admit.'

Marion did not answer for a moment. She turned the letter over delicately in her hands, then she said, 'I suppose not,' in an uncertain tone that made Colin, who was already half-way up the ladder, turn and look down at her curiously.

'You don't think it's interesting, do you?' he asked, surprised.

Marion made up her mind. 'Well, yes, I do,' she said. 'It's not just that it's addressed to a member of our family, although that's interesting in a way. Charles Ramsay must have lived in this house, sat in this very room, sixty years ago. Perhaps some of the books we've been handling belonged to him. Then there's this other man, Alan Farquhar — I'd like to know about him too. I know he probably wasn't anyone very important, but his letter

15

makes me want to ask so many questions that can't be answered. I'd like to know what his work was, and who was making plans for him, and what happened to him in the end. I'd even like to know whether he got his trunk back, or whether Charles had to open it. It's all a sort of history, isn't it?'

Colin stared at her. He had never heard Marion speak in this way before. He did not know quite what to think.

'I didn't know you were interested in history,' he said.

'No,' said Marion quietly, as she folded up the letter, and slipped it back into its envelope. 'I don't suppose you did. Nobody expects me to be interested in anything. Take this book off my knee, please.'

Colin took the book, and restrained himself from pointing out the unfairness of this remark. He could have reminded her that her mother spent hours every day trying to interest her in knitting and drawing and collecting things. Only last week she had brought home from the library a book which explained how to make pictures from leaves and seeds and pieces of bark, and had offered to collect these things in the gardens so that Marion could try to make one. But Marion, after only the briefest glance at the book, had said no, thank you, she didn't think she would, and that had been the end of that. Colin had been brought up to be very patient with Marion, but just occasionally in recent months, he had found himself thinking that never being contradicted was doing her no good. It was simply making her unreasonable. He swept up a pile of paper-backs, prised out five dominoes and a Christmas tree decoration from the back of the shelf, and applied his sponge vigorously to the dingy wood. Marion began to dust William Wordsworth. The clock on the stair struck nine, and Mrs. Ramsay arrived with three cups of cocoa on a tray.

'Well, I've finished with Dr. Woolf, I'm happy to say,' she announced conversationally, laying down her tray at the edge of the table, away from all the clutter of rejects from the bookcase. 'He must spend his whole life writing theses — this is the third one I've typed for him. Marion, when he comes to collect it, remind me to give him his umbrella. It has been in our umbrella stand for weeks, and it will be winter any day now.' She sat down on a convenient chair, looked around her and went on, 'I see you've been busy. That's splendid. I'll go over all this rubbish tomorrow, and see if there's anything worth keeping. Did you find anything interesting?'

'Only an old letter,' said Colin briefly, descending to floor-level and coming to fetch his cocoa. 'Marion think it's interesting.'

Mrs. Ramsay was so overwhelmed with delight and relief at the idea of Marion's being interested in anything that she completely over-reacted.

'A letter?' she said eagerly, turning to her daughter. 'What kind of letter? Where did you find it, darling? Is it something exciting?'

Marion eyed her uncertainly. She was aware that her mother was overdoing her enthusiasm, without understanding why. It was only quite recently that she had begun to notice the false brightness which people put into their voices when they were speaking to her, and to realize that for some incomprehensible reason they were doing it for her benefit. It was not how they talked to each other. At first it had only bewildered her, then she had begun to resent it. So now, instead of warming to her mother's interest, as she would have done when she was younger and less observant, she withdrew yet a little further into herself, and answered dully, 'It's just some old letter. It fell out of one of the books. Look at it, if you like.'

She heard her own words, leaden and ungracious and as encouraging as the slap of cold water on stone, and told herself she didn't care. But when Mrs. Ramsay said nothing, Marion raised her head, and looked at her, and for one unguarded second she saw the expression in her eyes, tired, worried and utterly disheartened. Remorse and shame swept over her.

'I'm sorry, Mother,' she said quickly. 'I want you to look at it, really I do. It is very interesting.'

She lifted Alan Farquhar's letter to Charles Ramsay, and pushed it into her mother's hands.

Mrs. Ramsay also thought that the letter was interesting, and Marion, with her ears so attuned to discern sincerity, knew this time that she really meant it. They discussed the speckled sheet of paper, spreading it out on the hearthrug, in the middle of their tiny circle, while they finished their supper, and spent the last half-hour before bed time together round the fire. Even Colin, catching something of the interest of the other two, began to think that there might be more of a mystery in it than he had at first believed. But even if that were so, they had to agree regretfully, it was a mystery which seemed to have little chance of ever being solved. Mrs. Ramsay had never heard of Alan Farquhar either; she had never heard of Charles Ramsay for that matter.

17

'1914 is such a long time ago,' she said. 'Even if he were a young man of twenty, let's say, it means that he was born away back in the last century. I suppose he might be an uncle, or a cousin — people had such enormous families in those days. That's why they had all these bedrooms I never have time to dust.'

'Mother,' said Marion, 'are we really the only Ramsays left? Are they all dead except us?'

Mrs. Ramsay looked startled; she had never thought of it in quite this way before.

'There are some in Australia, I believe,' she said. 'After the shop was closed, some went to Australia, but I don't know anything about them. They never corresponded in my time. But as for the Edinburgh branch of the family, yes, we are the only ones left.'

'I wonder about Charles Ramsay,' said Marion. 'Are you sure you've never heard him mentioned, Mother?'

'Yes, quite sure. I didn't even know that Charles was a family name — all the Ramsays I ever seem to have heard of were called Colin or John. It didn't give me much of a choice when you were born, Colin, but at least I was allowed to give my favourite name to my daughter.'

She smiled at Marion, and Marion smiled back. She could not have said why, but in some strange way the finding of this old but quite unimportant letter — only a note from a man about a suitcase — as Colin said — seemed to have kindled a tiny flame in the darkness that had become her mind, making it a little less dark.

'Mother,' she said, half-hesitantly, 'do you suppose that I might keep the letter? I would be very careful with it.'

Mrs. Ramsay looked at Colin, then nodded in agreement.

'Yes, of course you could,' she said. 'I don't think Colin minds, do you, Colin? And it isn't of interest to anyone but ourselves.'

'It's yours,' said Colin. 'You found it, after all.'

'Well, thank you,' said Marion. 'I'll keep it in my lacquered box.'

She picked up the letter, and began to fold it up with careful, caressing fingers. And Mrs. Ramsay, watching her, felt a fleeting, absurd but not unnatural regret that she could not thank an unknown man, who had happened to ask a friend to look after his luggage on the twenty-fourth of January, 1914.

3

Shadow People

Marion did not sleep well that night. She was always very tired
long before she went to bed, and by the time she had gone
through with her mother the exhausting routine of undressing
and bathing and hair brushing, and actually getting to bed, she
always felt a most wonderful relief, and the conviction that
tonight she would sleep and sleep and sleep. But it rarely happened that way, for her tiredness was not the healthy tiredness of
mind and body experienced by people who lead normal lives that
take them out to exercise every day in the sun and the wind and
the rain, but rather the unnatural, aching tiredness of immobility,
which afflicted her body but left her mind wide awake. The result
was that although she sometimes slept a little on first going to
bed, the least noise would be sure to wake her, and then she
would be unable to get to sleep again. And so she would lie for
hours in her little bed, alert to every sound in the house and on
the street, hearing floorboards creaking and dogs barking, footsteps passing on the pavement, clocks striking endless quarter-
hours, unable even to ease herself by changing her position in the
bed. She never told anyone, or complained of the misery and
loneliness of these sleepless hours, but for herself, she knew
them as the worst trials she ever had to bear.

Her mother knew how it was, because often she did not sleep
very well either; Marion could see her in the half-light, tossing
about in her bed on the other side of the room, and knew that
sooner or later she would sit up, switch on the light, peer at her
alarm clock and say softly, 'Marion, love, are you awake? Would
you like a cup of tea?' And then there would be warmth and
movement, and company for a while.

After the tea, usually they both slept, but it was not unknown
for Marion to lie awake through the ash-grey dawning, seeing the
mysterious night-forms of the furniture sharpen into their
detailed, day-time shapes, waiting until the fresh, unlikely beat
of a horse's hooves, the wheel-rattle of its cart along the street,
the cheerful clinking of milk bottles on the doorstep, told her that
another day had begun, and the city was shaking off the sleep she
had not shared. Sometimes, after a succession of bad nights, Mrs.

Ramsay would give her a sleeping pill, but reluctantly, because generally she disapproved of these, agreeing with Dr. Atkinson, who said that it would be unwise for Marion to form a habit now, in her teens, which she might find difficult to break later, when she had recovered. So for Marion, wakeful nights were a part of life, and although she had come to hate and dread them, she was also used to them, and had learned to devise ways of her own of passing the time.

On the night when she had found the letter from Alan Farquhar, Marion had heard midnight strike, then one, two, and three o'clock, without having slept at all. She was wide awake, but for once she was not playing her usual game with the shadows, the game she had invented when she was younger to pass the time, and now continued partly from habit, and partly as a more pleasant alternative to thinking about the truth of things.

Mrs. Ramsay always pulled back the curtains before she got into bed, and that was how Marion liked it. She liked to see the feeble light from the street lamp at their door, shining in through the twelve window-panes, dividing into elongated pools of whiteness across the carpet, the lower ones spiked by the shadowy spearheads of the railings outside. Then on some nights the moon would rise, lemon and sharp at its rim, rolling beams across the roofs of Mayferry Street and down into Marion's room, dropping short, paler shadows in front of the long ones, so that it seemed to her that every object in the room had three shapes, the bulk of its reality, its earthly shadow from the lamp, and the moon-shadow from another world far away. Sometimes people passed in the street, a solitary night-walker, a boy and girl holding hands, a group of people returning from a party, their shadow gliding across the shadow-window; sometimes a car went by, so quickly that the shadow-car was gone almost before Marion could see it pass. Then she would begin to make up stories about the shadow-people in the street, giving them names, and imagining their appearance and their houses, and how many children they had. She went to work with them, and took them to wonderful parties, and on holiday to Italy and the Riviera. Sometimes they had wilder adventures and left Edinburgh to explore the Amazon, or to go and live among the Eskimos; one small shadow-woman and her dog, named by Marion Miss MacGonnigle and Mustard, who should have gone peacefully home to bed in India Street, instead became famous detectives, and solved a hundred dastardly crimes worthy of Burke and Hare. It depended a lot on what Marion and Colin had been watching on television. Of course it was all a great deal of nonsense, and Marion knew that; it was also a waste of a mind and an imagination which were capable of much better things, although that was something she had yet to realize. But it gave her something to do, as well as providing a refuge from the distresses and fears that are always more dreadful at three o'clock in the morning than they are at any other time during the daylight hours.

Much later on, when she was able to look back from a distance over the days and nights which were now her present, it would strike Marion at first as strange that she had lived so long in a house tense with reminders of the past, yet had never given the least share of her thoughts to the people who had lived in it before her. Only on reflection would she realize that this is the way with prisoners; however interesting the prison may be in itself, it is the place they want to forget, and the outreach of their hopes and longings is naturally to the world outside. It does not matter how shadowy and ill-defined that world may be, it can only seem a thousand times more desirable than the world within. Certainly that was the whole of Marion's experience, up until the time when she learned the names of Charles Ramsay and Alan Farquhar. After that, nothing was ever quite the same again.

Mrs. Ramsay had fallen asleep almost as soon as she went to bed. She had had a particularly exhausting day. Marion could see her, huddled up under the blankets, her head a dark smudge against the whiteness of the pillow, and for once she did not feel the little stab of self-pity which tends to come involuntarily to those who believe themselves to be alone sleepless in a sleeping world. Tonight, Marion was quite content to be alone with her thoughts in peace and quiet. For the rest of her life, she would often wonder what instinct it was that told her, at the very moment of discovery, that Alan Farquhar's letter was vitally important to her. It could not have been anything in the letter itself, mundane, workaday and stilted as it was; it did not come from anyone famous, it did not say anything important, it was not even very old. And yet nothing altered the fact that from the very instant when she drew it out of the envelope, she did know that it mattered terribly, and that the finding of it was in some obscure way an event of significance in her life. And five hours after that moment, as she lay in bed, she still felt the strong, mysterious pleasure, an inexplicable lifting of her spirits, which she had felt when her mother had said she could keep the letter. When she had come to bed, she had put it away safely in the shiny red lacquered box which Jake and Jen had brought her two summers ago, when they had taken their little blue van all the way to Morocco. They had sent lots of postcards, and that had been a thousand times more exciting than any of the adventures of the shadowy people, because it was real. The box had had sweets in it, which Colin had eaten, but the box itself Marion had kept, loving its glassy scarlet skin under the stroking of her fingers; it stayed always on the little table beside her bed to hold all her treasures, her savings in a brown leather purse, a round and tawny pebble from the beach on Jura, where they used to go on holiday in the old days, a little gold key which she had found years ago in an empty drawer in the attic, photographs of Colin when he was a baby, and of her father and mother on their wedding day. And now, the letter from Alan Farquhar.

From the first time of reading it, Marion had had the letter almost by heart, and now, as she lay in the stillness of the night, she knew it so well that she was able to take the points in it one at a time, and consider them, without needing to refer to the letter itself at all. Very softly, she began to whisper the words of the letter to the wall.

"'My dear Charles, It is a matter of regret to me that after all I must leave Edinburgh without seeing you and thanking you in person for the kind hospitality I have enjoyed in your house over the past months".'

It would be just as well, Marion thought, to begin at the beginning. Alan Farquhar had been Charles Ramsay's friend, perhaps his best friend, because it was a very affectionate letter, in spite of its formality. And also, Marion supposed, you would only have somebody to stay in your house for months at a stretch if you really liked him a lot. When Aunt Phyllis came north from Ipswich to stay with the Ramsays, and give them advice, they were all agreed that a week was as much as they could stand. Not that she came so often now, since Mrs. Ramsay had written to suggest that she stop sending them food parcels — she said because of the postage, but Colin and Marion really knew that it was because she objected to their being treated like refugees. On the other hand — returning to the letter — it did not sound as if Charles had been at home all the time Alan was there, which probably made things easier than they were on a visit from Aunt Phyllis, whom you could never shake off for five minutes, unless you locked yourself in the bathroom, or went to bed. Even Colin had been known to lie down with a headache when Aunt Phyllis was in the house, which amused Mrs. Ramsay and Marion vastly, since they knew perfectly well that Colin had never had a headache in his life. Anyway, if Charles had been at home, Alan would not have had to write to him. Perhaps he had been away on business, or on a holiday, and had allowed Alan to stay in his house — this house, presumably — while he was gone. Marion began to wonder what Charles had done for a living, and why he was not called Colin or John. But then she thought that if people had huge families, as her mother had said, all the sons could not be called Colin or John. Probably Charles had been a younger son. But if so, the house would not really have belonged to him, it would have belonged to his father, or his elder brother, Colin or John. Marion puzzled over this for a while, then, realizing that she had no evidence to help her, and that it was not a very important point anyway, she sensibly left it, and returned her mind to the letter, wondering next why it had been deliverd by hand, instead of being put in the post in the usual way. Eventually she came to the conclusion that Alan and Charles had just missed each other, that Charles had perhaps even been on his way home when Alan left, and didn't have any address, so Alan had left the letter with Charles's servant, to whom he had already entrusted his trunk. She was tempted to give the servant a name — Angus, perhaps, or Hugh, both of which seemed to her very trusty names — but she resisted, reminding herself severely that this time she was dealing with facts, not playing with shadows.

'"It will, I think, please you to know that the work I have had in hand is now completed",' she said to the wall.

This, of course, was the really interesting part. What was the work that without Charles Ramsay's encouragement and interest would never have been completed at all? Marion knew that there was no way of telling this for sure, but as she allowed her memory to scan the rest of the letter, it came to her that there was in fact one clue. It was in the last sentence of the first paragraph: '. . . I leave it to you with my most affectionate remembrances.' She worked it out like this.

Alan was going to Paris, because there he had friends who might assist him in bringing his work to the attention of the public. Whatever it was he had been doing in Charles Ramsay's house, it was something he wanted people to know about, which made it unlikely that he was studying for an examination, or just working on papers he had brought home from the office, as Marion's father often used to do. What kind of work, then, did one want people to pay attention to? Was it possible that Alan Farquhar was a scientist, like Pierre Curie, or Sir Alexander Fleming, working night and day on some terribly important theory, which one day would turn itself into a discovery, and change the whole course of medicine? On the whole, Marion thought not, because if he had been, surely he would have worked at a hospital, in a proper laboratory, not in a room in a friend's house. She also rejected the pleasing idea that he was an alchemist, who discovered the Philosopher's Stone, or even the Elixir of Life, as unfortunately too fanciful when one was committed to dealing with facts only. Which left — what? Marion thought for a while, and decided that Alan had been either an artist or a writer. These were the kind of people who would be glad of the shelter of a friend's roof, while they were working on the masterpieces which were going to make them famous. But which? At first Marion inclined to the idea of an artist, because it pleased her to imagine Alan, tall and handsome in an artist's smock, covering huge canvases with wonderful pictures of sea and flowers and sky — and children, as in the paintings of Hornel and MacTaggart, which she had seen once at an exhibition, and thought she could have put out her hand and pulled handfuls of dry sea campion and thrift, and felt the salt wind blowing on her face from racing, cloud-lashed skies. She was drawn away to the paintings for a while, and on from them to memories of past summers on Jura, sun and thin rain and the smell of the open sea, and soft water swishing over her bare feet. But there was pain in these remembrances as well as pleasure, and a longing that soon was beyond endurance, and when Marion turned her mind back to Alan Farquhar, it was to the safety of someone more real than shadows, but not so real that it broke her heart to give him a face. If Alan, then, was an artist — but he was not an artist. There was an argument against that, Marion realized, concentrating very hard to shut out other thoughts, and it was in Alan's own words, 'I leave it to you with my most affectionate remembrances'. I leave it to you. If Alan did not come back from wherever it was he was going to after Paris — Marion hurried over this thought too, because it was an uncomfortable one — he was leaving his work, whatever it was, to Charles. Of course he might have meant that he was leaving it in his will, but from the way the letter was phrased Marion thought it was more likely that he meant that he was leaving it behind him, and if he should not return, Charles was to have it. Now it said in the letter that Alan was leaving only one small trunk, and the key, so that Charles could get into it, if necessary. So that disposed of the idea of huge canvases, which would not have fitted into it, and which surely would have been mentioned separately. The work was something which would go inside a small trunk, and from that piece of information Marion deduced that Alan Farquhar was a writer. He had written a novel, or a book of poems, and he was going to dedicate it to Charles Ramsay, who had let him stay in his house while he was writing it. A masterpiece had been born at 17, Mayferry Street.

Marion was feeling very pleased with herself, and with the results of her thinking, when a sad thought occurred to her. Whatever Alan's work had been, it did not seem that his hopes for it had been fulfilled. Her mother, who had been a librarian before she married, and had read hundreds of books before she became too busy to read at all, had never heard of Alan Farquhar. Surely, if his book had been a success, a librarian would have heard of it, because it was her business to know the best books available so that she could recommend them to other people. And — it had to be faced — Marion felt that she had wrung the last drop of information out of the letter, yet she had no idea whether the book had ever seen the light of day at all. There was no way of knowing whether Alan had ever come back to claim his trunk, or what Charles Ramsay had done with it if he had not. Unless . . . there were other letters. . . . But Marion did not stay awake any longer to think about that possibility. Dealing with facts must have been more exhausting than playing with shadows, because she fell asleep, and the next thing she knew was her mother's coming to wake her with a breakfast tray, and telling her that it was nearly ten o'clock.

4

A Face from the Past

It was Marion who insisted on finishing their work on the book-case, keeping Colin busy on nights when he would really have preferred to watch television, or go upstairs to gossip with Jake, and help him with his carpentry in the empty room on the second storey which Mrs. Ramsay allowed him to use as a workshop. Jake was Colin's hero; Colin admired everything about him, his muscular arms and his vast brown beard, his leather coat and his gigantic feet, and his omniscience. There was nothing Jake did not know. He knew the names of birds and the colours of football teams, the capacity of sports cars and how to breed white mice. He could take a clock to pieces and put it together again, and whatever leaf or flower or stone you put into his wide brown hands, he could tell you its name, and what family it belonged to, and as often as not where you had found it. He was a post-graduate student of Mathematics at the University, and he was able to do Colin's homework algebra in his head, while he was helping Jen to wash up. Jen pointed out that this was not really helping Colin, who might have to demonstrate at school next day how he had got the answers, but Colin said that was a risk worth taking, because it meant that the minute the washing up was finished, they could go upstairs and get on with the planing and the sand-papering and the knocking in of nails.

Marion, however, although she liked Jake too, said that he would have to get on without Colin for a while. The bookcase was urgent work, and Colin must put first things first. Colin might have been disposed to argue about this, except for one thing. Like his mother, he was overjoyed to see Marion taking an interest in anything. It was such a relief, after months of coming home to vague looks and apathetic remarks, to arrive at half-past four and find her looking bright and actually eager to begin. Of course Colin knew why, he knew that Marion was hoping that the bookcase, which continued to disgorge the most astonishing miscellany — everything from a dried-up piece of somebody's wedding cake to an envelope containing a golden curl of baby hair and labelled, 'Johnny, 2 years, 1890' — would suddenly throw up another clue which would help her to piece together the story of Alan Farquhar and Charles Ramsay. That was why she ran expectant fingers through the pages of every book she dusted, why she spent the last ten minutes every evening raking through the rubbish, to make sure that nothing had been missed. But it was also, sadly, why her animation only lasted for the nine evenings it took them to tidy the bookcase from end to end, for, although Colin complained that it was like painting the Forth Bridge, and that by the time they had finished it would be time to start again, in fact it took little more than a week, and at the end of it nothing that Marion considered important had been found.

'I'm sorry,' Colin said to her on the last evening, as he closed the final glass door, and prepared to take Jen's step-ladder back upstairs. 'I was hoping you'd find something else.'

'Yes, so was I,' said Marion despondently, 'although I don't know why I care, really. As you said at the time, it isn't important.'

But Colin, when he came home from school the following afternoon, and saw that the blank, weary expression had returned to Marion's eyes, and heard her blank, polite voice asking him what he had had for lunch, understood very plainly that it was important after all, although not to him in the way that Marion thought it was important.

'Would you like me to help you look for clues again tonight?' he asked her kindly.

Marion made an effort, and smiled at him. When her own unhappiness was not making her so self-centred that she found it difficult to consider anyone except herself, she felt troubled about Colin. He had wide brown eyes, and fair hair that wound itself into tight little curls on the crown of his head and at the nape of his neck, and in her seventeenth year, when she was being persecuted by an awareness of all sorts of things which she had never noticed before, Marion had come to realize just how intolerable the last three years would have been for her without his merriment and good humour. She knew that she should be grateful to him, and try to respond to the efforts he made to please her. The dreadful thing was that now she found it almost impossible to do this. For her new introspection, which she could not recognize simply as a sign that she had grown up, had not only made her aware of herself, it had also forced her to become aware of other people. She seemed to be alive to other people as she had never been before, and to be always watching them, and wondering what they were thinking, and what made them behave as they did. And with awareness came doubt. There was Colin, for instance. Was it really natural, she wondered, for an eleven-year-old boy to be as kind and pleasant as Colin always was to her? Would it not be more natural if they squabbled a bit? She tried to cast her mind back to the time before her accident — had they not always been fighting then? And if they had, did it not mean that he was only so kind and friendly now because he felt sorry for her, and not, as she had confidently assumed for three years, because he liked her as much as she did him? Then, for the first time, Marion thought about pity, and that was the end of her peace of mind. For as she thought about it, and she had plenty of time for thinking, a fearful seed of suspicion took root and began to grow poisonously, damaging her inwardly. Suppose, said a cold little voice inside her head, that made the most desolating suggestions, and refused to be silenced, suppose that her mother and Colin and Jen and Jake and all her other friends did not really love her as much as she had thought they did, but only felt sorry for her? Suppose that behind the masks of their smiling faces they were really tired to death of being kind, but had to go on, out of pity? She was, after all, the reason why her mother was tired out and old at forty-one, the reason why Colin never brought any of his friends home to play after school. She was spoiling their lives. There was no reason why they should love her. Set alongside a horror like this, her other troubles, her boredom and insecurity and shame at her own lack of education, almost disappeared into unimportance. Nothing was as terrible as knowing that one was spoiling the lives of the people one loved. So she tortured herself, and the worst part of it all was that she could never tell anyone, never confide her fears to another human being, not to her mother, not to Jen, who, next to her parents and Colin, she loved more than anyone she had ever known. For while she kept them to herself, her suspicions were only suspicions, but she had a strange, half-superstitious dread that to speak them aloud would in some way make them come true. So while half of her was grateful to Colin for being patient and kind, and sad that he felt he must be patient and kind, the other half had stopped trusting him. She watched him from the private room of her own unhappiness, and blamed herself for the awkwardness between them. And now, when he offered his help, she said flatly, 'No. We wouldn't know where to look. There isn't anywhere else, is there? Just do what you like, it doesn't matter.'

'I'd like to help you,' he said, meaning it.

'It's very kind of you. But it doesn't matter.'

It did matter, but for a while, that seemed to be the end of that. In November, Colin began to have extra homework at night, because he had exams at the end of the month. When he was not doing homework, he was either upstairs helping Jake, or out playing with Thomas and Vincent from next door. Marion went back to watching television and looking out of the window, and although when she was in bed she still thought a lot about Charles Ramsay and Alan Farquhar, soon they had lost the connection with the factual world of which she had been so proud when she found the letter, and become mere shadow people like all the rest. By the middle of the month, when winter came pouncing out of the sky with a blatter of rain and rageful wind, Alan and Charles were on an expedition to the Antarctic, and Alan was going to write a book about their experiences when they got home. Of course it was only playing with shadows, and Marion knew that; it saddened her, because it was not what she wanted, but at least with the shadow people she did not have to be for ever watchful, and wondering what they were really thinking. She controlled their thoughts as well as their actions, and they gave her relief. And she did still have the letter. That was real, and when she took it out of the lacquered box, and spread it on the quilt, and smoothed it with her hands, she knew that it still kept its power to communicate to her that small, strong stirring of hope in the darkness which was the thing she most needed at the present time.

The last day of November was a Saturday, a pale, sad day with damp in its bones and a wet sun hanging like a flat cut-out behind frayed tatters of dirty cloud. Colin had to go out in the morning, to the Supermarket and the library — as a librarian's family, the Ramsays patronized their local library faithfully, despite the presence of their bookcase in the sitting-room. He came home at twelve o'clock with numb toes and chill right under his vest, feeling very glad that he did not have to go out again in the afternoon. There was a huge fire in the sitting-room, and he would curl up in front of it with *The Fury of Cape Horn*, which he had just brought home from the library, and could not wait to start.

The Ramsays' Saturday afternoon was not of the bustling, expectant, determined kind, squeezed dry of activity by people who play golf and go shopping and attend football matches, knowing that they will have to wait a whole week before they can organize another one. Theirs was of the other kind, the timeless, limbo-like Saturday afternoon of those who would really like to be idle, but rarely have the opportunity, an interval loosely slung between weeks, and distinguished only negatively by not being set aside for anything special at all. It is near enough to Friday to give that leisurely feeling of space which treacherously marks the beginning of every weekend, and in that way differs from Sunday afternoon, when one may do the same things, but with the flutter of urgency brought on by the knowledge that time is running out. There is no hurry on Saturday, only the pleasing illusion that Monday never comes. This was how the Ramsays liked it; even under other circumstances, they would all have preferred a book to a bicycle. What happened in practice was that Colin and Marion read, and watched a serial thriller on television at half-past four, while Mrs. Ramsay, if she had no work that she had to catch up with, gave herself a treat, and retired to bed with a cup of coffee and the newspaper. As often as not, she woke up three hours later with a cup of cold coffee and the newspaper never out of its folds. Today, however, things were not quite as usual. Marion, who had been to the hospital the previous afternoon for her six-monthly examination, and had come back tired out, was spending the day in bed. The report had been non-committal, and although she had not expected anything else, she was feeling low, and did not want to talk to anyone. Mrs. Ramsay was typing in the sitting-room, and after about an hour of trying to read through the infuriating rasp-clatter-tinkle of her typewriter, Colin gave up, and thought he might as well go upstairs and see whether Jake was needing any help. Muffled banging away in the distance had told him at lunch time that Jake too was having an afternoon at home.

'Put on your old trousers,' warned Mrs. Ramsay above the whacking of the keys. She did not have to ask where he was going.

Colin changed into an old pair of shorts, and went upstairs. The flight of steps to the first floor doubled back on itself half-way up, and the contrast between the Ramsays' hall and the Taylors' landing, sighted round the bend, was electrifying. Jen and Jake had a passion for scarlet, and all their walls were painted that colour. It was startlingly cheerful. Colin met Jen coming out of the kitchen. She was carrying a plate of cookies, and a lovely baking smell came wafting out behind her.

'Hi,' she said.

Colin liked Jen, who was young, and wore brown and purple

frocks that reached down to her ankles, and green stockings. She had long soft hair, the colour of a mouse's back, and a smile that reached into every corner of her face.

'I was on my way down,' she went on, 'to see if Marion would like a cookie. They're just out of the oven.'

'I expect so,' said Colin. He was too polite to stare at the plate, but he had the kind of nose that could not stop itself from twitching at delicious smells. Jen watched his nose, and laughed.

'I suppose you wouldn't like one yourself?' she asked.

Colin said he would. 'But I didn't come up because I smelt them, honestly. I came to see if Jake was in.'

'He's upstairs,' said Jen. 'You had better wait a minute, till I butter some cookies, then you can take them up with you. That way Jake won't have the trouble of coming down as soon as he smells them.'

The room which Jake had taken over as his workshop had been a front bedroom in days gone by, when number seventeen had sheltered a thriving community of Ramsays, rich, well-fed and idle. At least, that was how Colin imagined them, and there were none left to contradict him, to point out pompously that money had to be earned, and food paid for, and that idleness was sinful in the sight of the Almighty. The Ramsays had been Pillars of the Kirk, and Colin could also visualize them in that role, on the Sabbath, made of stone, and supporting St. Andrew's Church of Scotland on their heads, like the caryatides on the Erechtheum, which he had seen in a picture at school. Now their fires had gone out and their bedrooms were deserted, and whoever had once slept within the flower-patterned walls of Jake's workroom would have had difficulty in recognizing it today. It had no furniture in it at all, though faded curtains still hung at the windows; it had not occurred to anyone to take them down. The floor was bare and far from clean, and it was covered with sawdust and chips of wood, and long curly wood-shavings like blond ringlets. At one end stood Jake's work-bench, bristling with an awesome collection of planes, saws, hammers, chisels, pliers and awls. Connected to an electric point which he had had to fit up himself, since there were no power-plugs above the first floor, was his power-drill, a frightsome tool which tore the air with its noise as it tore the wood with its teeth; secretly Colin was afraid of it.

In the middle of the room, taking up at least a third of the floor-space, stood an erection which looked like a miniature oil-rig, a wide platform supported on four massive legs. This was Jake's latest project, which he had designed himself, and of which he was immensely proud, athough he always did his best to put a modest expression on his face when people said how clever it was. It was not an oil-rig. It was a housebed, or a bedhouse, what Jake grandly called an experiment in compact living, and was intended to put all previous beds firmly in their place, including the Great Bed of Ware, and the one round which Odysseus built his palace. It was, said Jake, kindly simplifying the concept of compact living for people like Jen and Mrs. Ramsay, whose faces tended to betray their astonishment, a space-saving device. The idea was that one slept on the platform, which was eight feet high, and reached by a small staircase, and lived, compactly, in the space underneath, which was later to be boxed in on three sides and fitted with a desk, a bookcase, two chairs and a folding table. If there were room, there might also be a cocktail-cabinet. Colin was far too loyal to think that it was anything but brilliant, but Mrs. Ramsay, after she had been dragged upstairs to admire it, had taken the opportunity of stopping Jen in the hall the next evening, when she was coming home from work, to tell her that if they were short of space, they could easily have some more rooms for the same rent. Space, she pointed out, was the one thing they did not have to save, at number seventeen. But Jen had laughed and rolled her eyes, and said that surely Mrs. Ramsay knew Jake by this time, which was her way of saying that it had nothing to do with saving space, and that there was no use trying to reason with Jake, when he had a bee in his bonnet, which was most of the time.

When Colin arrived with the plate of cookies, Jake was reclining on the floor under the platform, in his old denim jeans and a grubby jersey, having a rest and a think. Colin sat down beside him, and they shared the cookies in silence. Then Jake flicked some crumbs off his beard, heaved himself onto his huge feet, and said, 'Care for a spot of sandpapering?'

'Sure,' said Colin.

He and Jake never talked very much when they were working, but they were very companionable.

'The posts,' said Jake.

He brought the sandpaper, and showed Colin which bits needed rubbing up, then he left him, and returned to his bench at the other end of the room. He had decided that it would be fun to put louvered sides on the living compartment, and he was cutting the slats carefully with a small saw.

Colin sandpapered the top of the post first, standing on a stool to reach the highest part. He worked slowly and carefully, because Jake could get very tetchy if a job was not properly done. Then he did the middle, standing on the floor, and gradually dropped down into a squatting position, then on to his knees. This was the bit he liked least, because the floor was rough and cold, and sometimes he got splinters in his bare skin. He wished that he had put on long trousers, but he had grabbed the first that came to hand, and it was too much trouble to go all the way downstairs to change again. In any case, by working on the posts one at a time, he did not have to be too long on his knees at a stretch. He was at the bottom of the second one when he felt something sticking into his knee, not sharply, but at the reflex, which made it hurt in a funny way. He moved his leg and glanced down, expecting to see that he had been kneeling on a knot, or on a chip of wood, but instead he saw that he had actually had his knee over a crack between two floorboards, and that whatever it was that had jabbed him was protruding from the crack. He poked with his finger, expecting a nail, but felt instead the triangular corner of a piece of stiff cardboard. He tried to catch hold of it, but it slipped through his clumsy fingers, and dropped down suddenly into the floor, so that the corner still showing was too small to be caught by fingers at all. Colin squinted at it in perplexity, his curiosity roused. It was not that he thought it was likely to be anything important, but now he wanted to know what it was.

'Jake,' he said, 'can you spare a minute?'

Jake laid down his saw and came, squatting down so that his shadow fell over Colin like a cloak.

'What's up?' he asked.

'It's this piece of cardboard down here between the floorboards. The corner stuck into my knee. I tried to get it out, but I can't grasp it. My hands are too big.'

'No point my trying, then,' said Jake, putting his face closer, and peering down into the crack. 'Ah, yes, I see it. What we need is tweezers. Hold on — I've a pair on the bench somewhere — I use them for taking splinters out of my hands.'

He found the tweezers while Colin guarded the crack, and kneeling down again, gently fitted them over the edge of the cardboard. Then he nipped it with the precision of one catching a fly.

'Got you,' he said.

33

But the cardboard was not going to give itself up as easily as that, and when he tried to pull it out, nothing happened. He tried again, but it refused to budge.

'Going to be awkward, eh?' said Jake, threateningly.

'Can't we get it, then?' asked Colin anxiously. The cardboard's inaccessibility was increasing its value by the minute.

'Sure, we can,' said Jake easily. 'Keep calm. Now see — you hang on to the tweezers, and don't let go. If it drops any further, it'll go right down under the boards and then you can forget it, because I'm not going to lift the floor to please you. Whatever it is, it's caked around with dirt. If I can get some of that loosened, I think it will come out.'

He got up again, and went to get a knife and a screwdriver, while Colin, beginning to get really excited now, held on to the tweezers so hard that they made dents in his thumb and forefinger, like depressions in a bread roll. Jake returned, and for a few minutes there was intense silence, broken only by the gritty scraping of the knife, and the scuttering sound of tiny earthfalls as the loosened grime fell away and rattled down between the joists below.

'And they talk about modern workmen making a mess of things,' remarked Jake presently. 'Whoever lifted this floor the last time made a pretty hopeless job of it, and that wasn't yesterday. See where these boards have been sawn across and lifted out? They've just been stuck back and hammered down any old how. That's why there's a space here for things to fall down. The boards are all uneven. Must have worn holes in the carpet, when there was one.'

'Why would they want to lift the floorboards?' enquired Colin, not because he really cared, but because he liked to take an intelligent interest in all Jake's topics of conversation. He was holding on to the tweezers as if his life depended on it, and watching the huge hands plying the knife.

'Oh, I don't know. Probably to look at the joists, or when they were wiring for electricity. Hang on, though — we're nearly there.'

He gave the knife a couple of taps with the end of the screwdriver, and said, 'Now, pull.'

Colin pulled. He felt the card moving, more dirt fell away, and he began to draw it upwards out of the crack.

What emerged was a photograph, although for a moment Colin did not recognize it as anything he had ever seen before.

Then he saw what it was, very old, very faded, in tones of brown and white, and mounted on a piece of buff-coloured cardboard which at one time had been gilt-edged. Now damp and dirt had done their work of destruction so thoroughly that the gilt was barely more than a memory, and until Jake produced a paper handkerchief, and carefully wiped away some of the film of grime and mould from its surface, it was impossible even to guess at its subject. Then slowly it began to emerge, though patchily. It was not a snapshot, of the casual, outdoor variety, but a carefully posed indoor portrait, and it showed a young man, perhaps about Jake's age, but as different from Jake as it was possible to imagine. He was tall and thin, with shiny hair neatly parted, and a small moustache, and he was dressed in some kind of military uniform. He was wearing a kilt, with a hairy sporran, and a high-collared tunic with lots of buttons, and decoration on the sleeves. He had a belt, and a leather strap over his shoulder, which Colin thought meant that he was an officer. Apart from that, it was hard to be sure about anything. The bottom third of the photograph, where his legs should have been, was terribly defaced by damp, and most of the background was more or less obliterated in the same way, but by peering very closely it was possible to guess that the man was standing in front of a draped curtain with tassels, and to distinguish with certainty a small table at his side. It held a pile of books, and under his left hand was some kind of wooden box. About a third of this was lost in the mouldy part of the picture, but the rest was sharp enough, and the embossed metal decoration around the lock was very clear.

Jake looked at it over Colin's shoulder for a moment, then he said, in a bored tone of voice, 'Lord, that was a lot of work for nothing. Sorry, old son.' And he went back to his sawing. Colin sat on under the housebed, staring at the soiled, mouldering thing, not knowing whether to be disappointed or not. Certainly it was not of any value, and it looked sorry enough. Still, he would have liked to have a conversation about it, to discuss the soldier's uniform, and speculate with someone about why it was down in the floorboards. But a glance at Jake's broad back, hunched over the bench, told him that he was not going to get any interest from him. Then he remembered that disapproving of wars and the army was another of the bees in Jake's bonnet. He was — what was it called? There was a name for it. A pacifist. In which case, he was never going to be much use over the photograph. Then Colin had another thought.

'Jake,' he said, scrambling up, 'if you can do without me for a bit, I think I'll just run down and show this to Marion. She might be interested.'

If Jake had doubts about Marion's interest in a filthy, disintegrating photograph that had probably spent the last forty years at least under the floor, he did not spoil a kind idea by saying so. He looked at Colin intensely with his fire-blue eyes, and said, 'Yes, you do that.' Then he added, 'Jen says she isn't very well today.'

'No.'

'No good news from the hospital?'

'No. I'll come back and finish off the sandpapering later.'

'Any time,' said Jake.

5

Detectives

Marion was half asleep when Colin arrived in her room. She could never understand why it was that she always seemed to be wide awake during the night, yet if she stayed in bed during the day, she slept nearly all the time. It was one of the small, wayward things which of themselves were not particularly important, but which, added together, could make her life very frustrating. Yet today, it was a relief to sleep, and to forget, because all the time she was awake her depression was like a cold stone lying inside her, making her irritable and contrary when really she did not want to be either. When she was alone, she wanted her mother. Then when her mother came, she wanted her to go away and leave her alone. She thought she would like an apple pie for lunch, then when she got it, she couldn't eat it. But when Mrs. Ramsay, who had had to go out in the rain to get the apples, and had spent a good part of the morning making the pie, said, 'It doesn't matter, darling — don't worry a bit,' Marion thought she would have felt better if she had been cross. Then she began to brood again over people's reasons for never being angry with her, and when Jen arrived, with a hot buttered cookie on a saucer and two magazines which Marion suspected she never read, but had bought specially when she was out doing her weekend's shopping, she felt so ashamed of not wanting to talk to her that she ate the cookie, and had had a lump of pain in her stomach ever since. After Jen went away, she wanted to cry, but that was something she had never been able to do easily, and presently she fell into an uneasy sleep, lying just inside the door of unconsciousness, aware of the sounds of the waking world, dreaming, but knowing that she dreamed. When Colin came, she was dreaming that an enormous owl was hovering above her head, dark and watchful, ready to swoop down the minute she opened her eyes. But she knew too that if only she could have the courage to open her eyes, there would be no owl there. Then there was Colin, and she was not sure whether he was in her dream, or real, until she heard his voice say, 'Marion.' She opened her eyes, the owl vanished, and in the gathering darkness she saw him standing by the bed.

'I woke you up,' he said guiltily. 'Sorry.'

'It's all right. I was having an awful dream about an owl. Put the light on, Colin.'

Colin fumbled under the shade of the lamp beside Marion's bed, and switched it on. Brightness sprang out, and the window, which had been grey, went black. He looked down at Marion'spale face, frowning in the pain of the light, and her tousled brown hair on the pillow. He was not so sure now that this was a good idea.

'I found something upstairs,' he said tentatively. 'I thought you might like to see it.'

'What is it?' Marion asked. Her mouth felt dry and horrible, and her head was still fuzzy with sleep.

'It's an old photograph. It was down in the floorboards of Jake's workroom. We had to get it out with tweezers and a knife.'

He put the photograph into Marion's hands, and watched how her fingers shrank away instinctively from its unwholesome texture until it was gripped only in the tips of her fingernails. But as she held it up to the light, and focused her eyes on the picture, he saw her expression change; surprise and intelligence swept over her face, and he heard the sudden, excited intake of her breath.

'Help me to sit up,' she commanded.

Colin breathed again. He let her take hold of his hand with both of hers, and pulled her up into a sitting position, hastily stuffing the space behind her with pillows. Marion settled herself, thanked him, and gave her attention to the photograph.

'Sit down,' she said, 'and tell me where you found it.'

So Colin sat down on the edge of the bed, and told her everything that had happened from the moment he had felt the edge of the photograph sticking into his knee, until Jake had freed it with his knife. 'Then I thought of bringing it down to you. Jake didn't think much of it,' he added. 'Because he's a pacifist, I suppose.'

'He's daft,' said Marion, dismissing Jake and his pacifism. She gazed at the young soldier for a long time, and Colin watched her. 'I wonder who it is,' she said at last, then, longingly, 'I know who I'd like it to be.'

'Alan Farquhar.'

'I was thinking of Charles Ramsay, actually. I don't suppose there would be a photograph of Alan Farquhar down our floorboards, do you?'

'I wouldn't have thought there would be a photograph of anyone down our floorboards,' replied Colin. 'I expect it must have slipped down while they were spring-cleaning, or something like that. But in any case, we're jumping to conclusions. The chances are it isn't either of them. Why should it be?'

'I know.' Marion bit her lip in vexation, but she was looking so lively all of a sudden that Colin could tell she wasn't really vexed at all. 'Colin, do you know anything about soldiers' uniforms?'

'Not much. Why?'

'I wondered when soldiers wore uniforms like this one.'

'I don't know. I'm a pacifist too,' he said to tease her.

Marion ignored this remark. She preferred not to be provoked by red herrings when she was busy thinking.

'It's a pity it isn't in colour,' she said. 'I mean, if the tunic was red, there's a chance that it was taken before the Boer War, because that's when the British army started to wear khaki.'

'Was it?' said Colin, impressed. 'How do you know that?'

'I don't know. Probably Miss Parkinson told me. She was stuffed with useless information. But in any case, it wouldn't tell us so very much, because dress tunics are still red.'

'Did they have photographs before the Boer War?'

'Oh, yes, long before. The earliest ones were called daguerreotypes, and they were invented away back in the 1830's,' Marion informed him. 'And I think they had learned how to take proper photographs by the middle of the last century.'

Colin looked at her with respect. He often thought that for a person who had never really been properly educated, Marion knew an extraordinary amount about all sorts of things. But Marion had returned her attention to the photograph.

'I don't suppose there's anything written on it, is there?' she asked, more of herself than of Colin.

She turned the photograph over in fastidious hands, wrinkling up her nose in distaste, but Colin knew perfectly well that she would not have parted with it for anything. He leaned forward, and together they scanned the reverse side with eyes as keen as X-rays. There was a watermark, where damp had seeped across the cardboard and then dried up again, there was some queer, encrusted grime that looked as if it might once have been alive, and a hard smear of dirt which Colin took for a squashed fly, Boer War vintage. But there was no mark made by a pen, held in any human hand.

Marion threw herself back against her pillow in a rage, and Colin began to laugh.

'Oh, come on now,' he said, 'that would make it too easy, wouldn't it? We're solving a mystery, for goodness' sake.'

'Are we?' asked Marion, uncertainly.

'Of course we are. So if it said, "Charles Ramsay, Second Lieutenant, Highland Light Infantry", it would take all the fun out of it, don't you see? It's much better to have to work things out for ourselves.'

Marion thought she liked the sound of this very much indeed. Still — 'How are we ever going to find out?' she asked helplessly. 'Unless we find another clue —' She spread out her hands in a little gesture of despondency.

'Until we find another clue, you mean,' said Colin firmly. Then, seeing from her face that she didn't believe him, he went on, 'Look, you were the one who moaned and groaned and said there was no use looking for clues, because we didn't know where to look. Now here's a clue, popping up all unexpected out of a dirty old floor, and you're complaining because it doesn't have an explanation written on the back. We'll have to put our brilliant minds to work now, won't we, stupid?'

It was so pleasant to be called stupid, in such a natural, cheeky way, that Marion laughed. It was a round, hooting sound that Colin didn't hear very often, and he liked it. And Mrs. Ramsay, who just at that moment was opening the door of the bedroom, to bring in Marion's tea tray, could not believe her ears. Or her eyes, when she saw that Marion was sitting up in bed, with a shining, delighted face, waving a dirty piece of paper at her and saying, 'Mother, come quickly and look at this! Colin has found a mystery for us to solve. . . .'

Mrs. Ramsay was somewhat taken aback by the change of scene. It was difficult for her to recognize in this animated creature the same Marion who, three hours previously, had been lying huddled and miserable under the bedclothes, hiding her face and saying she wanted nothing and nobody. And at first, when she had brought a chair for herself, and looked at the damp, repellent piece of cardboard which was thrust so eagerly into her hands, she still could not understand its apparent power to work a miracle. Only when she heard the names of Charles Ramsay and Alan Farquhar being tossed from one of her children to the other did she grasp the connection, and looked at the young man closely, with interest. What she was not prepared for was the pain, always most piercing when it caught her unexpectedly, and for a moment she could see nothing at all. But a long time ago she

40

had schooled herself never to distress Marion and Colin with her grief; it was a discipline which proved useful now.

'I don't know who it is,' she said, passing the photograph over to Colin, since Marion was busy working on her fingers with a sponge and towel before beginning to eat her boiled egg. 'But I can tell you one thing about him. He is a Ramsay. It's the family face.' She made herself smile at Colin, and added, 'It will be your face when you're twenty.'

Colin squealed with alarm.

'No, it won't,' he said indignantly. 'I'm not going to look like that, with hair cream on and a silly moustache.'

He had already decided his appearance when he would be twenty; whatever else, he was going to have a magnificent beard, and hair falling in smooth waves around his neck. It was a private, cherished dream of the future.

'It hasn't anything to do with hair,' said Mrs. Ramsay patiently. 'It has to do with bones, and eyes, and the shape of the nose. Fashions in hair change. Faces don't.'

'So it couldn't be Alan Farquhar?' asked Marion, merely to eliminate the possibility.

'No, I don't think so. It's too like — like the Ramsays.'

'Do you suppose it might be Charles Ramsay?'

Mrs. Ramsay shook her head dubiously.

'Darling,' she said, 'I don't see how we can possibly say. You see, we don't know anything about Charles Ramsay.'

'We know that he was a young man in 1914.'

'No,' her mother objected, 'I don't think we even know that. I think you only assumed that he and Alan Farquhar were young. There was really nothing in the letter to indicate whether they were, or not.'

Marion frowned. 'I got the impression,' she said doubtfully. Suddenly she realized that she very much wanted them to be young.

'Yes,' Mrs. Ramsay agreed, 'so did I. But it was only an impression.'

She thought for a moment, then she added, 'However, there is one thing —'

'What?' snapped out two voices together.

Mrs. Ramsay smiled at this.

'What date was your letter, Marion?'

'The twenty-fourth of January, 1914,' said Marion promptly. She knew that date as well now as her own birthday.

41

'Well then — assuming that our impression is correct, and Charles Ramsay and Alan Farquhar were young men, it's very probable that only a few months afterwards they would both be soldiers. The First World War broke out in August of that year, and most young men had to join the army. In those times, lots of families had photographs taken of their sons in their uniforms, and this does look to me as if it might have been that kind of photograph. Of course I'm only guessing, and in any case it still doesn't prove that it's Charles Ramsay. It might be one of his brothers, or even his son.'

Marion finished scraping out the white of her egg, and ate it. She then turned the shell upside down, and made a hole in it with her spoon, so that a witch could not sail in it. She did it quite automatically, because her mind was not on witches at the time. Colin had another of his visions of the Ramsays, not as caryatides this time, but as a long column of black-haired, identical young men, in sepia kilts and jackets, marching away to France to fight for King and Country.

'Mother,' he said dreamily, 'who were the Ramsays in the old days? Were they very important people?'

'They were grocers,' said Mrs. Ramsay, with a kind of flat emphasis. Although she had been married for fourteen years to one Ramsay, and had loved him very dearly, she did get a little tired of the Ramsays in general, with their eighteen rooms, and calling themselves city merchants when they had really kept a rather unsuccessful grocer's shop in Hanover Street, and would not let her call her only son Simon, as she had always intended, ever since she was five years old.

All this was lost upon Colin, who was still very young, but Marion, being older, was beginning to understand amusing things, as well as painful ones. Being in a mood for laughter, she smiled teasingly at her mother over Colin's head. Mrs. Ramsay laughed, a bit shamefacedly, but she went on defiantly, 'Well, so they were, and not very good ones either, by all accounts. Semolina in the sugar during the War, so the Minister's wife informed me.'

'Ugh,' said Marion, this time missing the point completely.

'I wish they had been gangsters,' said Colin.

After he had had his own tea, he helped Marion to clean up the photograph with a piece of cotton wool dipped in vinegar. Then they pressed it between sheets of blotting paper, under heavy books, to dry and flatten it. Afterwards, it was to be put into the lacquered box, beside the letter from Alan Farquhar.

For the next few days, Marion enjoyed another brief period of optimism. She felt quite confident that there must be a link between the letter and the photograph, and on the superstitious and not very sound premise that clues, like broken dishes, must come in groups of three, she expected every minute that the third clue was going to present itself, just as magically as the first two had done. Indeed, she thought, it seemed even more likely, since this time nothing was being left to chance; active clue-seeking was underway. Of course it was frustrating that she could not go hunting for evidence herself — although Jake would willingly have carried her upstairs, Mrs. Ramsay vetoed point-blank the suggestion that Marion should spend her evenings sitting around in damp, unheated rooms, and in the month of December, too. Never, she said had she heard such a preposterous idea, and Marion, who knew a veto when she heard one, did not even bother to argue. Colin, however, was quite willing to carry out the search on her behalf, and spent the greater part of the next two evenings poking about in drawers and cupboards, examining floors and walls in all the upstairs rooms, while Marion waited in the sitting-room, hopeful that somewhere, somehow, another clue would be found. But it did not happen, and when, at the end of the second evening's hunt, Colin came downstairs, cold, dirty and rather disgruntled, Marion realized with sadness that his enthusiasm was ebbing fast.

'I have looked everywhere,' he assured her.

'I know.'

'The trouble is, I don't even known what I'm supposed to be looking for.'

'I know that, too.'

'I mean, it might be another letter, or a photograph, but it might be something quite different, don't you think?'

'Yes, I do. I don't know what we're looking for either.'

Her spiritless acquiescence in everything he said always perplexed Colin far more than an argument would have done. He looked at her impassive face, and felt uncomfortable.

'Well, then,' he said, 'perhaps we had better wait and let the next clue happen on its own. The last two did, so most likely the next one will too.'

'If it happens at all,' said Marion bleakly.

'Oh, it's bound to,' said Colin brightly, with far more assurance than he really felt. 'Things always happen in threes.'

43

Although this was just the piece of silliness with which Marion had been keeping up her spirits for three days, she felt unreasonably irritated when Colin repeated it. But all she said was, 'It doesn't matter,' as she always did when she felt the cold sea of despondency washing over her again. And Colin, as he always did when she said, 'It doesn't matter,' found that suddenly he had something very urgent to do in his bedroom.

So once again, Marion returned to telling herself that that was that, and that it would be wiser to put the whole thing out of her head. Which might have been true, but the fact that she did not find it at all possible was perhaps a sign that, despite her pessimism, she had not entirely given up hope. Perhaps too, it was because the mystery now involved a human face that she found it easier to turn aside from the shadows, and see it in terms of real people. For whoever the young soldier in the photograph had been, however long ago he had lived, Marion knew that he could never have anything to do with the lamp-light shadows on her bedroom floor. He had a face of his own. It was not a face she ever recognized as her father's, which was as well for her, but neither was it the face of the Antarctic explorer, the Roman centurion, the brilliant scientist, puppets into whose false characters she had been manipulating the faceless Charles Ramsay over the past few weeks. The young man's face held its own secrets, and that was what Marion found fascinating about it. He was a real person, and she felt instinctively that she would be betraying his right to be himself if she turned him into someone else for her own amusement. She watched him and thought about him, but she did not try to appropriate his face, as she had appropriated other people's shadows.

Nonetheless, the face haunted her. Every morning before she got up, every night before she switched off her lamp, she opened the lacquered box and took out the photograph, now flat and dry and as powdery as old bone, although by now she had no need to reacquaint herself with the features that had been hanging before the eye of her mind, distinctly, ever since she had first seen them. But she liked to look, and as she did so, she seemed to get closer to the young man, and it came to her that the stiff, self-conscious, camera-shy face was not in the least what it first appeared to be. It had wide, dark eyes, which were solemn, but looked as if they could dance with merriment if they chose, a firm mouth which looked as if it would like to smile, but thought it might be undignified, in a photograph, and thick, wiry black hair, oiled to make it lie down when it was obvious that nature had meant it to stand up straight. Marion had the feeling that the moment the shutter clicked, and the photograph was taken, the young man would have heaved a sigh of relief, run his fingers through his hair, and let his photograph-face relax into an habitual, good-humoured smile. It was a nice face, she thought, but whether it was Charles Ramsay's face was quite another matter. And it was equally uncertain, she had to admit, whether the letter and the photograph, referred to by Colin as clue one and clue two, had in fact any connection at all. For all they knew, each might represent a quite separate mystery, which made the task of detecting twice as daunting as it would otherwise have been. Especially if, as it seemed, one had to wait for clues to come out of the blue.

It was quite different for Colin, who had his separate worlds of school and play and helping Jake to divert him, and who in any case had never shared, or really understood, his sister's intensity of interest in either the letter or the photograph. He had only wanted to amuse her, and when no new evidence was forthcoming, and Marion's first, excited spate of speculation had trickled away into the dust of disappointment, he forgot the whole thing, and turned his mind to its usual preoccupations, the progress of the housebed, his exam. results, the possibility of the school's going on fire, and whether he would get a place in the School Orchestra after Christmas. He would have liked to find another clue for Marion's sake, but he did not waste time worrying because he did not.

Mrs. Ramsay had been true to her determination to clean up the house, and do all the outstanding jobs of tidying and disposal of rubbish, before the New Year. She worked steadily, and to such effect that each Tuesday, when the dust-cart came, the pavement outside number seventeen was edged with a rag-tag border of sacks and cardboard boxes alongside the dustbin, all packed with the rubbish that had poured out of drawers and wardrobes and cupboards which had not been opened for two decades at least. Her finds, as she remarked to Marion, would have fitted out a small museum; mothy old fur scarves with little fox-faces, ration books from the last war, hairbrushes, scent bottles, wedding invitations, old shoes, ornate and lethal hat-pins, lace handkerchief sachets, bottles of cough syrup, dresses from the nineteen-forties, babies' boots. It was obvious, she said, that the Ramsays had never thrown away anything in their lives. It was the story of the bookcase all over again, on a very much larger scale. Marion was somewhat cheered by the thought that the Ramsays had never thrown anything away; she insisted on having all the boxes of rejects brought into the sitting-room so that she could sift through them before they were removed, just in case, by any chance, she should recognize in one of them something that was linked with her photograph, or her letter. Mrs. Ramsay was pleased to humour her, and if she had not been so tense with anxiety, Marion would have enjoyed for themselves the smells that the boxes exuded, and the surprising textures under her hands, the gentle odour of old scent, the rustling elusiveness of silk, the scaly sharpness of sequins, the prickle of Harris tweed. She would also have enjoyed the sight of Colin, dressed in a feathered hat and a pink satin dress, with a patch out of its seat, mincing around the sitting-room with a bag over his arm, in a pair of high-heeled shoes. As it was, she was only miserable because she had once more drawn a blank, and as she helped to pack the best of the clothes into a box for Oxfam, and saw the rest being taken away to the refuse collection, she was near despair, because surely, she thought, if a cleaning of this magnitude could not turn up another clue, it was because no other clue existed.

At last, what Colin called the Great Clean was at an end; on its last evening, Marion was left alone in the sitting-room to watch television, while her mother and Colin went up to the loft to finish tidying up the things which Mrs. Ramsay had decided were worth keeping. Later, when she was in bed, and looking at her photograph, Colin came in to say good-night to her. He was wearing his dressing gown, and he had the pink, steamy, slightly crumpled look of small boys just out of the bath. His hair was wet and as curly as a lamb's neck, and he brought with him a strong aroma of carbolic soap. The loft had been very dirty, and Colin, who had refused absolutely to wear an apron and headscarf, had come down much the worse for cobwebs and grime. Marion sniffed him appreciatively for his carbolic smell, which she liked better than scent.

'Did you get everything tidied up in the loft?' she asked.

'Yes,' said Colin, sitting down gently on the side of the bed. 'I think that's an end of it now, thank goodness, although the place is still packed to the gunwales with the most awful junk.' He paused, and added with relish, 'You'd never believe what's up there.'

'What's up there?' asked Marion immediately, as he meant her to.

'Well, there's a stuffed buzzard, for instance, and a pickled snake in a wine bottle, and an umbrella stand made out of an elephant's leg.'

Marion reacted with suitable horror and astonishment. Her brown eyes widened, and her small nose wrinkled.

'How on earth could anyone make an umbrella stand out of an elephant's leg?' she demanded.

'Think about it,' suggested Colin, but Marion said she preferred not to.

'Why on earth is Mother keeping anything so horrid?' she wanted to know.

'We couldn't get it down the loft ladder,' replied Colin solemnly. 'Mother said she didn't want anyone to be killed by a falling elephant's leg.'

This was the sort of nonsense which Marion appreciated when she was in the mood for it, and she laughed a lot. Then she asked, 'What's happening to the buzzard, and the snake?'

'Mother's going to give the buzzard to Thomas next door, if his mother says he can have it. He's keen on birds. I'm going to keep the snake in my bedroom.'

'Disgusting,' said Marion, with a shudder.

Colin grinned. He would have been disappointed with any other reaction. Marion was being easy to talk to tonight, for a change, and when she was like this Colin enjoyed her company.

'I see you're still admiring your boy friend,' he went on amiably, stretching over and taking the photograph out of her hand. He had only intended to tease her a bit, and provoke her with rude remarks about the soldier's hair style. But as he looked down at the picture, familiar, faded and never very exciting, a most peculiar thing happened. The words stopped at his lips, and a strange, almost eerie sensation filled his head. Because as he looked, he knew without any doubt at all that he was looking at something very important, that the next clue, whatever it was, had already been discovered. But he also knew that he had not the least idea what it was.

6

About a Flute

Now it was winter in earnest, with none of those warm, freakish days of sun and blue spilt behind the bare branches in New Town gardens, deceiving days that raise briefly the ghost of another, kinder season. It was very cold; grey rain dropped down endlessly out of grey skies on to a grey city, and gusts of a scalpel wind shunted Colin erratically along Heriot Row, down Cook's Lane, round the corner at the pillar box into Mayferry Street. It was the time of year for Wellington boots, and paper handkerchiefs, the smell of clothes drying indoors, hurrying home to the fire.

Colin had not told Marion about the strange feeling he had had when he looked at her photograph, neither at the time, nor later. It was, after all, the vaguest of sensations, and one which he could hardly even put into words; whatever it was he thought he had recognized in the picture, it certainly was not something he could point to, and say, 'There is the clue we have been waiting for'. And that being so, he realized that it would be unfair to raise Marion's hopes with a story so indefinite and unhelpful, especially when she was in her present mood for clutching at the frailest of straws. For a while, the matter of what it was that his eye had seen and his brain failed to recognize, tickled and irritated his thoughts whenever they were not too busy with something else, but as the days passed with no burst of enlightenment, it moved inevitably to the back of his mind as more pressing problems began to fill up the front of it. For problems there were, problems such as he had never had to grapple with before, all centred on a disappointment so terrible that Colin seemed to go around from morning till night in an angry haze, aware of nothing but a tight knot of grief and outrage which seemed to be situated somewhere between his stomach and his heart.

What made it all doubly bleak and trying was the fact that this ought really to have been a cheeful, happy time of year, when the cold and the damp outside were forgotten in a blaze of gaiety and goodwill. Christmas was only a few weeks away, and Colin, like everyone else, should have been caught up in the special excitements of December, the gift-buying and gift-hiding, school parties and carol-singing, writing Christmas cards and the making of plum puddings. And indeed, physically, he was; Christmas was everywhere, loud and obtrusive, stringing out its spruce trees from the Mound to Leith, and somehow that was worse than it would have been if it had been possible to cancel the whole thing because Colin Ramsay wanted no part in it. It was terrible to be obliged to take part in celebrations for which one had no heart — no pleasure, no joy, only that knot of anger and discontent, souring every day.

It had all begun one Tuesday afternoon, two weeks before the end of term, when Colin had been summoned from class to his Headmaster's study, to be told that he had been allocated one of the coveted places in the School Orchestra. It was something he had been longing and hoping and working for, for more than two years, ever since the night when Jen and Jake had taken him to hear the Hallé Orchestra give a concert in the Usher Hall, and with Mozart's music still exploding wonderfully inside his head, he had persuaded his mother to let him take lessons on the flute. And now, his long dream had come true. For one exultant, enchanted moment, he stood staring speechlessly at Dr. Fowler, too happy even to be embarrassed, although he could feel his face turning scarlet, then, as inevitably as a pendulum on its return stroke, the dry, precise voice sliced his happiness away.

'I suppose,' it said, 'that you have an instrument of your own?'

Colin went on staring, delaying the fatal moment of his reply. It was not a difficult question to answer; its answer was 'Yes', or 'No'. The difficulties began behind the answer. Presently, after the Headmaster, thinking that the boy had not understood him, had repeated his question with the words varied a little, Colin explained that he did not have a flute of his own. His mother paid for his lessons, but he was allowed to use one of the school instruments, and take it home two evenings a week to practise on. Whereupon Dr. Fowler nodded gravely, and pursed his lips, and tapped with his dry fingernails on the edge of his desk until Colin wanted to stamp and scream at him for his indifference to this terrible thing that was happening. In fact, he did Dr. Fowler an injustice; as Colin spoke, the Headmaster was remembering him and his story, and the regret in his voice was genuine as he pointed out that this arrangement was really only made for beginners, and that they had to insist that members of the Orchestra provide their own instruments, since the school ones were of poor quality and in short supply, and it was necessary to practise oftener than twice a week. He said that of course he did not expect Colin's answer immediately; he had till January to make up his mind, and perhaps if he were to discuss the matter with his mother . . .? Colin had no intention of trying to explain to Dr. Fowler the reasons why such a discussion was doomed from the outset, so he said he would, got out of the study somehow, and returned to his Maths class, with his mind a whirling chaos and the knot of misery already pulling tight inside him.

That evening, he and his mother had a session in the kitchen which was very painful for both of them. Sitting at the table, twisting his feet nervously round the legs of his chair, Colin told Mrs. Ramsay what Dr. Fowler had said, explaining very carefully that unless some way could be found of letting him have a flute of his own, his precious place in the Orchestra would be given to someone else. And as he had expected, Mrs. Ramsay replied that the expense of buying a flute was such as to make it completely out of the question.

'I'm sorry, Colin, but you know I just don't have any money to spare for that kind of thing.'

Which, Colin knew, was the final statement, and where the subject should have been dropped, before things were said which would be regretted later. But disappointment made him cantankerous, and being hurt himself, he wanted at that moment more than anything to hurt someone else. That normally he would have done anything in the world to shield his mother from the kind of pain he was inflicting on her now made no difference, at a time when unhappiness was already beginning to twist him into the shape of a stranger whom soon neither of them would be able to recognize. He was cruelly determined not to let her out easily this time.

'You could buy me one for Christmas,' he said perversely, as if he had not heard a word she said. 'I'd much rather have a flute than Rugby boots and a new strip.'

He had been scattering hints about Rugby boots since August, and knew for a fact that they had already been bought, and hidden away in Jen's kitchen cupboard till Christmas morning. Mrs. Ramsay cupped her thin sallow face in her hands, and looked miserably at him across the corner of the kitchen table.

'It just so happens that I can afford to buy you Rugby boots,' she said, with a patience which Colin observed, and took amiss, 'but I cannot afford to buy you a flute. Do you have any idea what flutes cost, Colin?'

Colin said sullenly that he had, having called in at Rae Mackintosh's music shop in Queensferry Road on his way home to find out.

'Then in that case,' Mrs. Ramsay said, 'you'll understand why you can't have one.' She gave him a look that tried to appeal to the person she had known until this evening, and went on, 'Colin, you know that there's nothing I'd like better than to be able to indulge you in this, and I do think you might spare a thought for the way I'm feeling at this moment. Really, I don't know what else to say. I've never known you like this before. You never ask me for anything.'

Colin looked back angrily into her bewildered eyes, and thought how unfair it was that, just because he was asking for something now, she should use his past restraint to rebuke him.

'I've never wanted anything before,' he said.

It was true. He had thought he wanted things, but there had never in all his experience been anything to compare with this great, overwhelming longing that was not for the flute itself, but for the music, and the joy of helping to make it. He heard his mother go on talking, talking, filling the angry silence with words, repeating herself, saying how much she would like to say 'Yes', how much she hated having to say 'No'. She kept asking him to understand.

'We do have enough to make ends meet, Colin, enough to live on, and to pay for the extra things that have to be accounted for, like the rates, and your school fees, and the flute lessons, and mending the roof when it leaks. Only there never seems to be anything left over. Of course I knew when I said you could have lessons that eventually you were going to need a flute of your own, but I didn't expect it to be so soon, and in any case, two years ago, I thought that by now I'd be free to go out to work again. But things just haven't happened that way, and much as I'd like to give you all the things you've had to go without, I also have to consider Marion.'

Whereupon, because he was tired and angry and deeply upset, Colin said the unforgivable thing, the thing which must never be said, must never even be thought. He said it coldly and on purpose, which is not at all the same as saying that he meant it.

'Of course, of course. I might have known we'd get round to her eventually. You always have considered her before me, which is pretty unfair, when all this mess is her fault anyway.'

Then Mrs. Ramsay slapped him; for a shocked instant he saw

51

her face above him, flaming and with eyes like black stones, before her hand cracked down across his cheek, a stinging blow that made his head spin and his eyes water. He slid out of his chair, and bolted out of the room, leaving his mother crying silently between her fingers.

The next few days were dreadful. Mrs. Ramsay apologized to Colin; Colin would not apologize to Mrs. Ramsay. Hurt and ashamed, they looked at each other like strangers, while Marion, completely in the dark as to what had happened, watched them with frightened, solemn eyes. With a quite uncharacteristic obstinacy, Mrs. Ramsay determined to carry on as if nothing were the matter at all. It was Christmas, and Christmas was going to be celebrated in every particular whether anyone was in a fit condition to enjoy it or not. She bought the Christmas tree, rammed it relentlessly into the coal bucket, and commanded Colin to help Jen and Jake decorate it. She made a large plum pudding, with wretchedness in her heart. Paper streamers were unearthed from the back of the broom-cupboard, and hung in festoons across the hall, where they swayed and shivered in the cross-draughts from the doors, their garishness accentuating the dinginess of the wallpaper and brown varnish. Mrs. Ramsay and Colin both thought privately that they had never seen anything so hideous in their lives, but they did not say so to each other. They did not say much to each other except 'Thank you', and 'Please shut the door'.

For the second time, Colin had been chosen to sing in the choir at the school's Carol Concert on the night before the holidays began. It was one of the important occasions of the school year, and he had been looking forward to having his mother come to hear him sing, especially since this year he had a solo part, as the page in 'Good King Wenceslas'. She had come last year, and had taken him to the *Bella Napoli* in Grindlay Street for a huge Italian supper afterwards, while Jen stayed with Marion. They had been saying all year what fun it had been, and promising themselves that they were going to do exactly the same this time round. But when the official invitation from Dr. Fowler, which was always sent to the parents of performers, dropped through the letter-box among a scattering of Christmas cards, and Mrs. Ramsay passed it over to Colin with a look of questioning in her eyes, Colin, who hardly recognized himself any more, said stonily that he thought he would rather she did not come. Mrs. Ramsay said nothing, but she tore up the invitation card in front of him, and tossed the pieces onto the fire. The matter was not mentioned again.

The concert was on a Wednesday evening, and when Colin got home from school, he found his clean shirt laid out in his bedroom, his best shoes polished by the bed, and the money for his bus fares on top of the chest of drawers, between the bottled snake and his model of the *Golden Hind*. His electric heater had been switched on, so that he would not have to change in the cold. He had to hurry, because although the concert did not begin till seven o'clock, performers had to be in their places by a quarter-past six, so that Mr. Coombes, the music master, could give everybody a last harangue, and rehearse yet again the several items which were not to his liking.

Colin ate his tea, washed, dressed, pocketed his money and left the house without opening his sulky mouth to anyone. He knew that Marion was sitting by the window, as she always was when he was going somewhere special, to wave to him, but he would not look in her direction; only after he had walked twenty yards along the pavement did a sudden surge of remorse, the first decent feeling he had had for a long time, make him turn and run back to number seventeen. But he was too late, for the curtains had already been drawn across the window. So he told himself he didn't care, and made himself hard again, and walked up to Queen Street to wait for a bus.

The atmosphere in the school Hall was stuffy and cold at the same time, for although by ten to seven it was full of people, all breathing and using up the oxygen in the centrally-heated upper air, blasts of cold from the open doors circulated busily round the floor, numbing feet and legs while the rest of the body kept reasonably warm. It was a damp, foggy night outside, and it seemed that the audience was drawing the fog indoors with it, because as well as being dim, which it always was after dark due to the inadequacy of the hanging lamps to the task of lighting so vast a space, the Hall was misty and full of winter.

From his place in the front row of the choir, which was ranged on stage upon a perilously steep erection of battens and scaffolding, Colin listened moodily to the beloved cacophony of the Orchestra's tuning up below him, and watched the parents arrive — fur-coated, confident Edinburgh mothers, with coloured hair and fingerfuls of diamond rings, each accompanied by a discreetly successful Edinburgh father, going a little bald and wearing a plain dark suit with an Old Boys' Club tie. The fathers greeted each other with subdued heartiness, while the mothers compared fur coats, and smiled dazzlingly. Colin was bored; he had no one to watch for, and he could not even pass the time, as Marion would certainly have done, by making up stories about the fathers and mothers. They all shared the same story, and Colin knew it by heart already. The fathers were lawyers or bankers, or civil servants who worked in the Government Offices at St. Andrew's House, they drove Jaguars or Rovers, took their sons fishing on Sundays, and were past-Presidents of the Rotary Club. The mothers went shopping in their Minis and Hillman Imps, had rows with traffic wardens, had appointments every week at the hairdresser's, and were so tired of holidays in Tenerife and Corfu that really they thought they might try Bermuda this year for a change. They all lived in modern houses, in suburbs like Barnton and Fairmilehead, kept dogs, and were going to give their sons very fast cars on their seventeenth birthdays. They were as remote from Colin Ramsay as were the Aborigines, and a great deal less interesting. He watched them dully, and hungered for a flute in his mind.

At last the prefects were closing the doors, politely shooing the latecomers to seats at the back of the Hall. The boys stood up as Dr. Fowler and his party of important guests filed into the front row. Mr. Coombes, to the accompaniment of some sporadic applause, lumbered on to the rostrum, shifting suspiciously from foot to foot, as if testing its ability to bear his weight, and raised his baton. The preliminary cackle of coughing, as inevitable as music at a concert, subsided, and the proceedings of the evening were underway.

> *On Christmas night all Christians sing,*
> *To hear the news the angels bring;*
> *News of great joy, news of great mirth,*
> *News of our Merciful King's birth.*

It would have been a mistake to come to the Carol Concert expecting variety and innovation, but not a mistake which anyone who knew the school would have been likely to make. Indeed, great pride was taken in the fact that the programme never changed from one year to the next, from one decade to the next. It was called Tradition. From the 'Sussex Carol' at the beginning to 'Good King Wenceslas' at the end, from the

Overture to Handel's *Messiah* and Corelli's 'Christmas' Concerto, zestfully performed by the Orchestra, to the Scripture readings by the Head Prefect, everything was deliberately kept the same. 'Now, boys,' Mr. Coombes would say in the middle of every October, 'it is high time that we began to practise for the Concert. . . . You will have your music from last year. . . .' And in the Hall, on The Night, this year's fur coats and dark suits were like last year's fur coats and dark suits; even Dr. Fowler, in his black gown and red hood, accompanied by the Lord Provost of Edinburgh, seasonably hung about like a Christmas tree with his chain of office, and the Members of the School Board of Governors and their wives, might have been there since last year, petrified, occupying the front row for twelve months, unchanging, unchanged.

> *God rest you merry, Gentlemen,*
> *Let nothing you dismay,*
> *Remember Christ our Saviour*
> *Was born on Christmas Day . . .*

It had not occurred to Colin last year, or indeed in any of the previous years since he had come to this school at the age of seven, but it was very obvious now, that the carols were chosen deliberately to taunt the miserable with their cheerful tunes and constant, trying references to gladness, and joy and mirth. It was worse than having paper streamers in the hall at home, and a Christmas tree in the sitting-room, worse than seeing coloured lights in Princes Street or having to go to Thomas's and Vincent's party on Saturday. It was worse because Colin loved the bright picture-words and the dancing tunes, but the hatred and anger inside him, which should never have been allowed to touch anything so precious, were rubbing up against them, fouling their beauty, perhaps for ever.

> *The rising of the sun,*
> *And the running of the deer,*
> *The playing of the merry organ,*
> *Sweet singing in the choir.*

On the floor of the Hall, at Colin's feet, the members of the Orchestra, in white shirts, sawed and blew and hammered cheerfully, raising the music which soared blithely past him on its way to the ceiling, enjoying themselves. Automatically, he picked out the flute part, playing it over in his head.

> *In dulci jubilo,*
> *Now sing with hearts aglow . . .*

It was while the choir was sitting down, and the strings of the Orchestra were performing Handel's Largo, that Colin caught sight of his mother. The Concert had been underway for an hour and a half, and he could not imagine how it was that he had not noticed her before. Probably it was because it had never crossed his mind that she might be there. She was sitting about five rows from the back, at the left hand side of the Hall, her bare dark head and green tweed coat conspicuous in the welter of fur and exotic millinery which surrounded her. She was looking straight at him, and Colin knew, although he had just that minute spotted her, that she had been looking straight at him ever since she came into the Hall. She had not come to look at anyone else. So in spite of his rudeness and unkindness, although he had not said good-bye to her, or waved to Marion at the window, she had put on her coat, and come. . . .

Applause for Largo. There was a moving and a rustling in the Hall, and with a sense of having been caught out, Colin started into awareness that it was time for 'Good King Wenceslas', the carol in which he was to sing a solo part. Afterwards, when he thought about it, it would seem to him strange that up to this point he had not felt a single twinge of nervousness, but he supposed that it was because, during the terrible days before the Concert, he had been too preoccupied with his grief over the flute to spare attention for anything as trifling as a solo part in a Christmas carol. He had sung at all the rehearsals, but that was quite a different matter from singing at a performance. And now, belatedly, in the very instant when the choir rose to its feet, a flood-gate seemed to burst open, and a panic washed over him as dark and cold as the sea. All the natural nervousness which should have been spread thinly over many days bore down on him thickly, suffocating him. He forgot his flute, and his quarrel with the world. He was one small boy, standing on a stage in front of fifteen hundred people, and they were actually expecting him to sing. It was not believable. Far away, he was aware of a sighing little stir of anticipation. This was the carol that the boys had been waiting for, the one they liked best, because it announced that Christmas and the holidays had really come at last. That was all it meant to them, whereas to him. . . . Mr. Coombes raised his hands. The drums rolled, the Orchestra played, the voices passed his head like thunder.

> *Good King Wenceslas looked out,*
> *On the feast of Stephen,*
> *When the snow lay round about,*
> *Deep and crisp and even:*
> *Brightly shone the moon that night,*
> *Though the frost was cruel,*
> *When a poor man came in sight,*
> *Gathering winter fuel.*

> *'Hither, page, and stand by me . . .'*

Robinson of the fifth form was singing Wenceslas. From the bass section in the rear, his deep, full voice penetrated confidently into the Hall, routing its vastness. A band of iron seemed to be encircling Colin's chest, and every second it was pulling tighter and tighter. He thought he was going to faint. With stretched round eyes, he watched Mr. Coombes' face, white and pear-shaped and perspiring, shining featureless in front of him, going a little fuzzy towards its rim. Then, just as he knew for certain that his tongue was glued to the roof of his mouth, that when he tried to open his mouth, no sound was going to come, and all would be disaster beyond repair, there moved into focus another face, beyond the music master's shoulder, and its dark eyes were looking calmly and steadily into his. Like someone grasping a lifeline, he fixed his gaze on the face he knew, took a great gasp of breath, and sang,

> *'Sire, he lives a good league hence,*
> *Underneath the mountain,*
> *Right against the forest fence,*
> *By St. Agnes' Fountain.'*

Colin heard his own voice as if it were someone else's, fresh and clear, rising through the air like the strong notes of an instrument, and one fear left him, never to return.

> *'Bring me flesh, and bring me wine,*
> *Bring me pine logs hither. . . .'*

That was Robinson singing again, then the choir, calling out all around him. The words were as familiar as a nursery rhyme, but to Colin it was as if he were hearing them now for the first time, so personal and important did they seem, and as the great song about kindness and caring for others pealed out of a hundred throats and echoed through the Hall, something inside him broke, but instead of injuring him, this breaking healed him, and brought him a kind of peace.

> *'Sire, the night is darker now,*
> *And the wind blows stronger,*
> *Fails my heart I know not how,*
> *I can go no longer . . .'*

It was not that in that moment he stopped wanting his flute, or that not being able to have it hurt him any less. That pain was continuing, but the anger and bitterness melted out of it, leaving it bearable. He stopped blaming everyone else for his misfortune, and at once his misfortune ceased to be the most important thing in the world. For he now knew with his understanding something which previously he had known by instinct, but had for a little while forgotten. People matter more than things. He was so tired, he thought he could not stand on his feet until the end.

> *In his master's steps he trod,*
> *Where the snow lay dinted;*
> *Heat was in the very sod*
> *Which the Saint had printed.*
> *Therefore, Christian men, be sure,*
> *Wealth or rank possessing,*
> *Ye who now will bless the poor*
> *Shall yourselves find blessing.*

Without actually knocking anyone over, Colin managed to slither and push his way through the slow, polite procession of parents and boys shuffling down the centre aisle of the Hall. He burst out at the head of it into the vestibule, and caught up with his mother, who had paused to turn up the collar of her coat before facing the creeping chill of the wet night beyond. Not caring now who saw him, Colin pushed his hand under her elbow, and together, leaving the lights and voices behind them, they walked away down the dark, shrub-fringed verge of the drive. Not till they had passed through the school gates, and crossed the road to wait for a bus, did either of them speak. Then Mrs. Ramsay said, 'You sang so beautifully.'

'I was scared.'

'I know.'

'Was it obvious?'

'Only to me.'

'I was all right when I looked at you.'

'Yes. I'm glad.'

There was frost in the air, yet dampness lay thick and brown over the city, sticking to their coats and hair in a million pinhead drops. Holding themselves together stiffly, and moving their feet because of the cold, they watched the column of headlamps moving slowly down the drive opposite, piercing the mist with their beams. One after another, cars nosed through the gate, slowed, and swung out into the stream of traffic with important little spurts of speed. The wet surface of the road gleamed like phosphorous under the neon lights, and the faces which flashed past, framed momentarily in car windows, were an ill shade of green. A few other boys and their parents crossed the road to join them at the bus stop. Colin glanced at his mother's face, expressionless under the strange light, and he wondered what she was thinking. Of course he could be wrong, but just in case, 'I'd hate it if you were one of these furry women with hats,' he said. 'I would, really.'

Mrs. Ramsay laughed, and said she didn't think it would ever have been her style. Then the bus came.

'Would you like me to take you somewhere for supper?' she asked him, as they trundled along between buildings all blurred and distorted through the streaming windows of the bus. 'We have time, if you'd like it.'

'I'd rather go home,' Colin said.

They got off the bus in York Place, and walked downhill in friendly silence, with half the lights of the city hanging softly before them in the haze, like tumbled golden stars. Then round the corner into Mayferry Street, shadowy and private in its night-life, with its own lamps surrounded each by a thin halo of rainbow flecks, dying out at the edges into darkness. There was no one about; only a little brown cat, high-stepping on fastidious, velvet-slippered feet, crossed the pavement in front of them, and slipped through the railings of number twenty-three.

'I'm tired,' Colin said.

Mrs. Ramsay looked down at him on the doorstep, as she rummaged for the key in the bottom of her bag.

'I'm not surprised,' she said gently. 'There's nothing more tiring than a long anger, I think.'

'It's over now,' said Colin.

7

A Jig-saw Puzzle

On Christmas night it was Colin's turn to sleep badly, which was not perhaps surprising, since he had spent the whole day eating. Turkey, plum pudding, chocolate gateau, ice-cream, fruit, biscuits, cheese, toffees, had followed one another down his throat, and he had cheerfully accepted second helpings of everything offered by Jen, who had insisted on cooking the Christmas dinner to give Mrs. Ramsay a rest. Marion had watched him in uneasy fascination, as if anticipating an explosion, Jake had egged him on, and Mrs. Ramsay, feeling ashamed, had warned him tartly that if he were sick he need expect no sympathy. He was not sick, but when he eventually went to bed, long after his usual time, he found that sleep had deserted him. He was wide awake; his stomach felt as large and as hard as a football, and however he tried to position himself in the bed, he could not get comfortable. So he wriggled and twisted and tossed in the darkness, hearing with a sense of grievance the church clock boom out twelve, one, two, three, and the irritating, tinny echo, two minutes later, of the clock on the stair, too silly even to tell the time properly. Then at last he fell into a restless, uneasy sleep. But troubled dreams came to him; through them he seemed to be searching endlessly for something which all the while eluded him, and indeed he had no idea what it was he sought. He was alone, and cold, wandering silent and ghostly through the empty, moonlit corridors of the school at night, gliding into the murky, church-like vastness of the Hall, stumbling over chairs, afraid to glance up into the unthinkable darkness of the roof, hearing breathing, sure that the black air was thick with eyes. Then, with the peculiar illogicality of dreams, he seemed to pass out of the Hall and find himself in the loft of his own house, a tent of gloom and cobwebs high above the places where people lived; the elephant's leg was on the move, the buzzard was ruffling its feathers, fixing him purposefully with its wild and bitter eye. Jake was standing at the foot of the ladder, telling him to hurry, hurry, but he was searching among the dust and spiders. . . . Now it was time to go, for he heard the thump of the leg approaching, but the ladder had disappeared, and Colin was kneeling by the edge of the trapdoor, looking down a deep well at Jake. Only as he gazed, it was not Jake any more, it was the other young man, the one in the photograph, in his kilt and soldier's jacket, and he was calling up to him, 'Turn round, turn round. . . .' Colin turned, but as he did so he lost his balance, and fell backwards through the hole. He was falling down the well of the staircase, from the top of the house to the bottom, down, down, into darkness. . . . Colin woke with a start, and in a split second knew what it was that he had not been able to remember, three weeks ago, when he looked at Marion's photograph.

His first impulse was to jump out of bed, and run through to Marion's room to tell her, but a moment's reflection changed his mind. He had no idea how long he had been asleep, and for all he knew it was still only four o'clock in the morning. And even if, as he thought quite likely, Marion was awake, she was in a room which she shared with her mother, and Colin could just imagine what Mrs. Ramsay would have to say if he came prancing in for a chat in the middle of the night. Liberties were given and taken at Christmas, but there was a limit, and Colin knew quite well what lay on the far side of it. Marion would have to wait until the morning. But meanwhile . . . Colin switched on his bed-lamp, slipped out of bed, and with his warm toes shrinking like curling starfish from the startling cold of the linoleum, he crossed the room to the little table where he did his homework and made his model ships. He searched around for a pencil, and tearing a sheet from his history notebook, wrote in large, untidy letters the two words 'LOFT BOX'. Then he hopped back to bed, pushed the paper under his pillow, and switched off the light. As well, he thought, to be on the safe side. He had forgotten once, and he did not want to forget again. He pulled the quilt up to his nose, and fell asleep.

Mrs. Ramsay was an early riser. Even on mornings when she did not have to prise Colin out of bed for school, and spend a frantic hour frying bacon and making toast, and seeing to it that Colin had washed his neck, and put on a clean shirt, and remembered his books, and his music, and his lunch money, she was always out of bed by half-past six, because, she said, she enjoyed the contrast of having the quiet, early-morning time to herself. Not that she ever did very much with it, except sit in the kitchen with a cup of coffee, glancing at the newspaper and doing calculations in her head over the bills which all too often arrived in the morning post. Sometimes she was joined for coffee by Jake, who also liked to get up early and go walking, enjoying the silver stillness of the town in the empty hour between night and day, when the tall houses stood enchanted, and birdsong pierced the glassy air.

So when, on the morning of Boxing Day, Colin heard their voices through the wall which separated his little back bedroom from the kitchen, he knew that it was safe to get up, and go through to Marion with the news. He did not need the piece of paper, for he had remembered in the very instant of waking, and had been lying for the last half-hour, burrowing cosily, revelling in his knowledge, and imagining Marion's face when he told her. Now he got up, put on his dressing gown and slippers, and crossed the hall under the quivering decorations to her room.

Marion was awake, and waiting for her breakfast; she had had a better night than usual, and was pleased to see Colin, which was not always the case first thing in the morning.

'Good morning,' Colin greeted her, with a heartiness which Marion at once found highly suspicious. Colin was usually at his worst at this hour of the day, grumbling and truculent, and looking, as Jen said, as if he had swallowed a lemon. Marion turned her rumpled head on the pillow, and looked at him thoughtfully.

'You're looking very pleased with yourself,' she remarked, then she giggled, and said, 'I rather expected to hear that you had died in the night.'

'Died in the night?' repeated Colin, mystified.

'Of over-eating.'

Colin dismissed this absurdity with contempt.

'I've got a marvellous digestion,' he said boastfully, conveniently forgetting his sleepless hours, and his nightmares. Then, unable to contain himself any longer, he went on gleefully, 'I know something you don't know,' and capered a little on the carpet.

Marion smiled.

'I can see that,' she said. 'I wish you'd hurry up and tell me what it is.'

But Colin had no intention of being drawn so fast. He wanted to spin out the preamble to his revelation, and enjoy himself. So instead of telling her, he said, 'Where's that photograph I found upstairs? The one of kilted Charlie?'

'It's in the lacquered box,' said Marion patiently, 'where it always is. Why?'

'Get it out. I want to show you something.'

Marion was beginning to look interested, but, 'You'll have to get it out yourself, Colin,' she said. 'I couldn't reach it from here.'

Colin opened the box, took out the photograph, which was lying on top of everything else, and shivered.

'Do you suppose I could get into bed beside you?' he asked. 'I'm freezing.'

The bed was narrow, and Marion was lying immobile in the middle of it, but she gladly turned back the bedclothes so that Colin could squirm down into the strip between her and the bed's edge.

'Only keep your icicle toes away,' she warned him.

Colin lay down, and help up the photograph in front of both their faces.

'Now, what do you see?' he asked.

'What do you mean, what do I see?'

'In this photograph. What do you see?'

'Is this a quiz?'

'It's a test of observation,' said Colin, adding honestly, 'I failed.'

Marion decided to humour him. He was only a little boy, after all.

'Well,' she said, 'let me see. I see a soldier, or at least most of a soldier. His legs are rubbed away.'

'What else?'

Marion looked at the photograph closely, as if she did not know it by heart already.

'A curtain,' she said, 'and a table.'

'And on the table?'

'Some books, and a box. You can only see part of it, but it's a wooden box, with a lock —'

'Yes, yes!' Colin bounced, so that the bed springs went up and down, then recollected where he was, and stopped abruptly. 'It is a box, and —' he made his voice into a thrilling whisper '— I know where it is. *It's in our loft.*'

The effect of this on Marion was all that Colin could have desired. Her eyes dilated, she clutched at his arm with eager fingers, and an expression of astonished joy spread over her face.

'*Colin*! Are you sure?'

'Yes, I am. At least, if it isn't that one, it's identical. I can tell by the decoration around the keyhole. I saw it the night I was up there with Mother, finishing the tidying up.'

'But that was ages ago.'

'I know.'

'Then why on earth haven't you told me before this?' demanded Marion, not sure whether to be cross or not.

'I couldn't remember,' Colin explained, and he told her all about the strange feeling he had had when he looked at the photograph, but how until last night, when a dream roused his sleeping memory, he had had no idea what it was he had recognized. 'I just couldn't help it,' he said. 'However much I thought about it, nothing happened. And for a while, I was always thinking about something else.'

'Yes, I know,' Marion said, with ready sympathy. 'Mother told me about your flute. You know, Colin, you could have the rest of my savings, if it would help. I had to give some to Jen, to buy my Christmas presents, but there's still a bit left.'

'How much?'

'Three pounds and twelve pence.'

Colin laughed, and whispered into her ear the price of a flute.

'Oh, Lord,' said Marion in dismay, 'you can't be serious. We'd have to find a treasure chest, or make a fortune on the Stock Exchange.'

'Not much chance of either,' Colin said.

After breakfast, while Mrs. Ramsay was helping Marion to wash and dress, and bringing her to the sitting-room in her wheelchair, Colin went up to the loft to fetch down the box. He supposed that Jake must be early at work on the housebed, because as he passed the door of the workroom he could hear music within; Jake often listened to the Music Programme on his transistor radio as he worked. Someone on the radio was playing a flute, and just for a moment, as he went on upwards, Colin felt a sharp thrust of longing, like pain, and wondered whether it would always be like this now, and he would never again hear the music of the instrument he loved without this sudden, sickening sense of deprivation. But the thought was fleeting, and his mind was filled again with a spidery feeling of anxiety which had first assailed him at breakfast, and grew in intensity as he climbed the dark flights of stairs to the top of the house. Perhaps he should have looked first, before he told Marion, instead of trusting to anything as fickle as a dream. Suppose it was all a mistake, and the box was not really there at all? Suppose he had had some kind of hallucination? Marion's disappointment was going to be terrible. His feet passed from carpet to linoleum at the second floor with a clatter that startled him, so loud and sudden did it seem in the stillness of forgotten rooms and passages. Above him were the attic bedrooms, where once servants had slept, but long deserted now, opening out of a low, shabby passage with a small, uncurtained window at one end. At the other end, opposite the top of the stair, was a cupboard, very narrow and high, with a ladder which disappeared some ten feet up through a black, oblong trapdoor. This led into the loft, where the box was, or not. . . . Anxiously Colin climbed the ladder, and hoisted himself over the lip of the trapdoor into the mirk. He had brought a torch with him, because although a certain amount of faint, greyish light glimmered weakly through a dingy glass panel in the roof, it was too dark to see anything clearly. Memories of his nightmare of a few hours before returned to him, and although he was not usually a nervous person, Colin found the strange, half-remembered shapes looming around him just a little alarming. He flashed the torch around, and saw the shapes go by, transformed for a second to the reality which had been theirs in everyday use; ornaments, chairs, a bamboo plant-container, a white-eyed plaster bust of Calliope, Muse of Poetic Inspiration. She stared blindly at Colin, looking faintly displeased. He knew where the elephant's leg was, and did not let the torch-light touch it, but sent the yellow beam questing round the dim grey place, searching for the box. And the box was there. It was there, as he had seen it in his dream, as he must have seen it that night weeks before, before he saw it again under the soldier's hand. It was lying on top of a pile of old periodicals between Calliope and an enormous blue basin full of tarnished knives and forks. Colin snatched it up, snapped off the torch, and slid down the ladder in triumph. Banging the cupboard door shut, he flew downstairs, passing in a streak a sleepy, crumpled Jen, who was just emerging from her bedroom to go and make her breakfast.

'What on —' said Jen with a yawn, and 'What on —' said Jake, who was coming round the corner of the stair with a plank under his arm, but by the time they got to 'earth', Colin was already down in the hall. Gasping for breath, he catapulted into the sitting-room, deposited the box on Marion's knee, and collapsed at her feet.

'I knew it,' he said.

Marion stared at the box as if she were afraid to touch it. At last, however, she took courage, drawing her fingertips hesitantly over the dull, neglected wood, and since it did not disappear, she knew that it was real. But as often happens at such a time, what she said was feeble and inadequate, expressing nothing of all the wonder and excitement within her.

'I didn't think it would be so big,' she remarked.

Mrs. Ramsay, who was sweeping up the shower of Christmas tree needles from the carpet with a dustpan and brush, got up from her knees and came over to look.

'That isn't a box,' she said. 'It's a desk.'

It was a box, and it was also a desk. When Marion's trembling hands opened it — it was not locked — she saw that the rosewood box was cut through almost diagonally, instead of straight across, making a base and a lid shaped each like a cut-off wedge of cheese. When the box was opened out completely, the lid swung right back on its hinges to reveal inside a slanting writing-surface, covered with fraying, ink-stained red velvet. At the top was a long, divided compartment, holding a silver-capped ink bottle with curly flakes of dried ink still sticking to the inside of the glass, an india-rubber, and a curved tray for holding pens. The tray came out when its end was pressed, and underneath it was a little drawer, containing two stumps of pencil, a paper clip, a piece of green sealing wax, and a tiny silver key, belonging of course to the desk itself. The pen, if there had been one, had been removed.

Storage space in the desk was uncovered by lifting up the two halves of the writing surface, which were separately hinged, and came up independently of each other. The inside of the lid was empty, but when Marion opened the other compartment, she found to her delight that there were several things inside. She lifted them out slowly, one at a time, and passed them to Colin, who made a tidy row of them on the hearthrug. First came a few sheets of plain writing paper, wrapped around three white envelopes. Then there was a strip of five ornately designed postage stamps, bearing a bearded head which Mrs. Ramsay was able to tell them had belonged to King George V, and valued at one old penny each. Next came a bundle of unused bill-heads, engraved in curly, elaborate lettering, *J. & C. Ramsay & Sons, Licensed Grocers, 61-63 Hanover Street, Edinburgh. Estd. 1846.*

'But none of this tells us anything,' Colin was beginning, when Marion interrupted him in a voice that was tight to squeaking-point.

'Wait a minute, Colin. There's something else.'

And as she spoke, she lifted out a brown manilla envelope, of

67

the kind that has a small transparent window in its front. She pulled out the flap, and removed a folded piece of white paper. Colin got up, and went to look over her shoulder as she spread it out on the red velvet. Together they read what was written there, in perfect black copperplate writing, under the printed heading.

CHARLES JENNER & COMPANY
47-49 Princes Street   Edinburgh

To Charles Ramsay, Esq., 17, Mayferry Street.

To 2 doz. White Collars,	*£0-12-6d*
„ *6 prs. Wool Hose,*	*£0-18-6d*
„ *3 Silk Shirts,*	*£3-11-6d*
„ *1 Wool Waistcoat,*	*£2-0-0d*
	£7-2-6d

Payment received with thanks, 16th November, 1913.

Marion looked from Colin to her mother with happy eyes.

'So it was Charles Ramsay in the photograph,' she said. 'This is the proof.' Then, 'I was sure it was.'

Colin did not want to pour cold water, but still, 'It doesn't tell us anything else,' he pointed out. 'It's only a bill from his draper. Is there nothing else?'

Marion looked down into the bottom of the desk in perplexity.

'There's a lot of rubbish he should have put in the waste-paper basket,' she said. 'Pencil shavings, and bits of lead, and pieces of paper torn up small. I don't think he could have been a very tidy person by nature. Look.'

She lifted up a sample of the litter on the palm of her hand, and held it out for Colin to see. He flicked away the lead grit and tiny chips of pencil wood, and took up two of the shreds of paper, neither much more than a centimetre across. He peered at them closely.

'Marion,' he said, 'are there any more of these?'

'Yes, lots. Why?'

'Because they have writing on them. This one says "t-h-a", and this one has the word "more" and the letters "g-r-i" on it. I think these are pieces of a letter — either one he was writing himself, or one he had received from someone, and torn up.'

Marion watched him, realization of the possibility he was suggesting dawning slowly on her pale face.

'Colin, do you think — could we?' she asked, almost afraid to hope.

'Yes, we could,' said Colin firmly, then qualified his certainty, just a little, in case of disappointment. 'At any rate, we're certainly going to try.'

'It will be a jig-saw puzzle,' Marion said.

Half an hour later, Mrs. Ramsay left them busy by the fire, and went upstairs to thank Jen for their Christmas dinner, and join her for coffee in her scarlet sitting-room. Although there were nearly twenty years of difference in their ages, Jen and Mrs. Ramsay were very close friends. Jake was upstairs, working on the housebed, and Jen, after she had brought the coffee on a hand-woven tray, pressed Mrs. Ramsay to try a home-made biscuit, and sat down beside her on the sofa which she and Jake had built and upholstered themselves, remarked that she had been expecting Colin to come up and help, as he usually did when he had nothing else to do. To which Mrs. Ramsay replied that today Colin had, for once, found something else to do, and feeling that some explanation was necessary, she went on to tell Jen about the letter that Marion had found, and the photograph, and the desk which only that morning had turned up to link the two together.

'It's an interesting connection, in a way,' she said, 'although of course it can only be coincidental. A house like this is full of such things — that's what makes living in it such a nightmare. I've tidied it from top to bottom in these last few weeks, and you've seen what I've thrown out, yet I swear I could start again tomorrow, and still find as much to discard. It's all such useless stuff — not old enough to be interesting, but too old to be any good to anyone. And yet —' Mrs. Ramsay paused, smiling half at Jen and half to herself '— do you know, Jen, when they opened that shabby old table-desk, and took out all these commonplace, everyday things — envelopes, and little pencils, and old bill-heads from the shop — they looked at them as if they were — well, magic, I suppose. It's the only word I can think of.'

The two women looked at each other and laughed indulgently, lifting their eyebrows.

'Well, anyway, it's nice to think that Marion is taking an interest in something again,' said Jen, who was kind and affectionate, but had never known very much about the nature of magic. And

Mrs. Ramsay, who had once known better than most people that the best of all magic is rooted in the common, everyday things of life, but had since forgotten, accepted another biscuit and agreed with her.

At four o'clock, the early winter night breathed darkness over Mayferry Street, muffling its plainness in a cloak of mystery. The street lights came on, and lights in the houses opposite the sitting-room window of number seventeen, but Marion, who usually liked to sit at this hour in the firelight, watching the night arrive, today only noticed with impatience that she was having difficulty in seeing the snow-shower of paper pieces on the tray across her knee.

'Light,' she said tersely to Colin, and Colin, who knew as well as she did that this was no time for wasting words, rose without remark and switched on the lamp behind her chair. The soft pink light washed over them, touching flashes of gold in Marion's brown hair, defining the circle where she and Colin had been sitting spellbound since morning, patiently reconstructing the text of a letter which Charles Ramsay had torn up more than sixty years before. They had worked without rest, apart from one short, reluctant pause for lunch, and now, as the day drew towards evening, they were still at work. Colin was tired, and Marion was exhausted, but they were so engrossed in what they were doing, so buoyed up by their excitement and the certainty that at last they were on the threshold of a real discovery, that they did not even notice how weary they were.

The task had not been an easy one; indeed, had it not been for a desperation of curiosity to know what the letter had contained, and later on the spur of partial success, they would have given up a dozen times. To begin with, they had had to pick out every single scrap of paper they could find in the bottom of the desk, poking into every cranny, and lay them on the tray which Colin had brought from the kitchen. Some of the pieces were unbelievably small. As Marion said, it did not look as if Charles Ramsay had torn up his letter and tossed it aside in the usual careless way, but rather as if he had sat for a long time, shredding it into fragments, and dropping them down absent-mindedly into the bottom of his desk.

'The way you might do if you were thinking very hard about something else, and not really noticing what your fingers were doing,' she said perceptively to Colin.

Colin said that he would not have thought of that possibility for himself, and Marion replied that she had only thought of it because she had done it, or something similar, often.

'It's the easiest thing in the world,' she said, 'to let your hands do something, without paying the least attention to what they're doing. Things you do with your hands don't occupy your mind, they only help you to concentrate on quite different thoughts —'

She broke off abruptly, and Colin thought no more about it, but if Mrs. Ramsay had been in the sitting-room at the time, she might have found in these words an important clue to another mystery.

'We'll put the pieces together loosely on the tray first,' Marion had said, 'then we'll paste them all down onto another sheet of paper, so that they don't blow away the minute someone opens the door.'

Colin agreed that this was a sound idea, and went off to his room to fetch a sheet of stiff drawing paper, a glue-bottle and a brush, but when he came back it was to find Marion groaning, because, she said, she had just made a most horrible discovery.

'The paper is written on on both sides,' she said. 'That means it will be twice as difficult to fit the pieces together, and we can't glue it down, because if we do, we shan't be able to read what's on the back of it.'

She looked really crestfallen for a moment, but now it was Colin's turn to be resourceful.

'We need transparent paper,' he said, 'so that the writing will show through. If we get the front right, it stands to reason that the back will come right too. I know — I'll get a sheet of that thin greaseproof paper that Mother uses to wrap up my sandwiches when I'm playing away. There's some in the kitchen drawer.'

That problem solved, they began. The best idea, Marion said, would be to imagine that it was a jig-saw puzzle, with words instead of a picture, and proceed from there. Since usually, when making up a jig-saw, one began by making a border of pieces with straight edges, that was what they would do first. What they did not anticipate was that it would take more than an hour, and that there would be four pieces missing. Only one was found after another search of the desk. Colin eyed Marion uneasily.

'If there are lots of pieces missing,' he ventured.

But Marion had suddenly been overtaken by one of her moods of confidence and optimism, such as she had been experiencing spasmodically ever since finding the letter from Alan Farquhar,

71

away back in October. It would fade again, no doubt, but for the moment, her satisfaction in the very unexpectedness of what they were now doing enabled her to make light of difficulties. Had not the impossible already happened, and more than once?

'We must hope not,' she said encouragingly to Colin, 'but if there are —' she smiled at him humorously '— then we shall just have to read between the lines.'

Colin smiled back, reassured by her calmness. If only she were always like this. . . .

They toiled all day. Slowly but surely, letters became portions of words, '17, Mayf . . . . eet, Edinb . . . . 1st . . . . . My de . . . nk yo . . . . your le . . . .' and gradually, as the minutes of Boxing Day ticked themselves into hours, such fragments began to form themselves into disjointed scraps of prose.

'. . . . thank you for your letter of Monday last, but must confess . . .' and '. . . . which was to have been placed in my care until your return, and a le . . . .' This sounded familiar, and therefore hopeful, but the most exciting moment of the whole day came when two scraps of paper, one with the letters 'r Al', and the other with the letters 'an', were slotted into place, and they were able to read 'My dear Alan'. They said nothing, but hugged each other wildly, almost overturning the tray.

From then on, the letter unfolded itself under their eyes. Despite the difficulty of having to try both sides of every piece of paper against both sides of most of the other remaining pieces of paper, and the additional trial of the letter's being much blotted and scored out, enthusiasm drove them on, and progress of course became more marked the nearer they got to the end. By half-past five, when Mrs. Ramsay began to bring in the tea, with the observation that they had done quite enough for today, and must stop now, before their eyesight was ruined, the whole page was assembled, and only the last five lines remained to be pasted down. Six pieces were missing, but it was not difficult to deduce what had been written on them.

'Mother, you have to let us finish after tea,' pleaded Marion. 'We're so near the end, and I couldn't bear to have to wait till tomorrow. Please.'

'Yes, do let us,' urged Colin. 'Honestly, Mother, it won't take half an hour, and then we'll be able to tell you what the letter says.'

Mrs. Ramsay looked from one eager face to the other, tried to be firm and say 'No', but instead found herself saying 'Yes'.

'But not more than twenty minutes,' she warned. 'You must both be tired out.'

Then they realized that they were, but it was the first time they had noticed it.

After a large tea of Christmas left-overs, which Colin enjoyed to the full, and Marion more than usual, Mrs. Ramsay said that for today she would wash up without Colin's assistance, while he and Marion finished pasting down the letter.

'But that is to be all for tonight,' she said. 'Remember, Marion, I mean it.'

'Yes, mother,' said Marion.

Half an hour later the job was done, and with the door shut and the old velvet curtains drawn over the winter night, they were all sitting round the fire to read and talk over the contents of the letter. The greaseproof paper had worked well; the glue seemed to make it more transparent, and it was quite easy to decipher what was written on the back, in Charles Ramsay's rapid-running, old-fashioned hand.

'You can read it,' Marion offered, holding out the sheet to Colin.

'No, you,' Colin said.

So Marion began, in a voice that trembled a little with excitement, but steadied as she went on:

"17, Mayferry Street,
Edinburgh 2.
1st July, 1914

My dear Alan,

I thank you for your letter of Monday last, but must confess that its contents shocked and grieved me. Perhaps I should be more grieved than shocked, for there is no mystery at all in the matter — the knowledge that I had a dishonest servant in my employ is not new to me. What distresses me most is that you, while a guest in this house, should have been his victim. You say that six months ago you left with Watt Davie, my servant at that time, a trunk, which was to have been placed in my care until your return, and a letter informing me of this. I have to tell you that I received neither trunk nor letter. The facts as I know them are these.

I returned from Italy on 1st March, to find the house in a troubled state, as a result of several things having gone missing, my brother Colin's studs, a ring belonging to my sister Alice, and several pieces of silver plate being the most valuable items. At this time it was not known who was suspect, more than another, and indeed Davie would have been the last to be blamed, because of his family's long tradition of service and friendship with mine. We were, as you may imagine, reluctant to call the police, and while we vacillated, I myself, coming up quietly behind him in my room — your room during my absence — caught Davie in the act of pocketing my watch. The villain swore he knew nothing of any other theft, and had been overcome only by the temptation of the moment, and although we made all manner of threats, and searched high and low, he stood by his story, and nothing was ever found. For his mother's sake, we would not take the matter to the police, so there was nothing for it but to dismiss him at once and without a reference. For some days the bold fellow continued to make a nuisance of himself by hanging around the kitchen door and trying to get into conversation with the housemaid Jean. They were said to be friendly, but she denied it. Finally Colin got hold of him, and told him that if he did not remove himself the police would be informed. Davie said that he had only been trying to persuade Jean to let him in so that he could fetch down his coat, which he had forgotten to take in the haste of his departure. However Colin said he would not set foot in the house again upon any pretext, and sent him about his business. He has not been seen since.

I go this evening to Mrs. Davie's in the Cowgate, to find out what she knows of her son's whereabouts, and wherever he is, I intend to find him, and discover what he did with your property. I know that he took none of it with him when he left this house, and from that fact I assume that he must have disposed of it locally, for lack of opportunity to take it further afield. I intend to know what happened, if it should take a year.

Alan, I cannot express how much this affair distresses me. If the contents of your trunk are not recovered, the loss to you, to me and, I believe, to many others is incalculable. Be sure that I shall do all in my power to recover your property and bring this man to justice — please God I can.

I shall hope to have news soon.

Your sincere friend,
Charles J. Ramsay."'

There was silence in the room after Marion had finished reading. Into it she said longingly, 'If only he had said what was in the trunk.'

But Mrs. Ramsay's mind seemed to be working in a different way.

'May I see the letter, please?' she asked.

Colin passed it over to her, and after she had glanced through it, marvelling privately at the miracle of patience and cleverness its reconstruction represented, she said, 'Yes, I see. That explains it.'

'What explains what?' enquired Colin.

'Why he didn't send it. Hadn't you asked yourselves that question? It's so terribly badly written, all alterations and scorings out — obviously he made a fair copy afterwards, and tore this one up. Poor man, what a dreadful letter to have to write. No wonder he had difficulty in finding the words. He must have been so terribly embarrassed and upset.'

They both agreed with this.

'But — Mother,' said Colin, 'if Charles Ramsay never got Alan Farquhar's letter, doesn't that mean that Watt Davie must have stolen it too? It had "By hand" written on it, if you remember.'

'It seems likely,' agreed Mrs. Ramsay.

'Well, then — why do you suppose he hid it in a book in the bookcase — wouldn't he have been wiser to destroy it?'

Mrs. Ramsay looked at Marion.

'What do you think, darling?' she asked.

Marion pondered for a moment, then she said, 'I suppose he thought that if he put it in the bookcase, and it was found later, people would think that Charles Ramsay had received it, and had put it there himself. There would be nothing to connect Watt Davie with it, would there?'

'I think that's your answer,' said Mrs. Ramsay to Colin. 'But the truth is that you'll probably never know for certain. In a matter like this, you have to do a lot of guessing, don't you?'

'That's what makes it interesting,' said Colin.

'I wonder if Charles Ramsay really did spend the next year looking for Watt Davie,' said Marion thoughtfully. 'I must say he sounds determined enough, doesn't he?'

Mrs. Ramsay did not answer her for a moment, but went on looking down at the letter on her lap. Then she said, rather reluctantly, 'I suppose it's possible, but I'm afraid it's not very likely.'

Her tone alarmed Marion.

'Why isn't it likely?' she asked quickly.

'Because, I think, he had only a month, before he had to start thinking about even more urgent things. You see, this letter is dated the first of July, 1914. By the first week in August, Britain was at war with Germany. We know now for certain that Charles Ramsay was swept up into that War, probably very early, because the young were the first to go. I expect that Alan Farquhar was swept up into it too, and the wretched Watt Davie. Perhaps we'll never know what happened next, but Charles Ramsay didn't have time on his side.'

8

Treasure Seekers

That night, for the first time, the people in the jig-saw letter came to life for Colin. The gift of breathing life into the figures who pass to and fro in the imagination was not as strongly developed in him as it was in Marion, but now, either because Marion's enthusiasm kindled his, or because the letter's bright glimpse of a past incident fired his imagination independently of hers, suddenly Colin was able to see Charles Ramsay and Alan Farquhar as human beings, alive and warm, instead of as statues stricken into immobility by the wand of time. As he sat in the firelight with his mother and Marion, and afterwards as he washed and got ready for bed, he could not stop thinking about them, and long after he was in bed, with the light out, they were still passing before the eye of his imagination, they and a whole family of Ramsays, who, Colin supposed, might have lived in this house in Mayferry Street more than half a century before. They had been real people, not the stylized, two-dimensional figures which he had previously imagined; they had had names and faces of their own, had got up and gone to bed, put on their long skirts and frock coats, talked, laughed, quarrelled and made up, eaten meals, opened letters, fed dogs, in the very rooms where Colin lived every day. Colin, Charles, Alice — these were three of them, and Colin supposed that there would have been others, and probably a father and mother too. One of them might have slept in the bed where Colin was lying now, his table might have belonged to another, his chest of drawers to a third. Their feet had passed up and down the stairs, their fingers turned the handles of the doors, tapped the barometer, opened the bookcase. Things Colin touched every day, they had touched in their time. Then they had vanished — well, not quite without trace, as it happened. They had a kind of life, while Colin and Marion remembered them. Yet it seemed strange, and rather sad to Colin, as he lay in his warm patch of the night, with the dark house piled above him, that if Marion had not found, in a book she was dusting, a letter from a stranger who wanted his friend to keep his trunk for him while he was away, a mere sixty years would have covered these Ramsays so completely that their descendants would not even have known their names.

The next few days provided no opportunity for Marion and Colin to discuss the jig-saw letter again, much less take any action concerning it. Jen and Jake always tried to give the Ramsay children a happy time at Christmas, and succeeded; it was not their fault that this year Colin and Marion privately wanted nothing more than to go into the sitting-room by themselves, and close the door, and spend an hour pouring over the paper patchwork which had spent sixty years as shreds of waste paper in the bottom of an abandoned desk. However, in the last days of the old year there never seemed to be an hour to spare, so they had to contain their impatience, and wait until time was empty again. Then, as Colin sensibly pointed out, they could mull over the letter at leisure, and meanwhile it would be silly not to devote themselves to the enjoyment of treats too extravagant to come frequently. Marion agreed with him, so they did not allow frustration to spoil their appreciation of the film show or the Chinese supper, the indoor barbecue or the visit of Jake's friend Will, who was a conjuror in his spare time. There was also a treasure hunt, during which Colin had a very strange experience.

The treasure hunt was held every year, on the thirtieth of December, and it was the climax to the programme of entertainments. On New Year's Eve, Jen and Jake went away to spend a few days with Jake's parents in Perthshire, and although there would be more fun when they came back on the third of January, by that time the holiday was nearly over, and Christmas really in the past. So this was the last of the special treats, and always one of the best. The hunt was devised by Jake who made up new clues every year, although the rules were always the same. The treasure-seekers were divided into pairs, Jen and Marion, Colin and Mrs. Ramsay. One partner was given a list of clues, each of which led to a place in the house where Jake had concealed a piece of paper with a puzzle on it. These papers had to be returned to the sitting-room and handed over to the other partner, whose job it was to work out the puzzles, which had words as answers. When all the papers were collected, and the puzzles solved, the words provided the final clue which enabled the runner to find the treasure. The Ramsays' treasures were always wonderful: they were made by Jen, out of cloth for Marion and Mrs. Ramsay, and from edible ingredients for Colin. It was a most exciting way to spend an evening.

At eight o'clock, they were ready to begin. Jen and Colin were the runners, Mrs. Ramsay and Marion the 'sitting partners' who worked out the puzzles. Jake gave Jen and Colin their list of clues, and Mrs. Ramsay warned them not to fall downstairs in the dark. Then they were off, and for the next few minutes those in the sitting-room had nothing to do but listen to the thudding of determined feet as Colin and Jen raced each other upstairs, and laugh at the distant cries of 'Beast', and 'Ouch', and 'It's mine, blast you', as they both tried to get into the broom cupboard at the same time. Then the feet were clattering down again, and Mrs. Ramsay and Marion were too busy with crosswords and anagrams to notice what their partners were doing any more.

For a while, Colin seemed to be falling over Jen at every turn. In the dim light on the second floor he could see her, with her long brown frock hitched up around her knees, to make running easier, scurrying to and fro in the rooms where he was himself searching for strips of paper that were pushed under carpets and hung on light-switches, and concealed in the folds of curtains. Even when he could not see her, Colin could smell the scent which Jake had given her for Christmas, and which had hung around her like a dress of flowers all week, and hear her whistling little tunes under her breath as she delved in cupboards and peeped into drawers. But then her clues must have drawn her away from him; as he groped under the embroidered cushion of an armchair for the clue that must be 'buried beneath the scarlet rose', he saw her pass the door, and heard her light footsteps descending to the floor below. The light went out on the landing. Colin knew that Jen had switched it off downstairs to tease him, and he was not going to give her the satisfaction of hearing him yell, as she hoped. He drew out his clue, put it in his pocket beside the two that were there already, and began to feel his way with his hands across the dark bedroom where he had been caught out when the light went off. He was not in the least afraid. The outline of the open door was in front of him, a grey rectangle against the blackness of the wall, and as his eyes became accustomed to the darkness he was able to see and avoid the shapes of furniture in his path. He moved towards the door, wondering whether it would be possible to creep downstairs, and pay Jen out by jumping on her from behind. But before he reached the door, in the complete silence which she had left in her wake, he heard a sound, so familiar and beautiful that a moment elapsed before its strangeness impinged upon his mind, and his body shuddered to a halt. Next door, in Jake's empty workroom, someone was playing a flute. Muffled by the wall, yet clear, the plaintive notes ran on Colin's ear, a tune he knew but could not name. He whispered to himself in the dark, 'Someone is playing a flute in the workroom.' And for a while, he could not move. Then the pure notes died, and in the returning silence, Colin's limbs sprang to life again. He leapt towards the landing and the stair, but before he could set his foot on the top step, another shock awaited him. Glancing to his right as he passed the workroom door, he saw a yellow ribbon of light shining out beneath it. He came downstairs so fast that he could scarcely stay on his feet. Jen came out of her bedroom and caught him in her arms; he held on to her, forgetting that he was twelve, and that this was not dignified.

'Steady on,' said Jen, wonderingly. She held him back from her, and peered into his white, startled face. 'What's the matter, love? Colin, I'm so sorry — I didn't mean to frighten you like this.'

Colin tried to tell her, but his mouth was so dry and his lips so rigid that the words would not come out. He was gasping like a fish on dry land as Jen drew him into her sitting-room, and made him sit down on the sofa. If he had been grown up, she would have poured him a whisky from the bottle Jake kept in the sideboard, but since he was not, she sat down beside him, put her arm around his shoulders, and said kindly, 'All right. Take it easy. Then when you're ready, tell me what happened.'

This time, Colin managed to say the main words. 'Upstairs. Someone upstairs.'

'Who?' said Jen.

'I don't know. Someone. In the workroom. Playing a flute.'

'Playing a flute?' said Jen. 'In the *workroom*? Oh, *Colin*!'

Her disbelief steadied him.

'I know it seems impossible,' he said. 'But I did hear it, quite clearly. And I saw a light, under the workroom door.'

Jen hugged him, then pushed him away from her.

'You're a silly ass,' she said. 'It would be the MacPhersons' television you heard — you always do, if they have their sitting-room window open. I think they must all be deaf in that house. As for seeing a light under the door, well of course you would, if it was dark on the landing. There's a street light outside the window, for heaven's sake.'

Colin tried to protest.

'It was brighter than that.'

'Of course it wasn't. It only seemed so because of the darkness. Really, Colin, you'll have to stop taking flute lessons — you're getting flutes on the brain.'

Colin wanted to believe her. His head had stopped reeling, and his terror was no longer like a drum beating in his chest. The cheerful commonplace of Jen's sitting-room was soothing him into believing the things her matter-of-fact voice was saying. He sighed deeply, blowing out his cheeks.

'Well, I suppose so,' he said.

'Of course,' said Jen firmly. 'Now come on — I'll come up with you, and we'll look, just to make sure, shall we?'

By now Colin was sufficiently recovered to find something humiliating in this suggestion. He was grateful to Jen, who had been there when he needed her, but her assumption that he would feel safer upstairs with her skirt to hide behind offended him. He went a little red.

'There's no need,' he said gruffly. 'I'm all right now. It was the McPhersons' telly, like you said. It couldn't have been anything else.'

Jen looked relieved.

'Then we had better be getting a move on,' she said cheerfully, 'and find the rest of these clues, or they'll think downstairs that we're lost. Have you many more to find?'

'Three,' said Colin.

'Same as me,' said Jen. '"Where Leicester met Elizabeth —"'

'*Kenilworth*,' said Colin, proving that he was still not quite himself. 'It's in our bookcase.'

'Well, thanks,' cried Jen gratefully. 'That's very helpful of you. Fancy Jake knowing that. . . .'

She skipped out of the room, leaving Colin telling himself that he was indeed a silly ass, for more reasons than one. Still, he was glad that the rest of his clues, too, led him to inhabited parts of the house. He accepted Jen's explanations because, like her, he had the kind of mind that always fastened on the least complicated solution to any problem, and this one was very convincing. The MacPhersons were Thomas's and Vincent's family, and Colin had been in their house when the television was on. It could have been heard in Princes Street. But all the same, he did not want to go upstairs again in the dark, at least not that night.

Colin and Mrs. Ramsay won the treasure hunt, but since there were prizes for everybody, no one was disappointed. Next morning, Jen and Jake set out for Perthshire in the blue van, leaving Colin and Marion, in the quiet aftermath of their departure, to give their attention at last to other concerns. Colin had, he thought, quite got over his fright of the night before; he even told Marion about it at breakfast time, when they were together in the kitchen. Mrs. Ramsay had gone out early to do her shopping, because the shops would be so crowded later in the day, as people hurried to buy all the provisions they needed for the New Year holiday. Marion had got up early to see Jen and Jake off, and had decided to stay up, so that nine o'clock found her enjoying the novel experience of sitting at the kitchen table in her dressing gown, drinking coffee and eating toast and marmalade while Colin regaled her with the story of his alarm the previous night. He could tell a story well, and he mocked himself mercilessly to make her laugh, although pride made him omit the embarrassing moment when he had thrown himself into Jen's arms on the landing. But as a funny story, it was not a success, for Marion did not laugh. She fingered the edge of the table-cloth, and looked at Colin thoughtfully, with an intense expression in her eyes which somehow brought back to him a remembrance of the fear he had felt when the flute began to play. He shifted on his chair.

'You don't think there was anyone there, do you?' he demanded, more aggressively than was necessary in a person who was only awaiting a response to a joke.

Marion's silences could be more challenging than any argument, and Colin was never sure how to deal with them.

'You mean — someone who shouldn't have been there? Oh, no,' she said.

Colin was puzzled by this.

'I don't know what you mean,' he replied. 'Who could be there, except someone who shouldn't have been there?'

'I don't know,' said Marion, 'I wasn't the one who heard it.'

It was this kind of answer, seeming to invite argument, yet at the same time making it impossible, which exasperated Colin beyond words. He got up from the table abruptly, and went off to get dressed, leaving Marion to finish her coffee, and read the news in the morning paper.

Fortunately, however, Colin's annoyance never lasted long, and an hour later, when Mrs. Ramsay had returned from shopping, helped Marion to dress, and installed her in her chair by the fire, he was ready to sit down with her and give his attention to the topic which had never been far from their thoughts since the jig-saw letter was found. It was at once obvious from the expression on Marion's face that she had an idea, and was longing to tell him about it. Still, her first words were not what he had expected.

'Colin, would you be willing to go upstairs and do some more hunting?' she asked.

It was not altogether an easy question to answer. If she had asked him yesterday morning, when Jen was hoovering her carpets on the first floor, and Jake was hammering in his work-room on the second, and he had not yet heard a flute playing when there was no one there, Colin could have replied without hesitation. As recently as yesterday he would have gone upstairs without a thought, and clattered carelessly through the empty rooms, searing their peace with shrill whistling, scattering dust and dreams with the stamping of his clumsy feet. Now it was different. Now, although of course he knew that he had heard no flute, and seen no light, he realized that he did not want to climb the long stair alone, opening doors into forlorn rooms where the clocks had stopped so long ago. He remembered the nature of their stillness, a stillness that was not silence, but filled with sounds of its own, where the rain on the roof was like children's feet, a draught of air beneath a door like a human sigh. Of course it was a changed Colin who felt like this. He had not known how perilous a step he was taking when he had brought the past Ramsays to life, that once he had imagined the house as it had been when they lived in it, warm and furnished and full of the sounds of life, it could only seem to him now, by contrast, sad for the passing of old times, listening for voices that had whispered into silence, and footsteps that had long ago ceased to fall. Yet there was enough of the old Colin left to feel ashamed of such thoughts, ashamed of his fear of going upstairs in his own house, and brave enough to do it, in spite of being afraid. So when Marion said, 'Would you be willing to go upstairs and do some more hunting?' he answered, 'Yes, of course, if you think it will do any good.'

Then Marion told him what she had been thinking while she ate Jen's sweet and sour pork with chopsticks, and watched Will bringing pigeons out of a shiny top hat.

'It seems to me,' she said, 'that if you look back over all the clues we've found so far, you can see that each one led us on to the next one. I mean, the letter I found introduced us to Charles Ramsay, then you found his photograph. The photograph led us to the desk, and the desk produced the jig-saw letter. Now the jig-saw letter has told us of things we didn't know before, but it doesn't obviously suggest another clue, does it?'

Colin shook his head.

'It's a thoroughly frustrating letter,' Marion went on, 'full of hints and mystery. Of course it's interesting, but I do wish Charles had said what was in the trunk, instead of going on about "your property" in that pompous fashion.'

Colin grinned.

'They were both pretty pompous, weren't they?' he said.

'Yes.'

'Do you suppose everyone was in those days?'

'I shouldn't be surprised. It probably seems more so in writing. Anyway, this was what I was going to ask you — when you searched upstairs before, how thoroughly did you go through the attics?'

'The attics?' said Colin. 'You mean those little rooms where Mother says maids used to sleep?'

'Yes.'

Colin considered this for a moment, then he said, 'Not very thoroughly, really. I paid most attention to the bedrooms on the second floor, because I thought that was where Mr. Ramsay and Mr. Farquhar were most likely to have slept.'

'That's what I thought,' said Marion. 'And of course you were right — if they didn't sleep in Jen and Jake's place, where you can't search at all. However, that doesn't matter for the moment. You see, what I was thinking was this. Up till now, Charles Ramsay and Alan Farquhar have been the most important people in the story, as far as we're concerned. Agreed?'

'Yes.'

'But since we've found the jig-saw letter, that has changed. I really don't think there's any point in our trying to find out more about them at the moment, because according to that letter, they didn't know any more than we do. It was Watt Davie who knew everything. He stole the trunk, so obviously he knew what he did with the things that were in it. He knew what became of Alice's ring, and Colin's studs.'

'And the silver plate,' Colin reminded her.

'And the silver plate. So it's not Charles and Alan we should be trailing, it's Watt Davie.'

Colin began to see how her mind was working.

'And you think,' he said, 'that we'd be more likely to find traces of Watt Davie in the attics than in the bedrooms.'

'Yes, I do. Servants in a house like this slept in the attics and ate in the basement, so if they left any belongings behind them, they'd be most likely to be in one of these two places. I know you can't get into the basement —'

'Who says I can't?'

'Colin, you know you can't. It's let to that wine merchant from Leith who keeps his bottles in it.'

'I know that, don't I?' said Colin impatiently. 'I can get in all right, if I want to.'

'How?'

'Through a window at the back. It has bars over it, and he keeps it open a little to let the air circulate. I could squeeze between the bars quite easily.'

'Colin, you couldn't. It would be burglary, and anyway, suppose you got stuck.'

'I won't get stuck. I'm not stupid.'

Marion wished she had never mentioned the basement. She knew from experience that this argument could go on for an hour, so to divert Colin she said firmly, 'Well, with any luck, you won't have to try. If Watt Davie did leave anything behind, it's much more likely that he'd leave it in his bedroom. How many bedrooms are there in the attic, Colin? I forget.'

'Four,' Colin reminded her. 'Two to the back, and two to the front. I'll go up now, and have a look, shall I?'

Better, he thought, to go in the daytime, if he had to go at all. Better than to be alone in the dark. . . .

Marion smiled at him.

'Please do,' she said. 'There just might be something. You'll look carefully, won't you?'

'In every cranny.'

'I'll tidy my lacquered box while you're away,' Marion said.

Colin climbed to the attic, trying not to listen for the flute, reminding himself that all he had heard last night was the Mac-Phersons' television, forbidding himself to stop and listen outside the workroom door. For there was no one there, there had been no one there last night, there could be no one there. He told himself this over and over again, crossly, while the prickle of uneasiness moved between his shoulders, and the rain made a staccato drumming on the dirty roof-light far overhead. The stair was always dark, even in summer, and now, on a rainy winter morning, it seemed to be hung with shadows, soft and dropping like curtains down the stair well, which pierced the house like a pit-shaft from top to bottom. At its highest point, the stair opened out on to a small bare landing, so close to the roof that one could hear the wind making hungry, sucking noises under the slates.

From this landing, an archway led into the low, narrow passage which ran along below the loft floor. Someone had pulled the curtains over the window at the end of the passage, so that when Colin stepped into it, it was almost completely dark. He groped hastily for the light switch outside the loft cupboard door, but the light from the low-powered electric bulb only exchanged one kind of darkness for another, less intense. It ran down the tunnel-like passage, thrusting shadow in front of it, making the four low doors black marks against the walls, like the mouths of caves. Colin shivered. He felt that he was a thousand miles from the sitting-room, where Marion sat by the fire with her lacquered box in her lap. He stood for a moment with his back against the loft door, mustering courage and telling himself that he was getting his breath back, then he strode firmly down the passage, and threw open the first door.

It was the smell he noticed first, the smell and the presence of a large black spider, scuttling across the bare boards of the floor. The smell was of damp and dust, with mouldy overtones which made Colin wrinkle up his nose as he glanced round the cramped little room with its low walls and coombed ceiling, which could scarcely, he thought, have allowed a tall man to straighten his back. There would scarcely have been room for him to turn round either, for the place was crammed with furniture, nothing not strictly necessary, but in this confined space giving an impression of being full to bursting point. There was a knobbly brass bedstead, which could have accommodated three adults easily, with a black and white striped mattress folded back to reveal half of its sagging springs. There was a large wooden chest of drawers, two rickety chairs in the alcove of the tiny window, with its uninspiring view of the backs of the houses in Great King Street, and a wardrobe with a yellow, dingy looking-glass door. Colin could see his reflection in it, faded and looking as if he had suddenly contracted jaundice. There was no fireplace, and he felt a passing pity for the Jeans and Watt Davie who must have been frozen half to death in winter, while the Ramsays sat cosily by their coal fires downstairs. This thought reminded him that he too was frozen, and he began to search, looking carefully into drawers and wardrobe, running his fingers along the skirting board and the window frames, tapping the walls, examining the dank mattress for suspicious lumps, and places where the ticking might have been opened and sewn up again. It was as he was leaving that it occurred to him to try unscrewing the knobs on the brass bedstead, just in case Watt Davie, being as ingenious as Colin Ramsay, might have thought of hiding something in the hollow poles beneath them. So he tried, but either the knobs did not unscrew, or had been so tightly screwed on that they would not budge, for Colin could not move them. So, abandoning that room, he went into the next.

It seemed like the same old story all over again. The rooms were empty, and he could find nothing, because there was nothing there to find. Each room was like all the others, varied only by having, perhaps, a wooden bedstead instead of a brass one, or wicker chairs instead of wooden ones. By the time Colin got to the fourth and last room, he was beginning to have the familiar feelings of disappointment and disgust, and regret that once again he would have to go down to the sitting-room and tell Marion that he had drawn a blank. The fourth room, however, was different from the other three, if only because there seemed to be more floor and less furniture. Colin could not remember having noticed this particularly on his last visit to the attic, but now, after the terrible congestion of the other rooms, it was all at once remarkable. Then he saw why; instead of a large double bed, this room contained only a narrow single bed, pushed into a corner against the wall. Moreover it had only one chair, and Colin realized that in each of the other rooms, two servants had slept, while this room had only been occupied by one. He could not think of any reason in particular why Watt Davie should have had a room to himself, but nonetheless he felt a certain quickening of interest as he got down on his knees, and began to tap his way along the skirting. Automatically he examined the woodwork for loose spars, took out drawers from the chest so that he could peer down into the dark, web-festooned space inside, and turned his attention to the wardrobe.

When he first looked into it, it seemed to Colin that this wardrobe was as empty as the others had been. In its narrow, crudely finished interior, three wooden coat-hangers swung gently on a tarnished brass rail, set in motion by the suction of the opening door. Only when he put in his hand, to feel into the dark recesses on either side did he feel the contact of something soft, and pulled out what at first seemed to be a bundle of cloth tied up with string. He untied the knot, and shook out the bundle, which dropped down into the shape of a man's jacket, black, with a silk lining. It was as damp and unpleasant to handle as everything else in these damp and unpleasant rooms, it was riddled with moth holes and exuding a very unwholesome smell. Colin would have been inclined to drop it with a shudder, had it not been that at that moment he heard a voice speaking in his head. It was Marion's voice, musical and soft, its Scottish tones overlaid by the East Anglian intonation which she had picked up during so much conversation with her mother. But they were not Marion's words, they were Charles Ramsay's.

'"*Davie said that he had only been trying to persuade Jean to let him in so that he could fetch down his coat, which he had forgotten to take in the haste of his departure. However Colin said he would not set foot in the house again upon any pretext, and sent him about his business.*"'

Colin clutched the horrible garment to his chest, and made off downstairs as fast as his legs would carry him.

9

167, High Street

Mrs. Ramsay had just come into the sitting-room from the kitchen to ask whether Marion would like chicken or lentil soup for lunch, and was waiting for her to make up her mind, when Colin arrived. He was covered with dust from head to foot, his face was scarlet, in his arms he was carrying a dirty, mothy, mouldy jacket, and displaying it as proudly as one would an archaeological find of great beauty and importance.

'Watt Davie's jacket,' he announced, his voice squeaky with excitement. 'Watt Davie's jacket, Marion.'

'I don't know whether it's Watt Davie's jacket or not,' said Mrs. Ramsay, forgetting about the soup in her annoyance, 'but I do wish that some of the clues to this mystery of yours were a little cleaner. It's the grubbiest mystery I've ever heard of. You're filthy, Colin. Now I suppose I had better go and heat water so that you can have a bath — as if I didn't have better things to do in the middle of the morning.'

Colin scarcely heard her, scarcely saw her go. He was looking at Marion, and she was looking back at him, her eyes shining with delight. She too had sometimes thought that the clues to the mystery were the shabbiest things imaginable, even the desk, with its scratched varnish and worn velvet stained with ink. But that did not make the mystery any less exciting, and she looked now at the tattered jacket as if it were a treasure beyond price.

'Oh, Colin, if only it could be,' she said, her voice taut with doubt and hope.

While they examined it, spreading it out across the coffee table, so that Marion could reach it without having to take it on her knee, Colin explained how and where he had found it.

'And I'm sure it's his,' he said, 'because if you remember, in his letter Charles Ramsay told Alan that Watt Davie had been hanging around the house, trying to get back a jacket or a coat he had left behind him. Some people call a jacket a coat. This jacket was bundled up with a string round it, at the back of a wardrobe in one of the servants' rooms. It makes it likely, doesn't it?'

'It isn't likely,' said Marion. 'It isn't only likely, Colin. It's certain. Look.'

She turned back the left front of the jacket, and showed Colin the strip of facing between the edge of the material and the lining. There, under the inside pocket, a small strip of cloth was sewn on, and on it, in faded ink, were marked the initials 'J.W.D.'

'"J. Watt Davie,"' Marion said.

They went through the pockets in silence, too tense now for conversation. There was little in them — a box of matches, a few pence and half-pence, disfigured by a rash of verdigris, a railway timetable, which had provided the moths with an extra treat, and a thin wallet. At first Marion and Colin thought that it was made of leather, but when they opened it up they found that it was really a cheap kind of oil-cloth, textured in imitation of leather on one side, while the other showed the warp and woof of a closely woven material. When Colin emptied it, he found two postage stamps, like the ones in Charles Ramsay's desk, the return half of a railway ticket from Portobello to Edinburgh Waverley, and a small cutting from a newspaper. It was an advertisement, which Colin read aloud to Marion.

J. J. RICKERT
167, High Street, Edinburgh

•

Jewellery, Silver, Antiques, Curios Bought and Sold

Best Prices Offered, Enquiries Welcome

They looked at each other speculatively.

'So,' said Marion. 'Proof of guilt, wouldn't you say?'

'The next clue, I'd say,' said Colin. 'I'll just put it aside, shall I, till we've finished going over the jacket? Then we can discuss what we're going to do about it.'

'Haven't we finished with the jacket?' asked Marion. They had been through all the pockets twice, and her hands were as black as Colin's.

'I think we'll open up the lining,' said Colin cautiously. 'The thing's a ruin anyway, so we may as well take it to pieces now, before we throw it away. He might just have hidden something in the lining, I think.'

This sounded very exciting, and while Colin went to fetch scissors from the kitchen, Marion looked at the jacket with fresh interest. But when Colin had cut it to shreds, and covered the hearthrug with its remains, they would see that no treasure was hidden in it, and that it had no more secrets to reveal.

There was a pause then, while Mrs. Ramsay shovelled up the jacket and took it out to the dustbin, chased Colin into the bathroom, and laid the table for lunch. An hour or so later, however, when they were again gathered round the fire to drink their coffee, they were able to examine the row of sad little objects laid out at their feet. Mrs. Ramsay had recovered her temper by this time, but she and Colin had days, occasionally, when they always seemed to be rubbing each other the wrong way. If she was feeling low, it upset Marion, but if she was in a cheerful mood, as she was today, she thought it rather funny. This was one of those days, and within minutes, they were disputing again.

'I'm disappointed,' remarked Colin. 'I was sure that he had hidden something in the lining. Why else would he make such a fuss about getting the jacket back? It wasn't for a few coppers and a box of matches and a ride from Portobello in the train.'

'Of course it wasn't,' said Mrs. Ramsay, already with a trace of impatience. 'It was because he needed the jacket. If you were in Watt Davie's position in 1914, you just couldn't afford to lose a perfectly good jacket. The Ramsays were in the wrong. They should have given it back to him.'

Both Colin and Marion were rather taken aback by this. They were so used now to thinking of the Ramsays as injured, and Watt Davie as a villain, that it came as rather a shock to be told that he too had rights which the Ramsays had withheld from him. Colin tried to argue.

'Well, I don't think so,' he said. 'Watt Davie was a thief, and if he lost his jacket, he was only getting a taste of his own medicine.'

'Exactly,' said Mrs. Ramsay emphatically. 'That's just what I mean. If the Ramsays kept the jacket, they were no better than thieves themselves. In fact, they were worse, because they didn't need it, and Watt Davie did, and they had no temptation to steal, because they were rich, whereas he had, because he was poor. People like Watt Davie were always exploited by people like the Ramsays, and I think it was mean and petty of them not to give him his jacket back.'

Marion did not enjoy hearing the Ramsays put in the wrong over anything, but she was too fair-minded not to admit that her mother's was a just point of view. Colin did not think it was just at all, but he was overpowered by her vehemence, and did not know how to answer her. To him, the good were good and the bad were bad, and he had not yet got to the stage of understanding that good and bad are mixed in everyone. He said no more for the moment, and the conversation turned to the advertisement inserted in an Edinburgh newspaper by J. J. Rickert in 1914.

'It seems fairly obvious why Watt Davie cut it out and kept it, wouldn't you say, Mother?' asked Marion.

'Yes,' replied Mrs. Ramsay.

'So you admit he was a thief,' Colin could not resist remarking.

'I didn't say he wasn't a thief. All I said was that that doesn't excuse the Ramsays for keeping his jacket,' Mrs. Ramsay could not resist replying, and the argument would have been in full swing again if Marion, half laughing, had not broken in on it to point out something so obvious that Colin could not imagine why he had not thought of it before.

'What I can't understand,' she said, 'is why he was trying to persuade Jean to let him come into the house to fetch the jacket. Surely the sensible thing would have been to ask her to bring it down, and hand it over to him at the door. He didn't really have to get in, did he? Unless —'

She paused, and Colin, who could often pick up the thread of her idea, finished for her, 'Unless the jacket was only an excuse for getting into the house to collect something else.'

There was a long silence, while they digested this most interesting possibility. Then Marion asked, 'What do you think, Mother?'

Mrs. Ramsay looked cautious.

'You could be right, certainly,' she said slowly, 'It *was* odd that he insisted on going up to collect the jacket himself. It was dangerous, because he might very well have met one of the Ramsay's between the basement and the attic, and then there would have been a dreadful fuss. As you say, it wasn't necessary — unless there was more at stake than the jacket. Do you know, I believe this may be the answer. Only don't go thinking now that it's proved. It isn't. It's only conjecture.'

'Interesting, all the same,' brooded Marion. 'He took nothing out of the house with him — the Ramsays would see to that. But we've been assuming that he had already got rid of the things he had stolen. Perhaps that wasn't the case. Perhaps he had been hiding them, intending to sell them to J. J. Rickert later on.'

'Then was surprised by Charles when he was taking the watch, and put out of the house before he could,' added Colin.

'So there is a possibility at least,' said Marion softly, 'that he didn't take them away at all.'

It was a possibility, perhaps, but nothing altered the fact that for all Colin's searching and probing, not a trace of any hidden treasure had been revealed. Only defaced photographs, torn letters, tattered clothing. And, as Mrs. Ramsay, fearing for their disappointment, felt obliged to point out, for all they knew, this mystery had been solved years ago, the trunk recovered, the ring and the studs returned to their rightful owners. It was impossible to know what had happened afterwards. Marion and Colin knew that this was all true, but today they were feeling so pleased with themselves that nothing could disturb their optimism.

'The letter gave us the clue, the jacket,' said Colin, 'and now the jacket has given us the next clue, the advertisement. That's how this mystery works out — it's like one of Jake's treasure hunts. Each clue leads to the next. And there's always treasure at the end of a treasure hunt.'

He glanced at the chimneypiece, where stood an enormous jar of Jen's home-made toffees, which had been his prize the night before, as if that were the proof of his statement.

'What are you going to do with the advertisement?' asked his mother, half amused and half moved by his artlessness.

'Why, go and have a look at 167, High Street, of course,' said Colin. 'I don't suppose there's any point in going for a day or two, because all the shops close over the New Year, but I could go on Friday, couldn't I?'

'But, Colin,' began Mrs. Ramsay, then stopped.

Colin smiled at her, and said, 'It's all right. I know.'

He knew that it was absurd to imagine that even if the shop were still there, and even if Watt Davie had contacted the owner with a view to selling his loot, there was any chance of finding out about it sixty years later. He knew that in all probability the shop had been closed, like J. & C. Ramsay's, and J. J. Rickert laid in his grave, long before he himself had been born. But even so —

'I'd like to have a look,' he said. 'Just on the chance, you know.'

'I wish I could go with you,' Marion said.

Colin could scarcely believe his ears. He turned to her in delight.

'But you could,' he said eagerly. 'You could, easily. Jake would take us in the van, if we asked him. Do come, Marion.'

But already Marion had taken fright. She had spoken automatically, not really meaning what she said. She shook her head.

'No,' she said. 'No, I couldn't,' and Colin, catching his mother's eye as she rose to start clearing the table, did not press the matter.

'Then I'll go by myself,' he said, 'and when I come back, I'll tell you all about it.'

'Yes, that would be best,' agreed Marion, relieved. 'Perhaps I'll go out with you some other day.'

On Friday morning after breakfast, Colin put on his coat and scarf, tucked Watt Davie's advertisement into his pocket, and set off for the High Street. It had rained overnight, but at dawn the clouds had drawn back against the wind from the east, unscreening a cold sun in a washy blue sky. The sun was not strong enough to dry the ground, but the wind was, and the pavements were mottled wet and dry under Colin's feet as he pressed against the blast along Mayferry Street, his ears and cheek-bones already beginning to sting. But it was not a school morning, when grumbling about the weather was obligatory, and today Colin was so interested in his expedition, so full of hope that he scarcely noticed how cold he was. He could not have explained his optimism, and for the past two days he had been warning himself sternly that his errand was futile, and not worth the walk to the High Street, yet against all reason he was convinced, as he rolled about in the wind uphill to Princes Street, that he and Marion were on the brink of yet another discovery.

He was also looking forward to visiting the High Street. Although he had lived in Edinburgh for many years, it was not in a part of the town where he often had occasion to go, and it would probably be true to say that any of the tourists who prowled about it all summer, with their cameras and their guide books in their hands, were better acquainted with it than he was. He remembered the principal landmarks from walks taken years ago with his father and Marion on Sunday afternoons, but that had been at a time when he was too young and unimaginative to be impressed by it. But last night, when they had been talking round the fire about his visit, Mrs. Ramsay had begun to tell him and Marion something of the history of that narrow, cobbled street which tunnels downhill from the Castle, overhung by cliffs of high, cramped houses, where the past perhaps hangs more heavily in the air than anywhere else in Scotland. She told them how, until the fifteenth century, this street had been the whole of Edinburgh and how, until their own part of the city was built two hundred years ago, it had been the hub of the dirty, crowded little town that clung to the stony spine projecting from the Castle

Rock, its rickety houses piled so high that they seemed in danger of breaking through the middle and toppling into the bleak marshes that surrounded it. Mrs. Ramsay was a good story-teller; she described so that Colin and Marion could see them the lords and ladies in silk and velvet, picking their way daintily through the filth and garbage that lay inches deep in the street, thrown from windows by the inhabitants of the 'lands', which was the old Edinburgh name for tenements. The smell of the city was so terrible, she said, that it was carried on the wind as far as Dalkeith, ten miles to the south. She told them too about the ordinary people, who for the most part pursued their daily business doucely enough, earning their bread and rearing their children and going to church on Sundays, but who in the wink of an eye could be changed into a snarling, savage mob who more than once, ranging themselves behind their famous banner, the 'Blue Blanket', had taken the law into their own hands and changed the course of history. It was in the lives of these people, Mrs. Ramsay thought, that the real story of Edinburgh was unfolded, because they were its continuity. People like Mary, Queen of Scots, Montrose, Bonnie Prince Charlie, had been actors moving across its stage, never truly part of its life. Later, sensing Colin's and Marion's interest, she had brought out books about Edinburgh from the bookcase, and shown them prints and old watercolours that made Colin feel he could step into the page, and walk through that old, precipitous Edinburgh, with its dark wynds and gloomy stairways, and twisted houses pressing on the sky. He went to bed with his head full of history, and when he set out next morning it was with a feeling of venture not entirely explained by the scrap of newspaper in his pocket.

Colin had wondered, while his mother was speaking, whether he would still be able to recognize the Old Town as she described it, or whether modern shops and traffic would have altered it beyond that point. But as he crossed Princes Street and began to walk up the Mound, with the Old Town hanging before him against the sky, looking oddly flat, like a backdrop on stage at the theatre, he realized that although through the years the city has crawled outwards until it sprawls for miles around it, it has failed to swallow it up. At once sombre and beautiful, it stands apart, and as Colin pressed on and up, dodging the traffic hurtling down to Market Street and beginning the last steep, curved ascent to the Lawnmarket, he had a strong sense of leaving the present behind him and stepping into a place so old that it made the house in Mayferry Street seem new by comparison, and Charles Ramsay and Watt Davie his contemporaries. For not even the outrage of traffic lights and tartan gift shops, and the well-meaning removal of many of the more haggard aspects of the past, have been able to take from the High Street its atmosphere of grim magic, a brooding remembrance of terrible deeds done and sights seen but not forgotten. And Colin, so recently awakened to the permanence of past influences in his own house, was all the more ready to experience it. As he came out from the narrow walls of St. Giles Street, with the bells of the heavy, blackened Cathedral opposite sounding in his ears, the ambience of the High Street enfolded him, and he began to walk down the pavement like a person under a spell. Bible Land, Morocco Land, Peebles Wynd, World's End Close . . . he repeated the names to himself, peering down the narrow openings, wondering at the darkness at their ends. The noise of car engines, horns and screeching brakes faded, to be replaced by the clatter of horses' hooves, street sellers crying their wares, the roar of the mob advancing behind the Blue Blanket. On either side of Colin, a tide of figures ebbed and flowed, fine gentlemen in velvet doublets and silk hose, ladies in farthingales and shoes of green leather, women in rags, huddled in dirty tartan plaids. Then the mob was upon him, he was pushed and jostled, by people then, by people now . . . 'Mind whaur ye're gaun!' said a cross voice, and Colin came out of the sixteenth century into the present, and remembered why he had come.

'I'm sorry,' he said to a red face, topped with hair rollers under a nylon headscarf, 'I didn't mean to push you.'

The face withdrew, mollified, and Colin glanced at the number above the nearest shop. It was one hundred and sixteen. He crossed the street, and keeping his mind very firmly on the matter in hand, he began to count the uneven numbers, waiting for one hundred and sixty-seven. He forgot the mob, and the murders and hauntings and hangings that had filled his mind as the sixteenth century swirled around him, and thought instead of Watt Davie and J. J. Rickert, and his advertisement.

It was no easy matter to keep count of the numbers. The High Street had been the scene of 'preservation' in recent years; many of its most historic houses had been rescued from demolition as slum property and very beautifully restored, while others had been demolished and replaced, less successfully, by modern imitations of the original buildings. But in the stretch which

Colin was examining, nothing of either sort had yet been done, and the row of rather dilapidated shops was interspersed with lengths of rough boarding, tacked over the disfigured façades of empty buildings which might, or might not, be restored later on. The pavement was dirty, the boarding defaced by tattered election posters and gang slogans scrawled with felt pens and spray paint. It was ugly and depressing, but it did not depress Colin, whose principal fear had been that J. J. Rickert's one hundred and sixty-seven might have been swept away by bulldozers in the nineteen-fifties, and replaced by a little boutique. The High Street was full of little boutiques. As it was, of course, there was the possibility that it was nailed up behind one of the board fences, but equally the possibility that it was not. He counted 157 as a fishmonger's, estimated 159 and 161 behind a board, found the numbers again at 163, which was a bookshop, passed 165 which was empty, but not yet boarded up, and found himself outside an antique shop. Bright and freshly painted, set like a precious jewel in a string of tawdry glass beads, it fronted the street immaculately, its superiority underlined by the threatening presence of a very large burglar alarm beside its shiny glass door. Colin stared at it as if he were seeing a mirage. Even although it was what he had come to find, the surprise of its being there so conveniently was overwhelming, and he stepped back to the edge of the pavement to peer up at the number above the door.

'One, six, seven,' he said to himself.

The number was painted in black on a long white board, and beside it there was a name, *Alison Baxter*, and the words, *Curios and Antiques*. Colin stared, but it was not at Alison Baxter's name that he was staring. For the white paint had been thin, and underneath it faint ghost-letters spelled out another name, *James J. Rickert*. With pattering heart, Colin approached the window, and put his nose against it.

He thought it was like looking through a peephole in the side of a pirate's treasure chest. The interior of the shop was lined with a dull gold wallpaper, its floor velveted with a carpet of dark red, making a perfect foil for the wonderful things the room contained. There were old books in brown leather bindings, with titles in gold which the peering Colin could not read, but in any case these books were less for reading than for touching and smelling and marvelling at. There was china, lovely old painted plates and jugs with their glaze cracked through age, graceful figurines and blue Chinese bowls. There was furniture, rosewood tables on long curved legs that reminded Colin of Red Setter's, armchairs with velvet cushions, a mahogany desk with — Colin counted — eighteen wooden knobs on its eighteen tiny drawers, and a grandfather clock, with the sun and the moon smiling on its enamelled face while its long brass pendulum gravely made seconds and gravely wiped them out. There were prints of Edinburgh and London in days gone by, washed with pale colours that contrasted with the rich cream of oil paintings in heavy, gilded frames. There was a Persian looking-glass with glass so dim and grey that it brought into Colin's mind the verse of the Bible which he had learned at school, 'For now we see through a glass darkly . . .' and there was a shiny brass warming pan which he thought would have been much more fun than a hot water bottle. It was the most enchanting shop Colin had ever seen, and if he had only been passing by, and lured to the window by a glimpse of treasure, he would have found his gazing pure delight. But the more he looked, the more his heart sank, as he wondered how he would ever have courage to open the door, penniless, and go in, and try to explain to Alison Baxter why he had come. Probably, he thought, he would come out again faster than he had gone in. Still — so far, he reminded himself, everything had turned out a thousand times better than he had dared to hope, and he must not be defeated now. Mustering his courage, he prised himself away from the window, and opened the door.

There was a smell of furniture polish and old things, a warmth in the air. The door swung silently shut behind him, a bell above it tinkled a warning, and from the shadows at the back of the shop Colin heard a fresh voice, saying something very unexpected.

'I was just going to come out and ask if you'd like to come in and look — you've been outside for ages, and you couldn't possibly see everything through the window. Are you a looker, or a customer?'

'Not a customer,' said Colin, startled. He frowned into the gloom, and saw that someone had come out from behind a red velvet curtain on the back wall — the owner of the shop, presumably, although a less likely antique dealer he could not imagine. It was a girl, older than Marion but younger than Jen, rather fat with a broad, pleasant face surrounded by a lot of yellow hair. She was wearing red trousers and a white jersey. 'But not just a looker, either,' Colin added, as she emerged into the light. The girl grinned, and waited.

It is always easier to explain what you want if someone asks you what you want first, and gives you an opening, and Colin, left to take the initiative, was not sure how to begin. But he had to begin with something, so he asked, 'Are you Alison Baxter?'

'Daughter of,' said the girl. 'Janet. Did you want to see my mother? She's gone to Perth to an auction, and I don't think she'll be back today.'

'It doesn't matter,' said Colin, hiding his relief, which was not polite. He felt sure that it would be much easier to explain why he had come to Janet than it would have been to her mother, the antique dealer. He pulled up the tail of his coat, and fished in his trouser pocket for the advertisement, saying, 'I wanted to ask about this. I found it at home, in the pocket of an old jacket, and my sister and I think it must have been there since about 1914.'

Janet Baxter looked interested. She had not had a single customer all morning, and any diversion was welcome. She took the little rectangle of newspaper on her hand, and turned it towards the light.

'Well, fancy that,' she remarked, looking at it closely. 'Let no one say that advertising is in vain. 1914, did you say?' Let me see — yes, that would be my great-grandfather Rickert, who opened this shop in the eighteen-nineties. He was my mother's grandfather.' She laughed as she passed the advertisement back to Colin, and added, 'You can still see his name on the front of the shop. It doesn't matter how many coats of paint we put over it, it keeps coming through. Mother says he's protesting at being taken over by a woman.' Colin thought that this sounded very hopeful. He could scarcely believe that he was actually standing in J. J. Rickert's shop, talking to his great-granddaughter. Of course, whether she could help him unravel any of the threads of the mystery was another matter. However, encouraged by her friendliness, he took a deep breath, and told her all about Charles Ramsay and Alan Farquhar, and Watt Davie who had stolen the trunk and the ring and the studs, and had cut the advertisement out of the newspaper. 'I know it's an awfully long time ago,' he said, 'and probably there wouldn't be any record of it now, but we wondered if perhaps there was any way of finding out whether he did sell any of the things he stole to your great-grandfather. . . .' He tailed off uncertainly, wondering whether it was a mistake to suggest to a person that her great-grandfather might have had dealings with a thief.

But Janet was showing no sign of displeasure. She had seated herself while Colin was talking on a very delicate little drawing-room chair, which she overflowed alarmingly, and was looking at him with nothing but curiosity in her blue eyes.

'Well, well,' she said with satisfaction, 'and to think that I've been cursing all morning about the boredom of keeping a shop. You had better come into the office, and we'll see what's what.'

She got up, and Colin watched the buttoned velvet cushion rise slowly after her, as if breathing out in relief. Pink with excitement, he followed her behind the velvet curtain, into a small, cluttered room with one barred window looking out on a dirty stone wall. An unshaded light bulb shone down on a large desk, piled high with books and papers, a few shabby wooden chairs, a shelf containing cups and a jar of instant coffee, a carton of milk and an electric kettle, and the most enormous safe Colin had ever seen. The contrast between this unadorned room and the opulent red and gold shop was shocking, but Colin scarcely had time to notice before his attention was drawn away to Janet, who had pulled out a step-ladder from a corner, and was now standing with her head thrown back, looking up at a shelf which ran along above the window, about half-way up the wall. Colin followed her example, and saw that on the shelf was ranged a great number of large, green leather-covered books. Most of them were covered with dust, especially in the corner above the window, where they were festooned with cobwebs as well.

'What are they?' he asked.

'Records of sales and purchases,' replied Janet. 'You're lucky, because in this shop we never throw things away. If your thief sold anything to my great-grandfather, there will be a record of it, never fear.'

'I don't expect your great-grandfather would buy stolen goods,' said Colin, not very sincerely.

'No, I don't suppose he would, if he knew they were stolen,' agreed Janet, shrugging her shoulders. 'But a dealer can't have a police check on every customer, can he? Now — the problem is knowing where to start.'

'The dustiest books are probably the oldest ones,' suggested Colin, glad to have the question of J. J. Rickert's integrity settled with so little trouble.

'Yes, you're right. I'll try over here, by the window.'

She dragged her step-ladder in that direction, opened it out, and climbed up until she could reach the books.

The next five minutes were among the most nerve-racking that Colin had ever experienced. The first books that Janet handed down to him detailed the purchases J. J. Rickert had made in the years 1924-1925, and it was some time, working backwards from there, before she found the one which dealt with the years 1913-1916. By that time her hands and sleeves were black, she had a smut on her nose and a cobweb on her hair, and the front of her white jersey was grey.

'Just pray that there are no rich Americans in the Royal Mile this morning, looking for Mary, Queen of Scots' bedroom slippers,' she said, 'because if there are, you will have to serve them.' She came down from the steps, laughing at Colin's alarmed face, and said, 'It's all right. Don't get agitated. It's not the season. Now come on — this is getting interesting. Have you any idea of the date? Beyond its being in 1914, I mean?'

Colin said he thought it might be somewhere around February or March, although he couldn't be certain. 'The ring and the studs had been stolen before Charles Ramsay came home on the first of March,' he told her, 'and Watt Davie must have been dismissed quite soon after that. Of course he might have sold them after he was dismissed, but we don't think so, because it seems that he didn't take anything like that with him when he left.'

Janet sat down at the desk, and opened the book at random. The stiff pages, with their blue and green marled edges, fell open at the entries for April 1916.

'Only look at the left hand side,' she said to Colin, who was peering over her shoulder. 'The purchases are on the left, and the sales on the right.'

She turned back the pages until she got to one headed, '1914, 28th January'. Then she began to run her finger down the lines of flowing, old-fashioned writing, which reminded Colin of Alan Farquhar's. 'The Lord Quincey's Estate: four Meissen figurines, two chairs, Hepplewhite,' he read. 'Ewan Torrence, Esq.: one dinner service, Spode, 1800,' and, 'Mrs. Northbrook: one silver rosebowl, 1790.' Details of the purchases, and the addresses of the sellers, were meticulously recorded in a separate column on the right, but Colin did not even glance at it. He was not interested in antiques, except as objects to be marvelled at, and all he wanted to see in the book was Watt Davie's name.

But Watt Davie's name was not there, not in the entries for February, nor in those for the first half of March. It would be terrible, Colin thought, if after so much luck, now at the last moment it failed him, and he had to go home and tell Marion that he had come to a dead-end. It was having to tell Marion that mattered. But just then, Janet turned over a page, and they both found themselves staring at an entry which seemed to be jumping up at them from the paper. Colin felt a speculative shiver running down his back. He read, '15th March. D. J. Watt, Esq.: one dress ring, set three rubies; one set gold studs, with pearl; two salvers, silver, 1860: one dozen dessert spoons, silver, date uncertain.'

They both looked at it for a long time, then Janet drew her finger over into the column where the addresses were written. Colin read, '123, Ramsay Garden.'

'That's impossible,' said Janet. 'There isn't a one-two-three Ramsay Garden. It's that little cul-de-sac at the top of the Mound, overlooking Princes Street Gardens, and I doubt if there are two dozen houses in it altogether. It looks as if he muddled up his name, to hide his identity, and when he was asked for his address, said the first thing that came into his head, one, two, three, then his employer's name, and Garden.'

Colin felt quite weak with excitement, but he managed to ask what he knew was the most important thing.

'Did he sell anything else, round about the same time? Are there any other entries?'

But there were no other entries. Whatever Watt Davie had done with the contents of Alan Farquhar's trunk, he had not sold them here. A search of the right hand pages of the ledger, covering the next year or so, showed that the ring had been sold for thirty guineas to a Mrs. Moore, the studs for forty-five guineas to Sir William Scott, and the spoons for ten guineas to a Mrs. Wordsworth. They could find no mention of the salvers, which, Janet said professionally, might have lain in the shop for years. 1860 was too late for really good design in silver. Colin was not much concerned with the fate of the salvers; now he only wanted to get home to Marion with the news. He thanked Janet for her help, and said good-bye. Janet said it had been the most interesting morning she had spent in many a long day, and she hoped he would call again, when he had found the treasure, and tell her the rest of the story.

Colin sped back up the High Street, this time looking neither to right nor to left, blind alike to the swarming traffic and the mob with the Blue Blanket. He plunged down North Bridge to Princes Street with a flurry of hail stinging his face, fighting against the wind which was doing its best to catch him up in its arms and toss him over the parapet onto the bright railway lines far below. Storm clouds were massing at the edges of the sky, but he thought he was perfectly happy. Indeed several days were to pass before he and Marion realized that his visit to the antique shop, although a triumph of a kind, had failed in one very important respect. It had not provided the next clue in the sequence, which they depended upon, and had come to expect.

10

A Storm in January

A new year had come, riding to birth on the backs of wild winds that came roaring out of the North Sea, determined to tear heavy, solid Edinburgh from its foundations, and toss it away like chaff across the hills. But Edinburgh held fast, as it had always done, and Mayferry Street along with it, refusing to yield to the fury of the gale that thrashed and beat upon its front doors, drove the hard rain like pebbles against its windows, and howled with curses around its chimney pots. So eventually, seeing that all their shouting and bullying would not prevail, the winds dropped down into a discontented moaning, and blew away in a pique across the roofs. Then the snow came, and went the next day.

The sudden change in the weather seemed to foreshadow the change in Marion's life; after the clamour, silence. At the beginning of the second week in January, Colin went back to school, and Jen and Jake to work, leaving Marion alone, with no choice but to pick up the thin threads of her life in the bedroom and the sitting-room, and the small room of her own unquiet mind. Of course she had known that it was going to happen, known that one day the house would be full of voices and laughter, running footsteps and banging doors, and the next so quiet that from her chair in the sitting-room, she would be able to hear the clock ticking half-way up the stair. But even so, the abruptness of the transition, when it did come, took her by surprise. It had all been so pleasant while it lasted, the coming and going of the children from next door, the excursions upstairs, which could only be managed when Jake was on hand to carry her, to watch Jen baking a cake to take to her mother-in-law as a present for New Year's Day, and to help her choose new wall-paper for her kitchen (the choice had been red) and the easy, natural way they had of making her feel that perhaps after all she was not so strange and isolated a person as she had thought, but really much the same as everyone else. Indeed, while she had been in fits of laughter over Jake's imitations of Miss Parkinson and the Minister, or at Jen's expression of dismay when the top fell off the spice jar, and a pinch became a deluge which had to be winkled out of the cake basin with a salt spoon, she had sometimes forgotten completely that she should have been brooding over the old question of whether they were being nice to her because they pitied her, and simply accepted that they were being nice to her because she was their friend.

But then, one day, it was all over. They had all gone away to resume that other part of their lives which she could never share, and inevitably, as she faced the long, lonely days ahead, the anxiety and dejection which she had managed to hold at bay as long as Colin and Jen and Jake were in the house to divert her, returned with all their old persistent malice. From the moment she woke, knowing that she was miserable even before she got her thoughts well enough organized to remember why, and all through the day, depression enfolded her. Hour after hour, she sat in her chair by the fire, opposite the window screened with a grey mesh-curtain of rain, and looked fearfully down the tunnel of a year which, she felt certain, could bring her nothing but the confirmation of her worst suspicions, and the smothering of her last, flickering hopes. All the terrors about her future, now that she had convinced herself that she was not going to get better, the doubts as to whether her friends showed her their true faces, tormented her constantly, as did this other matter of Charles Ramsay and Alan Farquhar, which once had been a pleasure and a relief from other thoughts, but which now had become as much of a trial as everything else.

Of course Colin's return from the antique shop had been greeted with excitement and wonder, as he had known it would be. For days he and Marion had congratulated themselves on their powers of detection and their cleverness, and gloated over the new information now added to their store. Colin had been made to tell over and over again how he had found the shop, and what it looked like, and what he had said to Janet, and what Janet had said to him, and it had all seemed a marvel beyond words. The only trouble was, as they ruefully had to admit in the end, they were no nearer finding out what Watt Davie had done with Alan Farquhar's trunk than they had been before Colin set out. The most important piece of information which Colin had gleaned at the antique shop was of a negative kind. Watt Davie had not sold the contents of Alan Farquhar's trunk to J. J. Rickert. And all that that meant was that he had sold them to someone else, or had hidden them at seventeen Mayferry Street, so cunningly that while the house stood, no one would ever find them.

So what had seemed an incident full of hope and pleasure ended on a rather sour note. They did not know what to do next. And as soon as Colin went back to school, Marion realized that nothing was going to be done. It was not that he lost interest — too much that was unusual had happened in the holidays for that — only that as all his other concerns outside the house claimed him again, the mystery could no longer be of exclusive importance to him. He returned to his old talk about waiting for another clue to turn up, and began to make a model of the *Victory* in the evenings. Marion did not blame him. She knew that it was bound to be like this, that there would always be a conflict between her own single-mindedness, and the broad spectrum of Colin's interests. What made it hard to bear was that to her it all seemed so vitally important, and no matter how often Marion told herself that it did not, could not, ever make any difference to her what had happened to these two young men who had lived in this house years before even her mother was born, still her vague and unsatisfactory knowledge of their story irritated her mind till she thought she would go mad with the frustration of not knowing more. There were times when she wished she had never heard of Charles Ramsay and Alan Farquhar, but then, as soon as she had wished it she changed her mind, because — and this was the strangest aspect of it all, the one she could never explain even to her own satisfaction — she now felt more strongly than ever before that Charles Ramsay and Alan Farquhar were the most important names she had ever heard, and that if help were ever to come to her, it must come through them. It was no use telling herself that even if they were still alive, they were ancient men over eighty years of age, that she did not even know what Alan Farquhar looked like, that they could never even have heard of her existence. The feeling she had did not have anything to do with reason, it was instinctive. The life-line she held was of thin, fraying cord, but at the other end of it were Charles Ramsay and Alan Farquhar. They were as real to her as Colin, and sometimes they felt so close that she thought they were in the house with her. Of course it sounded ridiculous when it was put into words, so ridiculous that it became another of the things she could never tell anybody, not even Colin, without whose help she could never have found out even the few things she did know. Her feelings were private, and must be locked away in the secret cupboard of her own mind, which was not so full of fears and problems that, no matter how hard she tried to lean against it, she could not close the door.

The worst of it was that, despite so much effort and thought, Marion felt that they were as far from finding a solution to the mystery as they had been weeks ago. The sad story of the young man of 1914, whose dishonest servant had robbed him of a prized possession left to him in trust by his best friend, was as remote from Marion in time as the story of the Great War which had doubtless swallowed them up, master and servant and friend. She had seen films on television about that war, with its horrors of mud and trenches and barbed wire, haunted young faces under steel helmets, fields of stone crosses at its end, and it horrified her to think that that was what was waiting for Charles Ramsay after one month, the last, sand-trickling hours of peace, which surely he must have spent in pain of mind, trying to trace the villainous Watt Davie, who had stolen — well, what had he stolen? That was the kernel of the mystery, the one piece of information which Marion felt sure was vital, and was equally, sadly sure she could never obtain. It was not idle curiosity on her part; it mattered terribly, only she did not know why. She began to hate Watt Davie, and to wonder how she could ever have been so misguided as to imagine him a trusty servant called Angus or Hugh.

It was dreadful to have to sit still. Any activity would have helped, and if she had been able to get up, and go upstairs, and wander through the empty rooms, opening cupboards and looking in drawers, it would have been a relief, even if she had found nothing. But of course it was out of the question, and no amount of thinking, no number of appeals to the grave, mute, photographed face of Charles Ramsay to speak to her and share her secret, could make any difference at all. And when, by a great effort of will, Marion was able to shut Charles Ramsay and Alan Farquhar out of her mind and think of something else, all she could think of was her own future, and how that future could possibly be affected by the long-forgotten past of Charles Ramsay and Alan Farquhar. The shadow people had now deserted her, their adventures no longer worth the effort of invention. Nightly they crossed the lamp-lit floor unheeded, going their way, not wanted any more.

And then, Marion began to hear music. The first time was on a Tuesday afternoon, when her mother had gone out to do some shopping, and Marion thought little about it, supposing that Mrs. Ramsay had left the radio on in the kitchen. She knew the tune,

107

and that it was a flute playing it; she was used to hearing Colin practising in his bedroom on Monday and Thursday evenings, and often, when he thought he had got some piece to perfection, he would come into the sitting-room to play it over, and have it applauded.

A rosebud by my early walk,
A-down a corn enclosed bawk,
Sae gently bent its thorny stalk
All on a dewy morning.
Ere twice the shades o' dawn are fled,
In a' its crimson glory spread,
An' drooping rich the dewy head,
It scents the early morning.

Without thinking, Marion fitted the words to the melody that floated to her through the half-open door of the sitting-room; she did not at the time notice that the pure, woody notes died away into silence long before Mrs. Ramsay returned to switch off the radio. She had heard it several times, on different days, the same tune on the same instrument, before it occurred to her to say to her mother, 'Isn't it strange how they keep playing that same tune on the radio every day? I do wish they'd stop — I can't seem to get it out of my head, I hear it so often.'

'Do you, darling?' said Mrs. Ramsay. 'I didn't think we'd had the radio on so often lately.'

Whether they had, or not, Marion kept on hearing the tune. She did not mention it again, but it became one more thing to worry about. So, as the days passed, Marion grew paler and thinner than ever, but when her mother, who was, Marion could tell, in a quiet frenzy of anxiety, touched her hair, and said, 'What is it, my love? Can't you tell me what's the matter?' Marion shook her head, and said, 'Nothing,' or, 'I'm tired.' Once she heard Mrs. Ramsay saying to Jen in the hall, 'I don't know what to do. This just can't go on.' And then she wanted to call her into the sitting-room, and blurt it all out, and share with her mother the terrible loneliness of knowing that it had to go on, day after day, perhaps for ever. But in that she was wrong, and Mrs. Ramsay was right. There was a breaking point, and it would be reached. It was only a matter of time.

Colin too, during these dismal January days, was encountering difficulties. On the first day back at school, he had had to go to dry old Dr. Fowler, and tell him that he would not be able to play in the School Orchestra, because he was unable to obtain a flute. Even although he had come to terms with this necessity as long ago as the night of the Carol Concert, and had known all through the holidays that he would have to accept his lot without grumbling, it was only now, with Christmas over and the staleness of the New Year's aftermath upon him, that Colin began to realize the continuing cost of having to turn his back on so much happiness. Every time he saw a senior boy hurrying to Orchestra Practice with his instrument case in his hand, every time the Orchestra played at Morning Assembly, and he had to sit in the row with the rest of the first formers, a sense of the unfairness of everything overwhelmed him again, till he despaired of ever being able to overcome this recurring wretchedness. True to his resolve, he did not allow his mother and Marion to see how he felt, but told them only that Dr. Fowler had said there would be other opportunities as older boys left school, and he would keep Colin in mind. This seemed to please Mrs. Ramsay, who had, Colin knew, got into the habit of hoping for miracles as a way of rescuing herself from despair, but he himself was sure that when the next vacancy in the Orchestra occurred, and the next, and the next, he would have to go through all this disappointment again. It was a melancholy prospect. He knew that Marion was unhappy — one only had to look at her to see that — and he felt mean because he was not taking more interest in the mystery which was so important to her. But he was honestly at a loss to know what to do next, and in any case, he was not in the mood. Preoccupied with his own troubles, he did not want to have to think about hers. So he ignored her, and sat in his bedroom in the evenings. There was nothing else to do; Jake was writing a thesis which had to be finished by the end of the month, so work on the housebed had been temporarily suspended, while he sat at his desk with his Anglepoise lamp shedding light on the most terrifying calculations, which he was transferring from tattered notebooks onto fresh foolscap sheets. It was a very tense business, and visitors were not welcome. He had said, however, that if Colin wanted to work on the bed on his own, there were several little finishing jobs he could do, but Colin made excuses, said he had extra homework, was going out to play with Thomas. The truth was that now nothing would have induced him to go upstairs on a winter night, without Jake. He, too, was hearing music, and he had stopped believing in the MacPhersons' television.

And then, one Saturday morning, the breaking point which Mrs. Ramsay had anticipated was reached.

Colin had been out shopping at the Supermarket, for no matter how tragic and misused one felt, and uneasily aware that the commonplace at seventeen Mayferry Street was being gradually overlaid by the singular, life flowed on in its accustomed channels; one went to school, and did homework, and practised on the flute, and went to the Supermarket on Saturdays. And if there were no carrots left at the Supermarket, one went to the greengrocer's in Broughton Street, and if the greengrocer's was shut, one came home, and asked Mrs. Ramsay what was to be done about it, before taking off one's coat and boots. One still behaved as if carrots were important.

Colin had expected his mother to be in the kitchen, preparing the lunch and available for a consultation about the carrots, but she was not. She had gone upstairs a few minutes earlier to ask Jen to lend her her electric food-mixer, and had been delayed, because Jen wanted reassurance about a new coat which she had bought on impulse the previous day at the January Sales, and had hated from the moment when she took it out of the parcel at home. Mrs. Ramsay thought it was a frightful coat, but did not like to say so outright, and so had been detained, because it always takes more time to be diplomatic than it does to state one's true opinion. So when Colin came home, she was still hovering in Jen's bedroom, clutching the food-mixer, and trying to think of something useful to say, while Jen paraded gloomily to and fro, garbed in the most un-Jen-like garment of checked tweed and artificial fur, the effect of which was not enhanced by its being worn over old denim trousers and furry bedroom slippers. She kept saying, 'It seemed like a bargain at the time,' and, 'I know I look awful,' while Mrs. Ramsay tried kindly but feebly to disagree with her.

Colin was not in a good temper. It was a windy day, and he hated wind, and he was unreasonably annoyed about the carrots. He looked for Mrs. Ramsay in the kitchen and the pantry, and the little yard behind the house, and was unreasonably annoyed because she was not there. He was unreasonably annoyed about a lot of things these days. He went into the sitting-room, where Marion was sitting as usual, resting her head on her hand, and staring into the red heart of the fire.

'Where's Mother?' he asked her abruptly.

Marion did not reply, so Colin repeated his question in a

louder voice, which apparently did not penetrate her thoughts either. When he saw that she was still paying no attention, Colin stepped towards her, brushing her arm tentatively with his fingers. His touch seemed to rouse her, for now she turned her head, and looked at him. But her eyes were empty; they stared at him blankly, without question or interest or even recognition, and as he looked back, Colin had the sick, lurching sensation of a person who unexpectedly finds himself looking down into the blackness of a pit. It was not that Marion's eyes were black, for they were clear and beautiful and the colour of autumn, but their fixed, expressionless gaze communicated darkness in a way that frightened Colin more than anything he had ever seen in his life.

Of course he had known for a long time that there was something very far wrong with Marion, whose whole personality had changed in a year while he watched her. Often he had thought he would like to help her, but even while he thought it, a feeling of complete helplessness had overpowered him. He could not make her walk again, and since that was her problem, surely she was beyond any help that he could give her. From day to day, she involved him in a turmoil of contradictory feelings. Naturally he felt sorry for her, and tried hard to remind himself how terrible it must be to spend all one's life in a chair in the sitting-room, instead of going to school and playing in the park and going to the library, and doing even just the small things that one did without noticing, like getting up to switch on the television, or walking across the hall to the kitchen to take an apple from the basket on top of the washing-machine. So terrible to have to ask for everything, to have to be grateful all the time to other people for doing the things which one would much rather do for oneself. Colin could see all that, and understand it up to a point; he never for a moment thought that if the accident had hapened to him instead of to Marion, he would have been any more pleasant to live with than she was. But that did not alter the fact that she was the one who had to be lived with, and often she was neither easy nor pleasant. So even while he pitied Marion's plight, Colin could not always suppress the feelings of exasperation and impatience which she aroused in him, and then he felt guilty because he had felt exasperated. The unfair thing, of course, and the one which caused most of his tensions, both with Marion and within himself, was that whatever happened he must not quarrel with her. No one had ever actually told him this, but it was something he had picked up without being told. If Marion was unreasonable, it was because she was ill; if she was unpleasant, allowances must be made, because she had so much to bear. So Colin was patient, and held his tongue, but often recently, when he felt secretly that he had as much to bear as anyone else could possibly have, he had several times been on the verge of giving way to the temptation to shout at her, and tell her to pull herself together, and stop making everybody else's life a misery. Only today, as he looked into her eyes, he saw for the first time something to which he could not give a name; he only sensed that Marion had gone away into a world so remote and terrible that he could not even begin to imagine what it was like, a buried world that might claim her completely if he did not try to pull her back. He touched her arm again.

'What is it?' she asked dully.

'Where's Mother?' Colin repeated, as if it mattered any more.

Marion seemed to consider this for a moment as if it were a very difficult question, then she said, in the same flat voice, 'I think she went upstairs.'

She would have turned away from him then, because the truth was that now she was so deeply immersed in her own misery that she thought nothing else was of any importance, and she resented the intrusion of people who came rousing her from her thoughts to ask humdrum questions, breaching the walls of her isolation, when all she wanted, it seemed to her now, was to be left alone. She had said it a hundred times in the last few weeks, 'I just want to be left alone'. Which was very odd, when her thoughts were so dreadful, and of all possibilities that was the one of which she was most afraid. So when Colin, instead of going away upstairs to look for Mrs. Ramsay, went on standing in front of her, looking nervous, and said in that bright, unnaturally cheerful voice she hated, 'I've been thinking, it's really time we were trying to find some more clues to that mystery of ours,' Marion felt irritation welling up in her before she had time to notice what he was talking about. When she did, she felt more aggrieved than ever, because he was the one who had said that the next clue was bound to turn up on its own, and that there was no use going looking for it. She did not understand that he had picked on this topic because he could not think of anything else that might possibly interest her. She looked at him suspiciously, and wondered at the knack people had of smiling with their mouths while their eyes held quite different expressions, dark expressions which she could not read. She only knew that the two halves of the face did not match, and sensing yet again a tension which she knew she caused, but could not understand, she felt afraid.

Colin was afraid too, but very anxious to help, so he persevered a little longer. Thinking that yet again, Marion had not heard him properly, he began to repeat himself, but this time he had barely got started when she interrupted him.

'No,' she said, 'I don't want to. None of it is any use. It doesn't matter.'

Of course it mattered, of course it mattered more than anything in the world, only now, at this moment, she thought she would prefer anything to another period of futile searching, and more disappointments, hopes raised only to be dashed again the next day. She knew she sounded peevish and ungrateful, but that seemed of as little importance now as everything else.

'It doesn't matter,' she repeated. 'Just forget about it.'

Which normally Colin would have done, happily enough, but today it was different. He was no longer trying to provide Marion with a diversion, out of kindness, because he felt sorry for her. He was trying, in the only way he knew, to prevent her sliding away from him into that darkness of mind which he had just glimpsed so terrifyingly. So ignoring the warning, he tried again.

'It wouldn't be any trouble,' he said more brightly than ever to the face that was about as encouraging as a mask of stone. 'Honestly it wouldn't. I could go through the loft again, and if there isn't anything there I could try the cupboards on the landings.'

He went on and on, hopefully listing all the places he had ransacked already, and was willing to ransack again, if only Marion would reward him with one small expression of interest. But the more he said, the more annoyed and obstinate Marion became, the more determined to have none of it. She waited till he had run out of breath and places to search, then she said again, rudely and unpleasantly, just to make him stop, give up, go away.

'I've told you, so you needn't bother going on about it. *I don't want you to look again.* I'm sick of the whole thing. Why can't you get it into your head that all I want is for you to run away and play, and leave me alone?'

It was the sheer unfairness of it that took Colin's breath away. So this was his reward for evenings spent in cold empty rooms, looking in cupboards and drawers for clues to a mystery which until recently had scarcely even interested him, for days of his holiday gladly given up to the jig-saw letter, and the jacket, and sleuthing in the High Street. Yet even so, at another time he might still have spoken softly, because it was the custom of the house. But now, because he was frightened and upset, and completely out of his depth, the provocation of these words was too much for him. He seemed to feel something hard expanding inside his head, then a kind of explosion, and he was shouting above a strange singing in his own ears, 'All right, then, have what you want. I don't care. Only don't ever expect me to help you again, because I won't. You'd never have found anything if it hadn't been for me, and I wish I hadn't bothered, because you're an ungrateful beast, and you're not worth it. I'm sick to death of your whining and feeling sorry for yourself. So I will leave you alone, with pleasure.'

This too, of course, was unfair. Marion had never whined, and she did not even feel sorry for herself, only scared and worried about what was going to happen to her in the future. But as she listened to Colin's voice, loud and hard and unfamiliar, and heard the incredible remarks he was making, her first feeling was not one of resentment because they were unfair, but one of astonishment that he should be making them at all. She had often wondered why no one was ever angry with her, and what it would be like if someone was. She had even thought that she would prefer anger to patience, as being more natural. But now that it had actually happened, and Colin was standing in front of her, his face scarlet, shaking and clenching his rough little fists as if he would like to hit her, it was so terrible that she was in no way prepared for the shock of it. For one moment she wanted to shout back at him, to tell him that she hated him too, and would never forgive him for saying such dreadful things to her. But she could not find any of the words she needed; she had no experience of quarrelling, and before she could say anything at all, her inadequacy swamped her. She put her hands over her face to shut out Colin's angry eyes and the sullen, ugly look of his mouth, and shrinking back into her chair, for the first time in three years she began to cry.

At that sound, Colin's rage left him like rags blown away in the wind, leaving only the despairing thought that once again he had done something that must never be done, and said what must never be said. And when all he had wanted was to help.

'Marion,' he said, 'don't cry. I'm sorry. I didn't mean it. Please don't cry.'

Marion drew away from his touch, and went on crying, not

loudly, but privately, behind her hands. Then Colin knew he had to have help. He left Marion, and ran out of the room, across the hall, and up the stair to find his mother.

11

Marion

With the recollection of one slap in the face still very fresh in his memory, Colin rather expected another one, because the circumstances seemed to him exactly the same. A law had been broken, and punishment should follow. But this time, when he had rushed upstairs, located his mother in Jen's bedroom, and gasped out his unhappy story, Mrs. Ramsay reacted quite differently. She listened, then she laid Jen's food-mixer absently on the bed, and came downstairs with her hand on Colin's shoulder. In the hall she paused, and said to him calmly, 'You really mustn't worry too much about this. I've known for a while that something was going to happen, because things certainly couldn't go on this way much longer.'

'I only wanted to help her,' Colin said.

'Yes, I know, and it may be that you have. Now listen — I want you to go into the kitchen, and light the gas under the potatoes. Then put the kettle on, and wash up my baking bowls — it will give you something to do. Don't come into the sitting-room till I call you.'

And with this she left him, went in to Marion, and closed the sitting-room door behind her.

Marion, finding herself alone, had stopped crying, but when she saw her mother she started again. Mrs. Ramsay sat down on the arm of her chair, put her arm round her shoulders, and let her cry for a while. Then she gave her a handkerchief, and said in a kind but firm voice, 'All right — that's enough now. Dry your eyes, and then we'll see whether we can sort out whatever it is that's making you so miserable.'

Marion took the handkerchief, blew her nose, and within a few minutes had sniffed and hiccoughed herself out of her crying. Her eyes and nose felt large and hot, but she felt better, and had no desire to begin again.

'I'm sorry,' she said.

Mrs. Ramsay had removed herself to another chair, so that she was facing Marion. She watched her gravely for a moment, then she said, 'There's nothing to be sorry about. I've often thought it would be easier for you if you cried more often. I also think it would help if you would try to tell me what's troubling you. I'm not going to try to force your confidence, but it does help sometimes to talk about things, and if you can't tell me, who can you tell?'

Her sensible, unemotional attitude was exactly what Marion needed at that time. It was as if, while she was crying, the door which she had for so long kept pressed shut on her secrets had burst open, and suddenly it seemed to her perfectly natural that she should be pouring out to her mother all the fears and distresses that she had been so sure she could never share with anyone. It all came tumbling out in a rush of words, her dread of being pitied instead of loved, her own pity for her mother and Colin, her conviction that she was not going to get better, her fear of a future that would never be any more than an extension of the empty, meaningless, useless existence she had now. It was a relief beyond believing; it was only long afterwards that she thought how painful it must have been for her mother to listen to these despairing revelations. But whatever she thought, Mrs. Ramsay made no comment, but let her talk on, without interruption, waiting quietly till at last the stream of Marion's new-found loquacity had dried up, and the silence of the room was once more broken only by the bright, sudden little explosions of burning coals in the grate. Then she ran her fingers through her hair, sat back in her chair and said, 'Yes. I see. Well, it seems there are a number of things needing to be straightened out, so we had better take them one at a time, hadn't we? Let's begin with the easiest one — this nonsense about whether we feel sorry for you or not. Of course we feel sorry for you — but what on earth makes you think that we could only love you or pity you? Don't you suppose that we might do both at the same time?'

It surprised Marion to hear that this was easy; she had found it so complicated that she could make nothing of it at all. She did not try to answer the question, but looked straight at her mother, who went on, 'Marion, can't you see that if we feel sorry for you, it's because we love you, not because we don't? Pity isn't an alternative to love, it's part of it. If Colin and Jen and Jake and I didn't love you, we wouldn't waste our time feeling sorry for you either.'

'I don't want you to feel sorry for me.'

'I should hope you don't. But that isn't the point. Surely you can understand that when you love a person as much as we do you, you can't help feeling sorry when things go wrong. You feel sorry for me, and for Colin. You said so. Is that because you love us, or because you don't?'

'Because I do, of course.'

'There you are, then. You're answering your own question. I don't think there's any problem when we feel sorry for other people — the real trouble starts when we feel sorry for ourselves.'

'I don't,' said Marion.

'I know you don't. Neither do I, nor does Colin really. We're just going through a bad patch at the moment, as everyone does at one time or another. When we say we feel sorry for one another, it's just a way — not a very good one, perhaps — of saying that we each care what happens to the others, and that's the proof of love, however we try to express it.'

Marion understood this; it seemed so obvious that she wondered why she had never thought of it before. Suddenly she felt so much better that she risked a question which had been troubling her for a very long time.

'Mother, why is it that Colin never brings any of his school friends home to play after school? Is it because of me?'

Mrs. Ramsay looked so astonished that Marion's peace came even before she answered her.

'No, it certainly isn't because of you. Why should it be, for heaven's sake? I've hardly thought about it, but I suppose it's because they all live out at places like Liberton and Fairmilehead — they'd never have time to come here and get home before dark. In any case, I don't think Colin cares very much — he has Thomas and Vincent, and he has played with them ever since we came here to live. What a silly thing to worry about. You are an idiot, Marion.'

Idiot or not, things were beginning to look simpler to Marion now, and she felt happier, to the extent of greeting this remark with a smile. But nothing that had been said so far went any way towards solving her main problem, and it was to this that Mrs. Ramsay now turned, with markedly less confidence. Marion, who had a lot of experience in watching people's faces, and interpreting their tone of voice, noticed this, and began to watch her mother carefully.

'Of course,' Mrs. Ramsay said, again pushing at her hair with nervous fingers, 'I've known that you were worrying because your progress has been so terribly slow, but I didn't like to mention it when you didn't. It stands to reason — at your age, three years is such a long time. It must seem to you that this has been going on for ever. But you're wrong, you know. No one ever said how long it would take, and if you have given up hope, I'm sure no one else has. The doctors did warn us that it would be a long, slow business.'

Mrs. Ramsay knew that she was being watched. She hoped that she was managing to inject enough confidence and brightness into her voice to cover over her own anxiety and grief; she was so afraid that Marion might guess that her thinking was sadly like her own. Then she heard Marion's voice say, 'They also told us, if you remember, that some people never recover at all. Have you thought of that, Mother?'

There was something in her tone, something cool and challenging, which startled Mrs. Ramsay. She looked up into Marion's unwavering eyes, bewildered for a moment before she realized what it was. It was the sound of maturity. It shocked her for a moment to think that Marion was sufficiently grown up to face possibilities which she herself had shunned, but it was to Mrs. Ramsay's credit that she was nimble-witted enough to cope instantly with the fact that she was no longer pacifying a child who must be shielded from the truth at all costs, and change tactics accordingly. She knew that from this moment on, only honesty would do. So she replied truthfully, 'Marion, I haven't dared.'

Marion felt relief sweep over her. She had been so afraid that her mother was going to try to fob her off with the old half-truths and vague optimism with which they had tried to comfort themselves through years of not being able to face alternatives. Now she felt completely calm.

'I haven't either,' she said, 'but the time has come when I know I must. And I think I could, if —'

'If what?'

Marion hesitated. She knew that she was about to take the final risk, and that everything was going to depend on her mother's response to what she was about to say. But she had come too far to back out now, so she replied, 'If I could find a way of filling in my days with something that would really interest me. It's having nothing to do that's so awful. Every day is just a kind of emptiness that I have to get through, with nothing to look forward to but other days the same. That's what I can't face.'

'Of course,' agreed Mrs. Ramsay, trying not to sound as puzzled as she felt. She did not point out that she had been trying endlessly, for many months, to provide Marion with something

119

that would interest her, and was now at the point of despair. But after she had thought for a moment, she did remark, 'You used to find things to interest you — knitting and sewing and drawing your flowers. You were so good at all these things. What went wrong with them?'

'They stopped being enough,' said Marion simply. 'You see, knitting and drawing were all right when I was younger — they kept my hands busy, and they helped to pass the time. But they stopped being enough, Mother. Now I want — I need more than that.'

'Tell me what you need, Marion.'

Perhaps if Marion had ever anticipated this talk with her mother, she would have prepared a statement to answer this request. In fact, she had never really put into words at all what it was that she needed, or exactly what it was that she wanted to do. Everything was so mixed up in her mind, her dissatisfaction with her former interests, her boredom, the aching awareness that precious years of her life were passing, while she watched third-rate films on television, and made up far-fetched stories about people who had no substance, only shadows. Yet now, as she began to speak, it was as if she had known all along; her mind cleared marvellously, the idea formed with the words, and she knew that she was only speaking out loud the desire that had been sleeping inside her through all these months of sitting still.

'I need to learn,' she said. 'I need something that will let me use my head, even if I can't use my body. Mother, do you realize that since Miss Parkinson stopped coming here a year ago, I haven't learned a single thing? I'm nearly seventeen, I haven't been to school since I was thirteen, and I've hardly learned anything that really matters. That's what I want. I want to learn — to read books, and know things.'

Mrs. Ramsay was stung by the yearning in her daughter's voice. She felt a complete failure.

'I didn't know,' she said miserably.

Marion hastened to reassure her.

'Oh, Mother, it isn't your fault. I'm not blaming you, not in any way. How could you know when I didn't tell you? You've tried so hard, and been so patient, and I've been so difficult —'

'I never thought you were.'

'I know I was. You've brought me books from the library —'

'You didn't read them.'

'No. You see, they weren't what I wanted to read — what I

want to read now. I want to read real history, not romantic novels about Napoleon and Mary, Queen of Scots. I want to read good novels, but I hardly even know what they are.'

Mrs. Ramsay made a helpless gesture with her hands, and shook her head in perplexity.

'But, Marion,' she said, 'we have the best novels right here in this room. If I had known you wanted to read them — darling, we only had to open the bookcase.'

Marion looked despairingly at the vast bookcase, with its yards of shelving, and books marching tightly along it by the hundred, waiting to be read.

'I didn't know where to start,' she said.

Mrs. Ramsay saw the point of this, and nodded slowly.

'It seems I've been wrong about everything,' she said. 'Only —' she gave Marion an anxious glance — 'Marion, why have you never told me of this before? Surely you could have told me. Did you think I wouldn't try to help you?'

'No, of course not,' said Marion quickly. 'I knew you would, if you could. Actually, I've never really thought it out properly till now — what I want, I mean. I think I was afraid to, and afraid to talk to you about it, in case you said it was impossible. Then I wouldn't have had anything left to hope for.'

Mrs. Ramsay understood this explanation perfectly. She also saw how important it was that she should say at once that it was possible, which she did.

'Yes, I see,' she said. 'Well, it seems to me that there's a lot left to hope for. I intend to go on hoping that you'll get better, and I think you should too. But in the meantime, I agree that we should perhaps be exploring other possibilities for your future, and whatever happens, education is never wasted. So if you really want to study, we'll arrange things so that you can. I don't think there's any problem — lots of people study at home. You can take a Correspondence Course, and even work for exams if you want to. I'll tell you what — after lunch, we'll ask Jake. He's likely to know about these things, and if he doesn't, he'll be able to find out.'

Marion thought there was nothing in the world she would like better than to work for exams, and she was just about to say so. But before she could open her mouth, the door flew open and Colin arrived, very red in the face and followed by a horrible smell of burning food.

'I know you said I wasn't to interrupt you,' he said, 'but it's twenty to two, and your soup has boiled all over the stove, and your potatoes have stuck to the pan, and I've broken a baking bowl, and the MacPherson's cat has been sick on the back doorstep. I thought you ought to know.'

Mrs. Ramsay groaned and fled, and Marion laughed and laughed. She thought she had never heard anything so hilarious in her life.

Now that she had found out at last what Marion wanted, Mrs. Ramsay lost no time in seeing to it that she got it. That very afternoon, after she had cleared up the mess in the kitchen, and given Colin and Marion their lunch, she went upstairs and asked Jake if he could possibly spare the time to come down to talk to Marion for a little while. Jake said that he was delighted to have any excuse for deserting his thesis, and shortly afterwards he came loping down to the sitting-room, where he sprawled on the sofa, with his hands in his pockets and his feet on the coffee table, while Marion explained to him about wanting to study, and asked his advice about how to begin. She found that, having once dared to confide her dreams to her mother, it was easier than she could ever have imagined to discuss them with Jake, especially as he showed no surprise, and listened to everything she said with his usual indolent expression. Jake was not at all what he seemed. Often he reminded Marion of a clever cat trying to trick a mouse by pretending to be asleep. He gave the impression of being a lazy, casual, good-natured kind of person, who would like to eat well and doze by the fire. But when one knew him well, one came to see the power beneath this show of passivity, and the alertness of his blue eyes gave him away.

And of course Jake, who knew all about everything, knew about Correspondence Courses and the exams one could pass as a result of taking one. He never talked about sitting exams, only about passing them, a positive attitude which gave Marion a wonderful feeling of confidence. It was incredible to her that after all these bitter months of anxiety and fear of telling the truth, everything seemed to be falling into place so easily, without any of the uncertainties and difficulties she had imagined. Within half an hour Jake had taken his feet off the coffee table, and was planning her course of study for her, raking his pockets for a scrap of paper on which to write down the address of a Correspondence School through which he had once taken a course himself. She was to write for the prospectus at once, he said, if not sooner.

'It's the best thing you could possibly do,' he told her, 'instead of sitting here moping by the fire all day. Pity you didn't think of it sooner. However, you have plenty of time. If you spend the next two years studying for A-levels, you'll be ready to go to University when you're nineteen, which is just about right.'

'And what happens if I can't go to the University?' asked Marion, more to test him than to obtain an answer.

Jake gave her his straight blue look.

'You can go to the University,' he said. 'Lots of handicapped people go to College nowadays, and many of them are much worse off than you are. What you have to do is rid yourself of this stupid notion that everybody is going to be staring at you and thinking you're a freak — people just don't think like that any more, Marion. Besides, in a University it's what you can do with your head that they're interested in, not whether you can stand up or not. So if you don't go, it won't be because you can't, but because you won't.'

This was not the reply Marion had expected, although when she thought about it, later on, she realized that she should have expected it from Jake. It was hard, but it was just, and any hurt she might have felt was lost in the relief of knowing that other people besides her mother were going to be honest, and that from now on she would never have to distrust the expressions on their faces.

'I feel like a completely new person,' she said to her mother that night, when she was getting ready for bed. 'I feel that whatever happens to me now, I shall never be afraid of anything again.'

Mrs. Ramsay said she was glad, which was not exactly what she meant. She too felt like a new person.

After that, everything happened very quickly, without problems or setbacks. Letters were despatched, and their replies eagerly awaited; within ten days the first lessons of the Correspondence Course arrived, and were seized upon by a Marion who was scarcely recognizable as the withdrawn, listless girl of only two weeks before. Jen and Jake brought gifts of notebooks and pens. Colin insisted on lending his Souvenir-of-London pencil, which was eighteen inches long, striped red, white and blue, and had a small plastic Beefeater on the end of it, while Mrs. Ramsay withdrew money from the Savings Bank to pay the fees and buy the text-books Marion needed, consoling herself for the diminished balance with the thought that she had never spent money in a better cause. Colin, although privately he could not understand why anyone would choose to do lessons who didn't have to, was delighted by the change that had taken place. At first, when he looked at Marion, he only thought that he had never seen anyone so altered. She had got back some of the old eagerness and hopefulness which had been quite blotted out of her in the past year, and for that Colin was thankful, both for her sake and his own. But as the days went by, perhaps because he too was growing up fast, he began to see that there was more to it than this. Without really being able to put his understanding into words, he perceived that her hopefulness was not of the old kind. The truth was, of course, that whereas before she had been hopeful because she was ignorant, and so weak, now she had a new strength from having faced facts and come to terms with them. So she, and Colin with her, as far as he was able, learned something very important, which is that one can accept the shutting of any door in one's life, however desolating the experience may seem at the time, providing that one still has the hope of another door opening. Perhaps that was why Marion found that after all she was able to take her mother's advice, and go on hoping for her recovery; at a time when hope had suddenly flooded back to her like the warmth of the sun, it seemed right and natural that she should hope for that one great thing, and bearable now that everything did not depend on that hope's fulfilment.

12

In the Firelight

During the next few weeks, Marion thought very little about the affairs of Charles Ramsay and Alan Farquhar, principally because she was so busy thinking about her own. It was not that she forgot them, only that her new, happy preoccupation with the present seemed to push the past back from a position of prime importance into its rightful, subordinate place in her scheme of thinking. And although the plaintive music of the flute continued to curl and wind itself around the house, its first, simple tune weaving other tunes around itself in variations of unforgettable loveliness, then running off into silence again, that too was something which had ceased to disturb her. She knew now that it did not come from any radio or record player, and therefore was not in a strict sense natural, yet it seemed so to her; she sensed that it belonged in the house and was good, so that there was nothing to be afraid of. The days melted one into another, full at last of interesting things to do; February passed, and most of March, and it was not until the pale winter grass in the gardens was speared with the darker green of daffodil leaves, the smoky trees were turning a woody green with a hint of coming leaf, and Mrs. Ramsay was beginning to mutter about spring cleaning, that Marion found out that she was not alone in hearing music.

It was a Friday evening. After tea, Mrs. Ramsay had gone next door with a recipe book which Mrs. MacPherson wanted to borrow, Colin had gone upstairs to see Jake, and Marion had settled herself in the sitting-room, with Charles Ramsay's little desk on her knee, to write an essay on the causes of the French Revolution. She was not often allowed to study in the evenings, because Mrs. Ramsay said that to work all the time would be just as bad for her as not to work at all, so usually, when tea was over, she played chess with Colin, or knitted, or painted some wild flowers; all the pastimes she used to enjoy, and had discarded, she was re-discovering with a pleasure born of the fact that she was no longer using them in a vain effort to fill the great blank of her existence. But that afternoon her studies had been interrupted by the arrival of Dr. Woolf, weighed down by yet another vast manuscript which he wanted Mrs. Ramsay to type for him. He had stayed to drink several cups of tea, while Marion told him all the new things that had been happening in her life, and had been so interested that he was still there when Colin came home at half-past four. The result was that Marion was now behind with her work, and had had to persuade her mother at tea to allow her to catch up while Colin was upstairs with Jake. But scarcely had she had time to write her name, and get her first two sentences down on the paper, when Colin appeared, and it needed only a glance at his face to tell Marion that he was very upset about something.

'What's the matter?' she asked, putting down her pen.

Colin sidled across the room, and climbed into the armchair opposite hers, drawing up his feet and resting his chin on his knees. He said nothing, but looked at Marion solemnly with round brown eyes, so that she knew that whatever was wrong was serious; the less serious Colin's troubles were, the more noisily he told the world about them. He stared silently for a moment, and not until she had repeated her question, in a coaxing tone, did he reply, 'I don't know whether I should tell you. You might laugh.'

'Do I usually?'

'No, but this is different. You'd probably think I was being silly.'

'I don't expect so. I promise not to laugh, anyway. And I might be able to help.'

Colin shook his head dismally, with an expression on his face which said that no one could help with such a terrible problem, but he had now got to the point where he had to share his experiences with someone, and he knew that if Marion said she would not laugh, she would keep her promise. Besides, he had followed his first impulse in coming downstairs to Marion, because — it was one of the things he had noticed recently without putting it into words — she had become recently the kind of person to whom one did confide one's troubles. There was a new calm about her which steadied Colin; if she could not help, at least she would never betray his confidence. Nevertheless, he did not begin at the beginning, but in the middle, so that he could shift ground and prevaricate, if in the telling the story became impossible to tell right through.

'You know about Jake's housebed,' he began.

Marion knew about Jake's housebed. Although she had never

seen it, she had heard every detail of its construction from the time when it was a heap of planks in the middle of the work-room floor until now, when it stood complete, furnished and curtained, wanting only an occupant.

'Yes,' she said.

'Well then,' Colin continued, 'as you know, it's finished now, and Jake has sold it to a friend from the University. He says we don't have to worry about compact living here, and he only made it for fun anyway.'

Jake had actually said, 'For the hell of it,' but Colin was officially forbidden to swear; it was something Mrs. Ramsay was very particular about.

'So?' prompted Marion, beginning to wonder whether she could possibly guess something of what was coming next. She told herself that she couldn't, but still. . . .

'So, on Sunday he's going to dismantle it, so that he can get it downstairs, then on Monday evening Philip — that's Jake's friend — is coming with a van, so that they can take it out to his place at Balerno, and put it together again there. Jake says I can go too, if mother will let me. But before it goes, he has invited me to sleep in it, to try it out. *Tomorrow night,* Marion.'

He hugged his knees, and his eyes grew even rounder.

Of course all this might have been mysterious to Marion, but it was not. She had not forgotten the story Colin had told her on the morning after the treasure hunt, and how vehemently he had insisted that all he had heard had been the MacPhersons' televi-sion. Sometimes, with the music of the flute in her ears, she had wondered whether he now knew, as well as she did, that it had been nothing of the kind, but had not liked to ask him. A little shiver of excitement went through her chest, but for the moment all she said was, 'That's very kind of Jake, isn't it? I suppose he wants to thank you for helping him so much.'

'Yes, I know,' said Colin miserably, 'but —'

'But what?'

'I don't want to sleep in the workroom by myself. I'm scared.'

He rattled it out, and dropped his head quickly, afraid to look at Marion, in case he had misjudged her, and might see incredulity and worse, amusement on her face. But when she did not answer, and he dared to glance up again, he saw just the opposite. Marion had an unexpected expression on her face, which he could not read, but Colin could tell that she was neither surprised nor amused.

'I suppose,' she said gently, 'you've been hearing things too.'

'Music,' said Colin.

'Yes.'

They could each feel the relaxation in the other. It was out, the secret they had thought they could never share with anyone, and the relief from loneliness was wonderful. Colin, who had thought that he was faced with the telling of an unbelievable story, felt his inside uncoil like a released spring. He slid down from the chair with a sigh, and curled up cat-like on the hearth rug at Marion's feet.

'I wondered if I were going mad,' he said frankly.

'Yes, I did too, at the beginning. I've been hearing it for ages, on and off. Always the same tune, but somehow different.'

'Variations on an air,' said Colin. '"A rosebud by my early walk, a corn enclosed bawk."'

'Yes, that's the one. I wondered sometimes whether perhaps you heard it too.'

Colin rolled over, and stretched out on his front, his small face shining golden in the fire-light. Marion could see tiny flames reflected in his eyes.

'I first heard it on the day when I went to fetch Charles Ramsay's desk from the attic,' he told her, 'although I didn't realize what it was. I thought Jake had the transistor on. It was only later that I realized that he wasn't in the workroom at all, because I met him coming upstairs as I went down. He'd been out at the Do-it-Yourself shop. Then I told you what happened on the night of the treasure hunt. Jen said it was the MacPhersons' telly, and I just had to believe her. What I couldn't stand was thinking I was the only one who heard it. Since then, I've heard it often — hey, Marion.'

'What?'

'I was wondering — if we've both heard it, that means we're not mad, doesn't it?'

Marion's wide mouth curved into a delighted smile.

'I expect it makes it a little less likely,' she said teasingly.

Colin smiled back at her, wondering at her composure. He knew that whatever she felt, she had no fear at all, and that puzzled him, until he recollected that she had not been upstairs in this house for three years, treading in emptiness and shifting shadow.

'It's very strange,' he said hesitantly. 'It's eerie, Marion. Upstairs —'

He shivered, and the sight of him shivering did more to remind Marion of what it was like upstairs than any description could have done. She had a sudden, sharp remembrance of a silence that was never absolute, but alive with whisperings, and little muffled sounds, of air stirring, and being afraid to look behind. She had not thought of it for years, and the memory did not frighten her now, but she understood how Colin felt. She ran her fingers through the tight fleece of his hair.

'I know,' she said. 'It is eerie, in a way. But I can tell you one thing about it, Colin. It's good. It's nothing we should be afraid of.'

He was finding her sharing a help beyond words, but it did go through his mind that she had not been asked to sleep in the workroom tomorrow night.

'How can you know that?' he asked.

'It's just something I'm sure about. I don't believe anything so beautiful as that music can be associated with anything evil. And in any case, whatever it is, it isn't anything that's happening now.'

She said this reassuringly, as if she were trying to comfort him, yet to Colin of all the aspects of the affair this was the most disquieting. He sensed that what she said was true, but it was something his mind found impossible to comprehend. He voiced his difficulty.

'I can't understand that. How can we hear something that isn't happening now?'

'That's the real mystery,' said Marion. She screwed the cap on to her fountain pen, and made her hands busy tidying up the desk, while Colin watched her, knowing that she was putting her thoughts in order too. Presently she went on, 'Look at it this way. If it's happening now, it means that there is actually some person up there, playing a flute. An intruder, if you like. We know there isn't — it's impossible that there should be anyone upstairs in our own house that we don't know about, and in any case I should think that the last thing such a person would want to do would be to play a flute. And besides, if that were the answer, everyone would hear it, which they don't. Mother doesn't hear a thing, because when I mentioned it, she didn't know what I was talking about, and all one gets from the Taylors is this nonsense about the television next door.'

'Then it's a ghost,' said Colin, hardly believing that he was saying such a thing.

129

But Marion took the suggestion very calmly.

'Yes, I think in a way it is a ghost. Only to call it a ghost gives a wrong impression, because one thinks at once of Hallowe'en-type ghosts — white sheets and green faces, and all that sort of nonsense. What we're talking about hasn't anything to do with that. It seems to me that ghosts, if you must call them that, aren't things which exist in their own right at all, but the memories of people and happenings that are past — I can't explain it any better than that, but I think this house is full of such memories, and that's why we feel about it the way we do. I'm convinced that what we are hearing is something that is coming to us out of the past. Once, long ago, someone played a flute in his house, and now, we're hearing it.'

Never before had Colin been so aware of the gulf which separated the thinking of twelve years old from the thinking of seventeen. Until now, when he had discussed things with Marion, he had felt that they were equals, and that he could contribute just as much sense to the conversation, although he was five years younger. Now, he felt that she had somehow leapt ahead of him, leaving him with nothing to do but ask questions, while she told him what she thought the answers were. He did not feel jealous or resentful, only surprised.

'I could never have thought all that out,' he said.

'Of course you could,' replied Marion, believing it. 'It's just that I have more time for thinking than you do. Do you think I could be right?'

Colin repeated her words inside his own head: '"Once, long ago, someone played a flute in this house, and now we're hearing it." 'Yes,' he said, 'but I don't understand it.'

'Heavens, no,' said Marion. 'We're never going to understand a thing like this.'

Colin asked another question. 'Have you thought why?'

'Why what?'

'Why we are the only ones in the house who can hear the flute.'

Marion had thought why. 'I can only think,' she said, 'that it's because we are thinking about — the person who is playing it.'

'Charles Ramsay, Alan Farquhar.'

'Yes. You see, Colin, until we found the letter, and started to ask questions about their identity, we had never given any thought to the past in this house. You had school, and your interests outside, and as for me, in all my daydreams I only wanted to escape it. I don't know about you, but over these past few months, the past has sometimes seemed more real to me than the present. That's what I mean by saying that I think ghosts are memories of people in the past — one somehow makes them real by thinking about them.'

Colin nodded slowly. Put this way, he knew exactly what she meant. The experience she spoke of had been his both in the house and out of it; he had seen Watt Davie creeping down the stair, dark and sinister, with a small trunk on his shoulder, and the Edinburgh mob, surging up the Lawnmarket by St. Giles, with the Blue Blanket waving at its head. He had made them real by thinking about them.

'And so,' Marion was saying, 'I feel it must be significant that we've heard the music only since we found out about them.'

'I'll tell you what I feel,' said Colin, twisting uneasily on the rug. 'I feel that this house is wakening up.'

Marion considered this for a moment, but disagreed with him.

'No, I don't think so. I think it has always been like this. I feel that we are wakening up to it.'

Colin immediately saw the truth in this. All these years he had lived in this house, and it had never occurred to him that it was anything more than walls and roof packing in empty rooms that no one had any use for. And he had been right, in a way, for that was what it was, still. The change was not in the house, it was in him.

'Marion, do you suppose all houses are like this?'

'Probably,' said Marion. 'Old ones, anyway. The older a house is, the more memories it must have hidden away. Whether they are ever stirred up must depend on the kind of people who are living in them.'

Colin liked this. For the first time, he felt that he and Marion must in some way be special people, and favoured, because the music played for them. Unfortunately, the memory of the music reminded him of where this conversation had begun, and he repeated loudly that he still did not want to sleep alone in the workroom tomorrow night.

Marion's first reaction to this was matter-of-fact.

'Then, dearie, you'll just have to tell Jake you'd rather not,' she said. 'You don't have to, you know.'

But no sooner had she said it than she knew it would not do.

'Jake will think I'm not brave,' whispered Colin.

'Oh, dear,' Marion said.

She felt that she was failing Colin completely. No one knew

better than she did how much he admired Jake, or the lengths he would go to in order to appear worthy in Jake's eyes. And no one else knew at all that Colin was having to cope with a situation astonishing beyond Jake's wildest dreams, one he could never explain to excuse himself. And he was only a little boy; just as he had looked at her earlier, and seen her grown up, now she looked at him and saw him a child, who could not possibly share her new found confidence that all the threads of life were twisting together into a strong, reliable cord, and that there was nothing at all to fear. She looked down into his unhappy little face, drooping in all the corners where it usually turned up, and bit her lip, trying desperately to think how she could save him. Then all at once, she knew.

'Colin,' she said, 'how would it be if I were to come up with you, and sleep in the housebed too? It wouldn't be frightening if you had company, would it?'

Colin felt her strength flow into him. He stared back at her, surprise, pleasure and despondency passing in quick succession over his mobile face.

'Would you?' he asked, but in the same breath, 'You'll never be allowed,' he said.

'Just tell me — would you be happier if I did?'

'Yes, of course I would. It would be an adventure with two. But you'll never be allowed,' he said again.

Marion leaned back in her chair and began to laugh, softly and gleefully.

'Oh yes, I shall,' she said. 'Just watch me. I shall look wistful, and say I should give anything to spend a night in the housebed, and it would be such a treat for me if Mother would only say I could. And Mother will say to herself, "Well, poor thing, she doesn't have many treats, and if a little thing like that will please her. . . . "'

Colin was shocked, and wanted to laugh at the same time.

'Marion Ramsay, you're wicked,' he said.

'Yes, I know,' said Marion unrepentantly. 'Do you want me to sleep in the housebed with you, or not?'

Colin said hastily that he did, of course.

'Then you had better not be so prim about my methods,' said Marion cheerfully.

Mrs. Ramsay came in at this point, shedding her coat and scarf as she came, and remarking, 'Guess what — Mrs. MacPherson isn't at all pleased with me. The buzzard has moulted since it went next door, and now she has a bald buzzard and a feathered carpet in her dining-room. I suppose it felt overdressed in the central heating. It feels like the tropics in that house.'

Colin and Marion looked at each other, and began to laugh. There was nothing so reassuring as this humorous, earthbound positiveness in their mother, a quality which made it possible for them to go on living in a haunted house without ever being completely overwhelmed by its strangeness.

In spite of her self-confidence, however, Marion did not find it as easy as she had hoped to persuade Mrs. Ramsay to allow her to occupy the housebed with Colin on Saturday night. Forced to give every reason except the true one, she admitted to herself that her story sounded feeble, and feared defeat in the face of her mother's objections that it was still only the month of March, that the workroom was bound to be damp, and that it was foolish for Marion to risk catching a chill, especially when she was feeling so much better. Not until Marion came as close to the truth as she dared, and said that she really wanted to do it because she thought that Colin was a little nervous about sleeping alone, so far away from everyone else, adding that for herself, she would enjoy it as the first opportunity of sleeping out of her own bed for three years, did Mrs. Ramsay give in, for much the same reason as Marion had anticipated.

Jen and Jake were delighted when they heard from Colin that Marion would also like to accept the hospitality offered in the housebed, and Jen remarked to Jake how nice it was of Colin to be so pleased. Very early on Saturday morning, she went up to the workroom with a coal-scuttle, to light the fire, and spent the day trotting up and down to feed it, so that the cold, bleak room would be properly heated, and the bed properly aired, before Marion went into it. Jake said that he would come down to fetch Marion at half-past nine.

'So long to wait,' sighed Colin, not because, deep down, he was anxious for bedtime to come. But it was like waiting to go to the dentist's; one did not really want the time of the appointment to arrive, but one knew that one would have no peace of mind again until it did.

'We must keep busy,' Marion said.

Taking her own advice, and disturbed only occasionally by cool little stirrings within her, which had nothing to do with fear, she wrote her essay on the French Revolution in the morning, and spent the rest of the day reading George Eliot's *Middle-*

march, which was part of the work she had to cover for her next assignment. She looked at the clock more frequently than usual, but managed to get through the day quite comfortably. She heard no music blown to her through the open door.

Colin got through the day too, although less contentedly. In the morning, he went shopping as usual; in the afternoon he rigged his model of the *Victory*, and later went out to play marbles with Thomas and Vincent under the lime tree in their back court. The old sock in which he kept his marbles came back lighter than it had gone out; Colin could not concentrate, and the MacPhersons beat him easily. His mind was a whirlpool of contradictions, with boldness, apprehension, pleasure, bravado and downright terror breaking its surface by turns. He had said the previous night that it would be an adventure with two, and he still thought so; no prospect is ever so daunting when one has a companion. Without Marion, he knew, he would never have had the courage to accept Jake's invitation, and he was very grateful to her for saving his face with his friend. He admired her calm, too, although he could not share it, or even understand it. Whenever he caught her eye, she smiled at him, and said something like 'It's all right', or 'Don't worry', then went back to her book. But he was not at all sure that it was all right, and he could not help worrying at the thought of spending a night in a haunted room. In a muddled kind of way, he realized that underneath her desire to help him was a desire for something else, for an experience which had nothing to do with him. The difference between them was that if nothing happened in the workroom that night, he would be overwhelmed with relief, she with disappointment. And that was very strange, Colin thought, very strange that a person should feel so little fear when facing a situation from which she could not even run away.

So the day passed, and at last evening came. When tea was over, Colin went over to MacPhersons' to play; he wanted to be out of the house, and among people who were ordinary, and had no secrets. When he had gone, Marion asked her mother to bring her lacquered box. She opened it, and took out all the treasures she kept there, laying them out lovingly on the velvet surface of Charles Ramsay's desk. There were the letters the two young men had sent to each other in 1914, the Jura pebble, Charles Ramsay's photograph, the little gold key. Marion had thought before, as she thought now, how unexceptional they were, the little important, worthless objects from her own past, the letters and the photograph which had come to her out of the past of two other people. She was as far as ever, she believed, from finding a solution to the mystery they had brought her, yet now here she was, caught up with them in another mystery, more extraordinary by far. She looked at Charles Ramsay, but strangely, it was the brown pebble from Jura that she took up, and held in her hand, until it grew warm like a living thing.

St. George's Church clock said it was nine, and after thinking about it, the clock on the stair agreed. Marion got ready for bed downstairs as usual, and at twenty-five to ten, Jake arrived in the sitting-room to carry her upstairs. Colin was capering around the sitting-room in his dressing gown, looking so flushed and bright-eyed in his excitement that Mrs. Ramsay looked at him suspiciously, hoping that he was not about to come down with measles, from which the MacPherson boys had only recently recovered. If not, she thought, his state was one of alarming over-reaction to the pleasure of spending a night in the housebed, and she began to feel guilty about the humdrum nature of his life. From the beginning she had thought, with Jen, that the housebed was the most ludicrous object she had ever seen in all her days.

Marion thought so too. After a half-hour pause for supper in Jen's sitting-room, the little procession mounted the second stair to the workroom, where the housebed stood in the middle of the floor, polished and immaculate, a white elephant the size of ten white elephants, which was bound to inspire wonder, of one sort or another. Jake had made a beautiful job of it, as he did of every-thing, but neither the perfection of the furnishings which he had made for the living compartment underneath, nor the fresh brightness of the curtains and quilt covers which Jen had sewn for the sleeping platform above, could compensate for the inher-ent ridiculousness of the thing. Marion did not want to hurt Jake's feelings by laughing, although she noticed that he did not seem to be at all put out by Jen's mirth, so she did not look at Jen, who was pouring them all imaginary drinks from the empty cocktail cabinet, and giggling openly. The amusement which was permissible in a wife, Marion thought, might be rude in a friend, so as Jake carried her up the little staircase, and deposited her among the red and white pillows and quilts, she told him politely how ingenious everything was, and how clever he had been — which was true, as far as it went. Jake, who was not unaware of the absurd aspect of his masterpiece, grinned widely, and putting his brown head over the edge of the bed, he called down to Jen. 'Do you hear that, Mrs. Taylor? Marion thinks it's very ingenious.'

At which Jen laughed more than ever, raising her imaginary glass to Colin.

'Cheers,' she said.

It seemed that Jen and Jake would never be ready to go away. Jen spent ages crawling about on the sleeping platform, which would have accommodated eight people easily, making sure that Marion was comfortable, and having a pillow fight with Colin, who had temporarily forgotten his alarm in the merry normality of his friends' company. She sent Jake down to boil a kettle and refill Marion's hot-water bottle, made up the fire, and sat for a long time dangling her green-stockinged legs over the edge of the platform, wrangling pleasantly with Colin about the merits of the rival Rugby teams they supported.

Marion tired of nonsense quickly. It jarred upon her mood of inner quiet and intense expectancy. She had not lost the ability, fostered during the darkest days of her unhappiness, to withdraw mentally from what was going on around her, and she did so now. Closing her ears to the sound of Colin's and Jen's voices, and blotting out the physical presences in the room, she retreated into her own corner, and began to observe intently her surroundings; part of the absurdity of the housebed was, she realized, accounted for by the incongruity of its setting. The room was sad and shabby enough, Marion thought, as she ran her eye over the sallow walls with their tracery of discoloured roses, and the faded velvet curtains, softer yet for the fur of white dust clinging to their snuff-coloured pile. The carpet was gone, the ceiling cracked and flaking, with one unshaded light bulb, at the end of a dusty flex, casting crude, undirected light into all the shameful corners of the room. Only the fire which Jen had made leaped orange and gold in the basket of the ornate iron grate, as it had done sixty years ago, when some other Ramsay had sat by it, slippered feet on the fender, enjoying its friendly warmth and liveliness before getting into bed. Lines from a poem she had read floated into Marion's mind, as she thought of that other Ramsay:

> 'But the tender grace of a day that is dead
> Will never come back to me.'

Well, perhaps. She thought that it had not been her experience. She looked into the fire, then and now.

Marion was recalled to the present by the rumpus going on on the other side of the platform. Jen was trying to kiss Colin good-night, while Colin squealed and writhed and burrowed under the covers so that she could not get at his face. She gave up, eventually, and flopped over to Marion's side of the bed.

'Good-night, honey. Are you comfortable?'

'Yes, lovely, thank you, Jen.'

'If you need me, send Colin down.'

'Yes, I shall. Good-night, Jenny.'

'Good-night, kids,' from below.

'Good-night, Jake.'

At last, the light was out, and they were gone, leaving behind a stillness that was the more intense for the noise that had preceded it. Colin and Marion listened to their feet descending the stair, his heavy, hers light, like an echo. Then firelight, and silence. A draught lifted the curtain, and laid it down with a sigh. Laughter drained out of Colin, and misgiving filled the emptiness.

'Marion,' he whispered.

'Yes, love.'

'Shall I bring my covers closer to you?'

'Yes, of course. You seem so far away.'

But it was not, he knew, that she needed him. There was movement, and Colin's shadow vast on the ceiling as he pulled his pillow and his quilt across the space on the mattress which separated his position from Marion's. He lay down again, wriggling in close to her back. Marion had managed to pull herself over onto her side, and she was half sitting up, supporting herself on her elbow as she looked over the edge of the platform into the fierce, rose-gold heart of the fire. Pink flickerings patterned the walls, and the ceiling above their heads.

'Marion.'

'Yes.'

'Do you think we're going to hear that flute tonight?'

'I'm sure of it,' Marion said.

Perhaps they slept, perhaps they did not. It was hard, afterwards, to tell anything with certainty, even the extent to which their experiences had been a kind of dream. They only knew that they had been in the thrall of something so beautiful that to the end of their lives, all beautiful happenings would seem like a shadow and an echo of it, attempts to know again the wonder of a single night spent camping in a shabby room. Marion thought the music came first, Colin that the beginning was movement, the formation of shapes in the firelight, shadows, yet with the seeming substance of life. Either way, it was not important, because both sound and shape were weaving themselves into a harmony which soon the eye and the ear absorbed without any sense of their separation. Pure and wild, a flute went singing, first the simple melody that Colin and Marion knew so well, then catching up other tunes that they thought they knew too, spinning them into a silver gyre of sounds, making harmony of the wind sighing, the sea birds calling, the waves breaking on a shore. Then they saw that the music was rising to them, wherever they were, from two boys sitting on the floor, dark silhouettes in the fireglow, one playing, one listening, surrounded by the shadow-forms of furniture which had stood in this room before Colin's father was born. But the flute sang on, its songs of longing and joy and sorrow, and Marion and Colin forgot the boys as they were drawn into the heart of its enchantment; the shadows that had for so long been the solace of Marion's life began to form upon the wall, but not now as she willed them, rather as the music invoked them. There was a deer leaping, horsemen riding among trees drawn black against the fire of the evening sky, and they were riding to the sea. Now morning came. The shadows lightened into shapes; Marion saw the blue-green branches of pine trees, and behind their sweet, resinous scent there was a strong, sharp smell of the sea. Now she saw, as the sun rose, a path through the trees, and it came to her that she knew the path, and she knew the trees. They were behind the little white-washed cottage near the beach on Jura, where she had spent her summer holidays with her father and mother and Colin, so long ago that it seemed to her now that she had become another person in another world. Half-way along, the path forked, and Marion remembered that the path to the right wandered off up a little hill, leading eventually through crumbly red soil and encroaching shingle to the beach, bordered all along by a bank of pebbly bracken and thin, wind-bent saplings which blocked out the silver movement of the sea. But not its sound; Marion heard its voice again in the music of the flute, and the crying of gulls and sea mews overhead. She could remember nothing of the path to the left, only that one entered it through a tangle of fern and bramble which scratched one's bare legs, making white scores on sun-burnt skin, and that further on, one came to a corner, where the path turned down an incline among the pines, and one walked in the dark on the spongy floor of fallen needles, with a sky of net overhead. Where the path went to after that, she could not recall; she was aware of an overwhelming desire for sleep.

She heard Colin's voice say, 'The unicorn is swimming in the waves,' and felt surprised; it was not what she had seen at all.

The fire leaped up in ribbons of golden flame, and fell apart, caving inwards and dying in a shower of bright sparks. Simultaneously, the walls darkened, the figures at the hearth dissolved, and the music faded away. Marion put her arm over Colin, turned her face to the pillow, and slept.

13

An Unexpected Visitor

Several days passed before Colin and Marion had an opportunity to discuss what had happened on the night when they had slept together in the housebed. They agreed, later, that this had really been a good thing, since to begin with, so strange had their experience been, they would not have known what to say to each other. Each needed time to think, privately, and to absorb the night's wonders alone; the course of events provided them with the chance to do so. From the moment they awoke, in the dusty morning, with the grey north light dripping coldly on to the floor through a chink in the curtains, and the dolorous clamour of Edinburgh's church bells telling them solemnly how late they had slept, for three days they were never left alone together for more than a few moments.

For while they were still lying half awake, smiling at each other without having said a word, Jen arrived, in patched velvet trousers and a pink Indian shirt, ushering back the world of every day with a laden breakfast tray, and the announcement that she could not step on the bedclothes, because she had wet varnish on her toe nails. Colin scrambled up and took the tray from her at the top of the little stair; Marion watched her strutting barefoot to the window, on her heels, in the half-darkness, and letting in a clear flood of light as she drew aside the snuffy curtains. She gave them a weather report, squatted down to test her nail varnish, and decided that after all it was safe to come up. By the time when Jake arrived to carry Marion downstairs, Jen had managed to eat at least two thirds of Marion's share of the breakfast, without having stopped talking once.

Colin felt obliged to spend the rest of the day helping Jake to dismantle the housebed. He found this task less disagreeable than he had expected, since Jake never intruded on his thoughts with chatter, and it had a steadying effect on him to see the workroom once more revealed as what it was, a dirty, uninhabited room, which seemed to have no connection at all with the enchanted places where Colin had been the night before. Only now and then, when his eyes strayed from his screwdriver to the cold grey honeycomb of ashes in the grate did he grasp, with a small shiver, that it had all happened here, and not in some wonderful firelit hall where he had never been before, nor would ever be again.

Marion spent the day with a book in her lap which she was too stunned to read. She did not think she was unhappy, yet every little while she felt scorching tears in her eyes, and a feeling of desolation swept over her. But the feeling passed quickly, and she could not recall it once it was gone. A greater problem was hiding from her mother the fact that she had the worst headache she had ever had in her life. Eventually Mrs. Ramsay found out, and packed her off to bed immediately after tea, which pleased Marion well enough. She intended to lie quietly, and try to recall what was round the corner of the path through the wood, but she found that she was too tired even to try, and when Colin came downstairs at nine o'clock, she had already been asleep for two hours.

Monday's school separated them again, and on Monday and Tuesday evenings, Colin was away at Balerno, helping Jake and Philip to wrestle with the problems of rebuilding the housebed in a cottage with a coombed ceiling. Jake was so unnerved by the task that he promised Colin, as they drove home on the second evening, that the next project would be the simple one of building a two-seater canoe, which they would take to Cramond on Sunday afternoons in the summer. Colin arrived home in such a state of rapture that his mother began fretting about measles again. On Wednesday night, however, when Mrs. Ramsay had retired groaning into the kitchen with her typewriter and Dr. Woolf's fourth thesis, Marion and Colin found themselves face to face across the chess board, and not many moves had been made before the game was forgotten, and they were once more talking, the kind of talk that is no more nor less than the telling of one's thoughts out loud.

'What I keep wondering and wondering,' Colin said, pushing his stool back, and pointing his feet to the blaze, 'is whether it was all a dream. I feel it must have been, but I know that if it was, then a dream has been the realest thing that ever happened to me in my life.'

Marion smiled appreciatively at this. It was exactly what she had thought herself.

'I know,' she said. 'Perhaps it was a dream, in a way, although I don't remember even feeling sleepy before it began. In any case, its being a dream wouldn't make it any less strange, would it?

141

Dreaming is usually a very private affair, yet we shared it — whatever it was, you and I felt and heard the same things. I don't think I can ever forget the joy that music brought me, yet it was a strange joy, because even while I was happy, it was hurting me. I saw Jura, Colin, and I thought Daddy was in the house.'

'I saw a white unicorn,' said Colin, 'running through the trees. It leaped out of some bushes on to a beach, and ran into the surf. I didn't know it was Jura — I can't remember much what it was like there.'

'Of course,' said Marion, remembering. 'When you were little, you had a book with a picture of a unicorn in it. You used to sit on Daddy's knee and look at it, before you went to bed. And when he went to London, you always wanted him to bring a unicorn home for you, from Regent's Park Zoo. Had you forgotten that?'

'Yes. I remember the book vaguely. But what did that have to do with Jura?'

'You thought unicorns lived in the forests there. In those days, everything had to do with Jura. I think we talked about it from one summer to the next.'

Marion knew that there was no point in asking Colin if he remembered the path through the wood. Colin hardly remembered anything of the old days. Sometimes she pitied, sometimes envied his forgetfulness.

There was a silence for a while, broken by the ticking of the clock, loud and immediate against the distant rumble of traffic in Princes Street and George Street, the background music of city life. The fire crackled cheerfully, without mystery.

'Marion,' said Colin presently, 'do you suppose we shall ever hear that music again?'

Marion shook her head sadly, knowing at last the reason for the tears that had been rising in her eyes at intervals, ever since Sunday.

'I don't know the answer to that question,' she replied. 'I think perhaps not — I haven't heard it again since that night, and it seems to me that then we were probably hearing it for the last time. But I can't be sure.'

'There's one thing sure,' said Colin, picking up one of the chessmen and fingering it gently, 'I shall never be afraid to go upstairs again, whatever happens.'

'No, indeed. Nothing so lovely could possibly do anyone harm. The two boys —'

'Charles Ramsay and Alan Farquhar.'

'Yes, I'm sure of it. Colin, did you see their faces?'

'No. They were in the shadow — no, I don't think I looked,' replied Colin, frowning a little, for there was a puzzle here.

Marion put it into words.

'It's very strange, isn't it, how all through this winter we've talked about them and thought about them, yet when we were in the same room with them, we hardly noticed them at all? We've no idea which of them was playing the flute. It didn't seem to matter — it was the music that was important. That was the link between us and them. I had convinced myself that we were going to experience something of the past that night, and so we did, but did you notice, Colin — the only part that wasn't in shadow was the part that had to do with our own past, not theirs at all.'

'He was a most marvellous flautist,' said Colin longingly. 'To be able to play like that —'

'You will, some day,' predicted Marion loyally. 'The flute is a bond between him and you.' She paused for a moment, then she went on, 'You know, Colin, I'm beginning to wonder whether I was right in thinking that it was the manuscript of a book that Alan Farquhar left in his trunk. Every thing now seems to be pointing towards something quite different.'

It took a long minute for her meaning to break upon Colin. His wide eyes grew wider.

'Marion! Do you really suppose —?'

'Well, use your head, Colin,' ordered Marion.

Colin used his head, and as a result spent much of the next two evenings upstairs, knocking on walls and opening cupboards in rooms which he had already searched from top to bottom and side to side, with the usual result. The music was not heard again; time went by, and the upstairs rooms returned to the dreaming stillness which had characterized them before the flute began to play. The night spent in the housebed itself became part of the past, and as the routine of everyday life at number seventeen wound them with firm threads into a protective cocoon of normality, the immediacy of that extraordinary experience faded, and they lapsed back into a way of life dominated by the commonplace. They did not forget, and Marion still felt occasionally the ache of being shut out from the place where she most wanted to be, but more and more they came to remember that night of magic as a peculiarly bright dream. They did not talk of it much, nor indeed of the other mystery with which at that time, oddly, they scarcely associated it, for now they were both convinced that some things could not be hurried; they could only wait, and trust that sooner or later the wheels of the mystery would start to turn again. In the meantime, there were lots of other things to think about.

After weeks of advancing and retiring and changing its mind, spring came like the crack of a whip. There was warmth in the sun; all at once the faint, tender fuzz of lime along the branches burst out in a plumage of bright leaves and pink blossom, and there were daffodils everywhere. In May the flowering currant reddened between the railings in Queen Street Gardens, and the long still evenings of the north were luminous with silver and green. And instead of having it all reported by Colin and Mrs. Ramsay, Marion went out to see for herself. Reluctant, as Colin had been, to have Jake think she was not brave, and tempted by the beauty of the lime tree in the next door yard, she went with him twice, on clear evenings to the library at the University, and the second time allowed him to take her for coffee on the way home. It was all a great deal less terrifying than she had imagined, and, although she watched very, very carefully, she did not see a single person staring at her. Indeed, apart from a red-haired waiter who winked at her, she did not see anybody looking at her at all.

'What did I tell you?' said Jake triumphantly, as they drove home in the leafy twilight, juddering over the cobbles round Moray Place and along Heriot Row, under a thin white slice of moon.

But such weather in Scotland never lasts for long; after ten days it changed, and the city went grey again. Without the sun, it became bitterly cold, with only the bent flowers and the leaves, thrashing about in the wind against a stale sky, to remind the shivering citizens that it was not still February. Mrs. Ramsay made Colin put on his overcoat, and he went back to grumbling every morning about the rain, or the wind, or both.

One wet and windy Tuesday afternoon, Mrs. Ramsay had to go to the dentist's, on the other side of the town. Her appointment was for four o'clock, and knowing that she would probably be delayed in the rush-hour, and that Colin would be home, starving, long before she would, she told Marion that she would leave some milk and sandwiches for him, and make a meal for all of them when she eventually got back. But Marion said there was no need for this; 'I can make the tea quite easily, if you leave things where I can reach them, and we have it in the kitchen. Then you won't have to bother about starting to cook when you come home — especially since you may not have any teeth left.'

'That isn't funny,' said Mrs. Ramsay, who was getting weary of jokes on this particular topic. 'However —'

She looked at Marion speculatively, and wondered whether to agree to her proposal. It was a miracle enough that she should be making it; Mrs. Ramsay sometimes had to shake herself into realizing that this was indeed the same girl who had huddled by the fire for months and months, moping and refusing to leave her chair. But cooking was one of several new interests that Marion had discovered recently, and she had been spending quite a lot of time in the kitchen, helping to make pies and pancakes and chocolate biscuits, which Colin scoffed and cheerfully pronounced poisonous. It seemed a pity not to allow her to put her new knowledge to use, but at the same time Mrs. Ramsay was reluctant to leave her working at the stove when she was alone in the house. She explained this to Marion, who was sensible, and said she understood, and so a compromise was arranged. Mrs. Ramsay would leave a pie ready, so that Marion had only to light the oven, and lay the table ready for Colin coming home at half-past four. She could put on the kettle, but Colin was to make the tea when he came in. Accordingly, when Mrs. Ramsay had departed with her umbrella in the rain, Marion put aside her books, and wheeled herself across the hall to the kitchen, where she began to lift the cups and saucers from the draining-board, and lay them out on the blue-checked tablecloth. She put on the kettle, refilled the sugar basin, and poured milk into a jug from a bottle in the refrigerator. Just as she was going to fetch the salt and pepper from the cupboard beside the stove, the door opened, and Jen put her smooth head round it.

'Boo,' she said.

'Boo to you too,' said Marion. 'You're very early today. Do you want a coffee?'

The rest of Jen quickly followed her head into the kitchen. She was wearing a pink and brown striped cloak, jewelled with raindrops, and purple boots. Her nose was red and shining.

'That's very civil of you,' she said. 'My office was closed early because the central heating broke down, and we were all blue with cold. It seemed like a blessing at the time, but then I had to stand for an hour at the bus stop, having a shower bath every time a car went by, then I got a ticking off from the conductor because

I didn't have the right money, and to crown it all, I was nearly trampled to death in the British Home Stores.'

She sat down at the table and shrugged off her cloak, revealing a pink pinafore underneath. Marion looked at it approvingly.

'What did you buy in the British Home Stores?' she asked, as she spooned instant coffee into a cup, and directed Jen towards the kettle.

'Nothing,' replied Jen, going to the stove, 'I couldn't get near to a counter. I was lucky to get out alive.' She always exaggerated wildly, partly from habit, and partly because she knew it made Marion laugh. She brought her coffee back to the table. 'Where's your Mama?'

'At the dentist's. I'm in charge.'

'So I see,' said Jen. She stirred her coffee, and watched Marion lighting the oven and bringing bread to the table from the bread bin. Mrs. Ramsay was not alone in finding it difficult to recognize the new Marion. 'What's Hilary having done at the dentist's?' asked Jen.

'Hilary doesn't know. She hoping for the best, and expecting the worst,' Marion told her, giggling hard-heartedly.

Just then, the doorbell rang.

'I'll go,' said Jen, getting to her feet.

Marion peeped into the oven, to make sure that the pie was not getting too brown, and began to put out forks and knives. She heard the front door close, and feet clipping across the linoleum in the hall, but not until Jen was actually back in the kitchen did she realize that there had been two pairs of feet, not one. She looked up, and saw, standing behind Jen, another girl, whom she had never seen before in her life.

'It's someone to see you,' said Jen.

It was a testing moment for Marion, and, had the stranger known it, a testing moment for her too. Both passed the test. Marion, recovering quickly from a panicky feeling of having been caught out, smiled at the stranger and said, 'Hello,' while the stranger, a stout girl in a red waterproof and head scarf, looked back at her without a flicker of curiosity or pity in her eyes.

She said, 'My name is Janet Baxter. We haven't met, but your brother came to our shop in the Christmas holidays. Perhaps you remember.'

'Yes, of course I do,' said Marion.

She could feel the quickened pattering of her heart under her jersey. The wheels of the mystery were beginning to turn again.

'Well, I'll be off,' said Jen, picking up her belongings and her coffee. 'I'll bring your cup back later.'

She nodded pleasantly to Janet and left, closing the door behind her. Marion was fleetingly surprised; she would have expected Jen to stay, just to make sure that she was all right. But then she realized, rather proudly, that Jen had gone because Janet Baxter was her visitor, and because now she was able to cope with things on her own.

'Would you like some coffee?' she asked Janet, not at all shyly.

'Yes, thanks. That would be lovely. It's a foul day out.'

She laid her briefcase on the edge of the table, and sat down on the chair Jen had just left. She took off her head scarf, and shook out her limp yellow hair. Marion brought another cup, and reached for the coffee jar.

'I wonder if you would pour the water in yourself,' she said. 'I'm not supposed to lift the kettle.'

'Surely,' said Janet, without fuss.

Politeness forbade Marion to ask Janet what she wanted, and somehow she managed to endure the seemingly endless ten minutes during which Janet drank her coffee, admired the china, and groused about the weather, at intervals explaining that she was a student at Heriot-Watt University, and lived quite near the Ramsays in Royal Circus, so that it was no trouble at all for her to turn along Mayferry Street on her way home, instead of going straight down Howe Street. Marion listened, and nodded, and was just beginning to form the unpleasant suspicion that this was only a social call after all, when suddenly Janet said, 'When Colin came to the shop, he was looking for information about a man called Watt Davie. That's right, isn't it?'

'Yes,' replied Marion, trying to look cool, and not let her excitement show.

Janet nodded slowly.

'I remember it well,' she said, 'because it was so unusual. It's an awful bore keeping a shop in the Royal Mile in the winter, and I liked Colin a lot. He was a nice little kid. I've often wondered whether he managed to solve the mystery of what Watt Davie did with the other things he stole. Did he?'

'No,' Marion told her. 'We haven't really found out any more about it since Colin came to see you.'

This was true up to a point; anything they had found out since was not for telling.

'I see. Well, you'll be surprised to hear that I have — found out something else, I mean. It's nothing marvellous, but it was such an extraordinary coincidence — a chance in a million, that really — I thought I must come and tell you about it.'

'Then tell me,' pleaded Marion, forgetting to be cool.

'Well,' said Janet emphatically, putting her elbows on the table and settling to her story, 'it was like this. Under our shop, we have a kind of strong-room, where we keep all the items we can't display, because the shop is too small. Some of them have been down there for years, kept just on the off-chance of their being asked for — everything from chopsticks to warming pans. It's an awful nuisance, because it has all to be kept clean, and I'm always having to go there to work when I'd rather do something else. However — one night last week, I was down in the store-room with Mother, and we were checking on a crate full of bits and pieces — china, mostly, but some brass and copper as well. All the items were wrapped individually in tissue paper, with a layer of newspaper on the outside. It was obvious that they had been there for years and years — the crate was ancient, and the china honestly wasn't the kind of stuff we can sell nowadays. However, Mother is very fussy about her stock, and when she saw that the newspaper was all yellow and falling to bits, she decided that all the junk would have to be re-wrapped — and just when I wanted to get home to see a programme on T.V. Anyway, she went away upstairs to the office to get some fresh newspaper, and I started to unwrap the stuff from the paper it was in. I had done one or two plates when I noticed that the old newspapers were dated September 1914, so it was no wonder they were past their best. I thought of Colin, just because it was the year he was so interested in, and while I was waiting for Mother to come back, I picked up one of the papers and started to glance through it. It was an *Edinburgh Evening News*, and it had a lot of local news in it that made you think Edinburgh must have been exactly the same then as it is now — what Bailie Wotherspoon said at the Town Council, you know, and complaints about the pigeons making free with the pavements in Queen Street. But there was a lot about the War too, especially about a battle that had just been fought on the Marne. Apparently the reports about it were still coming in. There was a list at the bottom of the front page, headed 'Edinburgh Casualties', divided into three columns, 'Killed', 'Wounded and Missing', 'Presumed Killed'. I let my eye run down the first column, quite casually, and there it was — look, I brought the paper with me.'

She unzipped her brief case, and took out a crackly yellow newspaper, which had had its crumples smoothed out, and which was now neatly folded. She passed it across the table to Marion, pointing as she did so to a name which she had circled with a red biro. Marion held it up to the light, and read, 'DAVIE, James Watt, Cpl. Argyll and Sutherland Highlanders, C/o 37, Cowgate'.

'That's the man,' she said. 'His mother lived in the Cowgate.'

When she was telling Colin and her mother all about it later, Marion said that it was just as well that Janet had warned her at the start that her discovery had been 'nothing marvellous'. So marvellous had the story been, that she would have expected to hear that Alan Farquhar's trunk had been advertised as lost property in the newspaper. Yet she had to admit to herself that that news could scarcely have been more dramatic than this. She looked at the paper in wonder, then she said to Janet, 'It's so extraordinary, I can hardly believe I'm seeing it. He must have been killed after only a few weeks in France. The War only began in August.'

'Yes. Well, maybe that was better than to go through hell, only to be killed at the end of it,' said Janet philosophically. She gulped the last of her coffee, and stood up. 'Marion, I must go. I only looked in to give you the paper. I thought you would be interested.'

'Oh, yes, I am. Colin will be, too. Can't you stay to tea, and tell him yourself?'

'Not tonight, unfortunately. I have an exam. tomorrow, and I really must look over some work. Better late than never, you know. But if you'd like to ask me to come another time, I'd love it. Maybe you'll have solved the mystery by then.'

Marion said there was not much chance of that, but she arranged that Janet would come to tea on Sunday, and remembered, as Janet was tying on her head scarf again, to ask two questions that had been in the back of her mind while they talked.

'Janet, how did you know where we lived?'

'Colin mentioned it. He said the Ramsays lived in Mayferry Street, not Ramsay Garden. I didn't know the number, but having a good Scots tongue in my head, I went to the first house and asked.'

'And when you came, why did you ask for me?'

'Because Colin said it was your mystery,' said Janet. 'Goodbye till Sunday.'

When she was gone, Marion took the pie carefully out of the oven, and listened for Colin's steps in the hall.

14

One Thread Breaks

All the Ramsays would have liked to sit down, as soon as tea was over, to discuss the incredible news which Marion imparted separately to each of the other two, almost as they came through the kitchen door; their open astonishment was a rich delight. But Colin had lots of homework to do that night, and Mrs. Ramsay, returned jubilant from the dentist's with her teeth intact, had rashly promised Dr. Woolf his thesis by next Saturday without fail. It would never do, she said, to disappoint a good customer like Dr. Woolf, so she must type a section of it every evening. There was a time, not very long before, when Marion would have felt hurt and aggrieved because they could not drop everything to pay attention to her and her concerns, but now, she too had work to occupy her, and agreed readily to her mother's suggestion that they should all bottle up their wonder and curiosity till supper time. So when Mrs. Ramsay had gone into the kitchen, and Colin to his room, Marion settled herself in her chair by the sitting-room fire, with *The Heart of Midlothian* on her knee, determined not to waste her time. Until recently, she would not have been able to concentrate with such an interesting question in her head; she would have sat there, letting her eyes skim the same paragraph over and over, absorbing nothing, while her thoughts went wandering through the house, following shadows. Now, however, she was learning to discipline her mind, discovering how to concentrate on one subject at a time, shutting out all others. And so, when her mother joined her in the sitting-room at half-past eight, she was surprised to find how quickly the time had passed.

Mrs. Ramsay always tried to find some time in the evening, when Colin was occupied elsewhere, to discuss with Marion the books she had been reading. It was a long time since she had been able to have this kind of conversation with anyone, and she was enjoying thoroughly this interest which she and her daughter had suddenly found in common. Marion, for her part, was delighted to discover how interestingly her mother could talk about books and history and all sorts of other subjects, and sometimes she felt rather ashamed that she had lived with her for so long, and had never taken the trouble to find out the kind of person she really was. She had taken her for granted, she realized, as the person who made the meals and cleaned the rooms and did for her all the things she was unable to do for herself, and had scarcely noticed that besides being a cook and a housemaid and a nurse, she was also an intelligent, educated woman, who had far more to offer her children than the making of pies and the washing of linen. But when she tried to tell her mother this, and to apologize for being so obtuse, Mrs. Ramsay laughed, and said that all children regarded their mothers as servants. If Marion had stopped doing so, it was simply another sign that she had grown up.

So while they were waiting for Colin to come, Mrs. Ramsay fell to discussing *The Heart of Midlothian* with Marion, and went on to tell her about Walter Scott and his friend Johnny Lockhart, and the strange house he had built on the Tweed at Abbotsford. She said that later in the summer she would take Marion to see it, and Marion, emboldened by her two outings with Jake, did not say no, that she did not want to go, but thought that it was a nice idea, and something to look forward to. Then Colin arrived, and no one wanted to talk about Abbotsford any more. Mrs. Ramsay brought in the cocoa, and with feelings of relief they sat down to give their attention to the most important event of the day. The soiled old newspaper was passed around, and the few fatal words, shut in by the circle of red ink, memorized amid wondering remarks from Mrs. Ramsay and Colin about the marvel of coincidence. Marion, who did not believe that anything which had happened was coincidental, said nothing. And, having remarked what an incredible coincidence it was, the other two did not seem to have anything else to say either.

'I don't really see that it's a clue at all,' said Colin eventually, poking his finger into his cup to draw aside the wizened milk-skin on top of his cocoa. 'It seems to me it's just a piece of information — it helps to build up a picture of what happened, but there's no way it can lead on to anything else. I mean, the man's dead. Full stop.'

'Surely not,' objected Marion. 'What have all the other clues been but pieces of information that have helped us to build up a picture of what happened? I admit that each one seems to have led to another, and that there's not much chance that this one can do that, under the circumstances, but it's the picture that's important. If we can reconstruct the picture, we should be able to solve the mystery.'

As she spoke, there came into her mind a Roman mosaic she had once seen in the Museum. More than half of it had been rubbed out by the indifferent hand of time, yet it was still possible to understand it, because the colour and form of the patches that remained, uneven areas of blue and rose and turquoise tesserae clinging to the ruin, still managed to suggest the whole. Marion thought that the best they could hope for was that the same would be true of the very different kind of picture she and Colin were trying to make. It was unlikely that they would be able to construct a whole picture, but they might be able to construct enough to let them guess the rest. And then. . . .

'I see what you mean,' said Colin. 'Only — there are an awful lot of gaps in the picture,' he added helplessly.

Mrs. Ramsay decided that it was time to intervene, although she was reluctant; she much preferred listening to Marion and Colin talking to taking part in the conversation herself. But sometimes, if she felt that she knew something that might help them, she offered her opinion.

'Actually,' she said, 'I think this particular piece of information helps to cover a larger part of the picture than you perhaps imagine.'

Two pairs of eyes fixed themselves on her intently.

'Go on, then,' urged Colin.

'Well, now — it appears that Watt Davie was killed in the first Battle of the Marne, which was one of the earliest engagements of the War.'

'Sixth to tenth September,' said Colin. 'It says so here, in this paper.'

'Exactly. Now, when the War began, in August, and young men from all walks of life began to enlist, they obviously had no experience of warfare at all. Poor things, I suppose they hardly knew one end of a gun from the other. So before they went to France, they had to be sent for several weeks to training camps in this country to learn — well, just the basic skills of soldiering. Even then, they were disgracefully ill-prepared, but they did have this training, and it must have taken some little time. So think of that, and tell me — even if Watt Davie had enlisted right at the beginning of the War, does it seem likely that he would have been sent to the front line by September?'

Colin and Marion shook their heads.

'Nor to me, either. So — what does that suggest to you?'

'It suggests to me,' said Colin slowly, 'that he was already trained when the War began, and that means he was a regular soldier, not a volunteer.'

'Yes,' agreed Marion eagerly, pointing to the newspaper, 'and there's another thing. If he was a new recruit, he would have been a Private, not a Corporal. He had been in the army long enough to be promoted, hadn't he?'

'Twice,' said Mrs. Ramsay. 'He would have been a Lance-Corporal before he became a Corporal. However blighted his career as a manservant had been, he must have been quite a good soldier. Now use your brains, Colin, and tell us what you deduce from that.'

Colin looked at the same face watching him from either side; his mother's questioning, Marion's wearing an expression which told clearly that she was restraining herself with difficulty from beating him to the answer. But he knew the answer too.

He grinned at Marion and said what she was thinking.

'When the Ramsays kicked him out, he went and joined the army.'

'Well done,' said Mrs. Ramsay. 'You see, it would be a sensible thing to do. He had no reference, so he wouldn't have been able to get another job as a valet. In the army, no questions would be asked. I expect he would want to get away from Edinburgh too, and start a new life somewhere else.'

'I wonder if Charles Ramsay found out,' said Marion, remembering the vow Charles had made in his letter to Alan. If Charles Ramsay had got to Watt Davie before the War broke out, then the mystery they were trying to solve had been solved already, long ago, in 1914.

Mrs. Ramsay shook her head.

'It's impossible to say,' she said, 'but I don't think so. He said in your jig-saw letter that Watt Davie hadn't been seen or heard of since Colin showed him off the premises nearly three months before. The only person in Edinburgh, who would have known what had become of him was his mother. Now whatever he had done, and however much she felt she owed the Ramsays, I don't think she would have given him away.'

'If I were a thief,' said Colin teasingly, 'wouldn't you give me away?'

'No. I would smack your bottom,' said Mrs. Ramsay, more Scottishly than was her habit, 'but I wouldn't betray you. It wouldn't be natural. I'm sure poor Mrs. Davie felt the same.'

'I wonder what connection Mrs. Davie had with the Ramsays,' said Marion.

'She was probably their cook, or their children's nurse,' said Mrs. Ramsay, 'and after she had given them the best years of her life for a few shillings a week, they let her go and end her days in a slum tenement in the Cowgate. But they still went on thinking that the Davies were in their debt.'

Colin and Marion exchanged sidelong glances. They had heard her on this topic before.

'Mother,' said Colin, 'you don't like the Ramsays, do you?' Mrs. Ramsay tutted.

'I don't like them, and I don't dislike them,' she said, 'How could I — I never met them. I don't suppose they were any worse than all the other people who were rich at the same time. I've nothing personally against the Ramsays — what I think was wicked was a system which allowed a rich man to make a poor man work ninety hours a week for a pittance, and to behave as if he were actually doing him a favour.'

'The Ramsays didn't go to the police about Watt Davie,' Marion reminded her. She did not care a bit about the Ramsays in general, but she was anxious that Charles should not appear in a bad light.

'That's true. It's something in their favour,' said her mother, without enthusiasm. 'I admit that Watt Davie was a scoundrel — it's Mrs. Davie I feel sorry for. First her son was disgraced by stealing from the family she had probably worked for all her life, and then he was killed in the first weeks of the War. For all we know, she was dependent on him.'

'Perhaps the Ramsays helped her after her son was killed,' said Marion loyally.

Mrs. Ramsay smiled at her.

'Well, perhaps they did,' she said, relenting.

'This is all supposition,' said Colin grandly. It was a new word he had acquired recently, and he had been waiting for an opportunity to try it out. 'We should stick to facts, in my opinion.'

Mrs. Ramsay laughed inwardly. She thought that Colin was becoming more like his lawyer father every day.

But Marion said with dignity, 'We're not supposing, Colin, we're deducing. And it's all very well talking about sticking to facts, but that isn't going to do us much good when there are so few of them.'

This was all too true, but still, as Mrs. Ramsay hastened to

155

point out before Colin's face fell, their deducing had been very fruitful, and after a long, thoughtful pause, Marion went on again.

'It seems to me that we can say three things fairly definitely. First, that Watt Davie had an ulterior motive for wanting to get into the house again after he had been sent packing, and the most likely explanation is that he wanted to take away something he had stolen, but hadn't been able to sneak out because the Ramsays were watching him. Second, that there's little chance that Charles Ramsay caught up with him before the War began, because his mother wouldn't tell where he was. And third, that if he didn't get in to collect his loot before he left Edinburgh, he certainly didn't come back for it later, because for the rest of his life he was away in the army.'

Another lawyer, said Mrs. Ramsay to herself.

'And so,' continued Marion, 'I think we can at least say that the chances of there being something still hidden in the house are greatly increased. We know that Watt Davie didn't sell the contents of the trunk to J. J. Rickert, and although there is a chance that he sold them elsewhere, it seems to me a lot more likely that he didn't get round to selling them at all. All things considered, they could still be here.'

'Yes, but where?' demanded Colin despairingly. 'I've looked everywhere.'

This was the truth. He had looked everywhere, except in the basement, and he no longer thought it was worth the risk of breaking in among the wine bottles there. Watt Davie would have found it very difficult, he reasoned, to remove anything from the basement during the day, with all the other servants around, and anyway, if he had only wanted to take something out of the basement, why would he have made such a point of going all the way up to the attic to find his coat? Watt Davie had wanted to go upstairs. But Colin knew there was nothing upstairs.

'And another thing,' he said, continuing his gloomy thinking out loud, 'where is the next clue to come from? We can't learn any more from Watt Davie. His story is finished. I don't see where another clue can come from now.'

'That's what we always say,' said Marion comfortably.

It was indeed what they always said, and yet, Marion thought, later that night when she was in bed, Colin was right in thinking that this time it was different. It did seem that with the death of Watt Davie on the battlefield, so many years ago, the thread they had been following had broken, leaving them, for the time being at any rate, to start again from some other point. She had taken the old newspaper to bed with her, and while she was waiting for Mrs. Ramsay to come from her bath and switch off the light, she had spread out its dry pages on her flowered quilt, and in the warm security of a quiet room had read the first chilling, tragic accounts of the War that was to go on for four more years, cutting away thousands and thousands of young lives as it had cut away Watt Davie's at its outset. Perhaps, as Janet had suggested, he had been luckier than some, yet Marion knew that if she had been in his shoes, she would have prayed to live every morning, and felt thankful every night because she had survived one more day. It was too easy, at the safe distance of sixty years, to shrug your shoulders, and say that someone else was better off dead. She had understood, earlier in the evening, how her mother had identified herself with Mrs. Davie in her love for her son; Mrs. Ramsay knew, because she had Colin. And now Marion found herself experiencing the same strong pity for the son, who had died far away among the filth and barbed wire, denied every young man's right to come home and marry and have sons of his own, and live in peace in his own land. It no longer mattered that he had once been a thief, and she had hated him; he was a human being whose life had been wasted, and Marion would never think of him again in any other way. Knowing his fate, however, she felt more anxious than ever for others, and she thought uneasily of Charles Ramsay and Alan Farquhar. Had they survived, she wondered, the long years of misery in the trenches, or were they too lying under little grey stones in military cemeteries, somewhere in France? She had always worried about this; although it had all been decided so long ago, she cared about them as if they had been her contemporaries, friends whose future was still in the balance.

'Mother,' she said to Mrs. Ramsay, when she arrived in her dressing-gown from the bathroom, 'if Charles Ramsay was killed in the War, it would explain why we've never heard of him, wouldn't it?'

Mrs. Ramsay came over to her, took away the newspaper, and helped her to lie down.

'Yes,' she said, 'but it would only be one of a dozen possible explanations. We had never heard of Colin or Alice either, and we've still never heard of any others of their generation. Do you know, it's my belief that they're the ones who went to Australia, and for all we know, they're alive and well, and camped by a billabong. Now go to sleep, and stop thinking about it. It's all over, long ago.'

It was good advice, had Marion been able to take it. Sleepless nights for her were largely a thing of the past; nowadays she was always genuinely tired by bedtime, and as likely to sleep soundly as anyone else in the house. But the events of this day had been unusually exciting, and now, after Mrs. Ramsay had kissed her good-night, and switched off the lamp, for the first time in many weeks she found that she could not close her eyes, turn her cheek to the pillow, and drift unthinkingly into sleep. Instead, for a long time, she lay wide awake, watching the familiar patterns of lamplight and shadow on the floor, spinning out in her mind once more the thread of the mystery, from one clue to another until, with the finding of today's clue, the thread seemed to break. It was, she realized, the finality of death that made it seem so; it was difficult to see, now that Watt Davie was dead, how anything more could come of that particular line of investigation. Not long ago, such a difficulty would have plunged Marion into a dark pool of despondency, but now her attitude was much more sensible and balanced. She no longer felt that her whole future well-being depended on finding out what Alan Farquhar had left in his trunk; that former conviction seemed to her now to have been hysterical and absurd, but nevertheless, she had to admit, she had never shaken off the belief that the solving of this mystery was of great importance for her. And now, she also believed that sooner or later it was going to be solved. So she could not give up hope entirely that one day the ends of the thread might be tied again, and another clue in the line be forthcoming. But at the same time, she felt very strongly that meanwhile she should be looking elsewhere. But where? Marion lay in the still night room for a long time, watching the floor and unaware really that she was thinking at all, then, just as the clocks of Edinburgh began to strike midnight, like the glass fragments of a kaleidoscope forming their pattern, everything fell into place. And it all seemed too obvious, she could not imagine why she had not thought of it before.

For there were, she now saw, two kinds of clue. There were the ordinary, everyday ones, the shabby things, the jig-saw letter, the jacket, the little advertisement, the ones her mother and Jen and

Jake knew about, and shook their heads over in a wondering way. Then there was the clue of the music, which, until now, she had never considered a clue at all, although only a few days ago she had told Colin that because of it she thought she now knew what the trunk had contained. She had thought of it only as something beautiful and magical, in no way to be connected with the tawdry evidence of a small thief's guilt, a gift that had been for her and Colin alone. And of course it had been that, but now she saw that it had also been at the centre of the whole mystery, and that when the ordinary clues had failed, it was the clue of the music that must be followed. The clue of music, that had come from — and led to — the dirty, second-floor room where Jake had made the housebed, and now was making a canoe. All the clues led into that room, the everyday ones, as well as the charmed one. Marion knew that it was Charles Ramsay's and Alan Farquhar's room, because she had seen them in it. There, at different times, they had written their letters to each other. There, Charles Ramsay's photograph had fallen down a crack in the floor. To that room, Watt Davie had access — it must have been there that Charles had surprised him trying to put the watch into his pocket, perhaps the pocket of that very jacket which Colin had found in the attic. Yet, because the room belonged to Jake, Colin had never searched there. He must, Marion decided sleepily, get Jake's permission, and search it now.

As usual, however, there was delay. Colin, when Marion told him the fruits of her thinking on the following evening, was most impressed, and said so between sneezes. He had caught a dreadful cold in the wintry summer weather, and when Mrs. Ramsay saw his streaming eyes, and nose the colour of a ripe strawberry, she ordered him to bed, and made him stay there for the next two days. On Friday he was allowed to get up, but forbidden to go upstairs to the workroom, and the same happened on Saturday, by which time he was feeling well enough to make a fuss about it.

'Tomorrow, then,' said Mrs. Ramsay, rather wearily. The attraction of the workroom was lost upon her. Colin and Marion grinned at each other, and nodded triumphantly, but meanwhile something interesting occurred, something which even Marion considered an amusing coincidence.

Jen and Jake had just bought a new stereophonic record-player, so wonderful that listening to it in the red sitting-room had all the advantages of being at a splendid concert in the Usher

Hall, with none of the disadvantages, like a hard seat, other people's coughing, and a strong wind whistling round one's ankles. Jen said they had been saving up for it for twenty years, which meant twenty months; naturally she and Jake had been playing their records every minute when they were at home, and the Ramsays had also been enjoying the music of Beethoven and Mozart and Brahms, which came to them through their open sitting-room door. Mrs. Ramsay did not care so much for the occasional thunderclaps of pop music which interspersed the classics, but Colin, coached by Jen, told her that he and Marion had less prejudice than she had, and therefore better taste.

'Bad logic,' said Mrs. Ramsay.

On Saturday afternoon, they were all three sitting round the fire after lunch, reading, and half-listening to the music in the room above.

'Someone is playing a flute upstairs,' said Colin to Marion, in a significant tone that meant more than 'someone is playing a flute upstairs'.

Marion raised her head, and listened sharply for a moment.

'But with an orchestra,' she said, and they both laughed, while Mrs. Ramsay smiled privately behind the newspaper.

There was silence for a time, while they listened to the flute weaving its threads of melody into the heavier texture of the orchestra. It was not like anything they had ever heard before, and yet, Marion thought, the very fact that there was a flute playing upstairs at all made it seem almost familiar. At least, that was how she explained to herself the little echoes in her mind of something she had heard once, perhaps.

'Mother,' she said, 'do you know what that music is?'

Mrs. Ramsay lowered the paper.

'Yes, I do,' she replied. 'It's a flute concerto by a composer called Alasdair Balfour — it's called *Edinburgh*, actually. The movements are named after places in the city — *Calton Hill*, and *Swanston Village*. The one that's just finished is called *Ramsay Garden*.'

Colin and Marion looked meaningfully at each other, and giggled; Mrs. Ramsay watched them, then lifted the newspaper, smiling to herself again. Of course she knew that they had secrets from her, and that it was perfectly right and natural that they should. She was also very glad to observe they they were still sharing them with each other.

Upstairs, someone changed the record, and a wall-and-floor-shaking blast of pop shattered their peace. Mrs. Ramsay winced.

'Close the door, please, Colin,' she said. 'There's a terrible draught, don't you think?'

15

When the Flute Sounds

On Saturday evening, Colin went upstairs to ask Jake's permission to search the workroom on the following afternoon. He had at first intended to do so in the morning, but Marion had reminded him that Janet Baxter was coming to tea, and said that if there should be anything exciting in the workroom, it would be fun for her to share it with them. Jake, who had just switched off the record-player, and settled himself to another stint of advanced Mathematics, said that Colin was welcome to do all the searching he liked, but, 'You won't find anything,' he warned, 'for there's nothing there. I stripped the place myself, before I moved in, so I know. If it's Tutankhamun's treasure you're looking for, you'll have to think again, old son.'

He did not say it to deflate Colin, but only because the eager gleam in Colin's eyes made him afraid for his disappointment. Colin understood this, and was not in the least offended. He grinned back at Jake, and thought that if Jake had ever spent a night in his own housebed, he might not be so positive about the emptiness of the workroom. But there were some things that could never be told, so he only said that he was not looking for Tutankhamun's treasure, and would be up to start his prowling at three o'clock next day.

'Then pass the door quietly,' said Jake, groaning, as he turned back to his terrible calculations.

'I shall,' promised Colin, and seeing that he was not being encouraged to linger, went. But when he was at the door, he suddenly remembered something, and turned back. 'Oh, I nearly forgot. Jen, you're invited to tea tomorrow, to meet Janet Baxter.'

Jen, who was sitting by the window, looked up from her sewing with a savage expression on her face.

'That's nice,' she said, in a growly voice. 'Very nice. Say I shall be pleased to come. I'll look forward to some pleasant conversation. Up here, I've been warned not to open my mouth until Wednesday.'

'You'll never make it,' said Colin seriously.

'She had better,' said Jake.

Sunday afternoon brought Janet, still in her red waterproof, and with a dripping umbrella. She had not been in the sitting-room for ten minutes before Colin realized that it was going to be a women's party, at which his presence would not be required. So he left his mother, Jen, Janet and Marion sitting round the fire, admiring each other's clothes and beginning to get on splendidly, and mounted the dark stair to the workroom. All the fear he had once felt of walking alone through the upper rooms had left him, but he had not returned into his old careless, unfeeling self. Now he trod quietly, hearing the breathing of the old house, sensing its presences, but calmly, because it all belonged to him. He passed Jake's door on tiptoe, and climbed on to the second floor.

Colin had never been able to equate the dismal, bare work-room where he worked with Jake with the enchanted, flame-lit place where he had once spent a night with Marion. When he entered, he did not look round the faded walls, wondering at the contrast their everyday appearance presented, for to him there was no connection or comparison to be made. The wonders he had seen, on the night passed in the housebed, belonged in his memory to some other time and place. He no longer expected to hear music; that had reached its climax in the firelight, and now had died away. He opened the door, slid round it, and closed it quietly behind him.

The workroom, which had seemed small with the housebed in it, seemed enormous since it had been taken out. There was still a vast rectangle on the floor, defined by fuzzy lines of dust and sawdust, marking the place where it had stood; the uneven floor-boards were slightly cleaner within the rectangle than without. At one corner, Colin could see the ill-fitting boards around the crack which had concealed the photograph of Charles Ramsay. The ceiling seemed very high. And, as Jake had said, the room was empty. Apart from the work-bench, and the trestle table which supported the skeleton of the canoe which they were now building, there was nothing in it at all, and Colin, who had been accustomed in other rooms to having the pieces of furniture to investigate, felt rather at a loss. He stood for a minute in the middle of the floor, wondering what to do first, then, for want of a better idea, he got down on his hands and knees and began to crawl round the perimeter of the floor, tapping the skirting board and trying to poke his fingers into the cracks between it and the floor. He knew that this was futile, that wherever he should be looking, it was not here, but he thought that if he covered every

163

inch of the room, he was bound to come upon something sooner or later. Although he did not share Marion's passionate certainty that in this room the mystery must be solved, he thought that it was probable, and he had his own conviction that now the days of the mystery were drawing to a close. So, while the wind soughed through the deserted house, rattling the doors, and the rain threw itself in short, ill-tempered bursts against the window, Colin edged around the room, examining the cold grey fire-place in passing, and came in a corner to a cupboard door.

There was one cupboard in most of the bedrooms, of the kind that one can walk into, with shelves in rows facing the door, and coat-hooks screwed to the walls on either side. Colin had investigated such cupboards before, in other rooms; most had a stale, camphor smell, and were full of hat boxes and cardboard cartons, old suitcases and discarded clothes, kilts and fur coats, evening dresses and opera cloaks of long ago. Even after Mrs. Ramsay's great cleaning effort, they still seemed to be full to overflowing, and Colin had heard her say recently that she was trying to pluck up courage to start again — and do the job properly, this time. But the cupboard in the workroom was different; when Colin opened it, there seemed to be nothing in it at all. So, as he told Marion later, it was all the more strange that as he stepped into it, he felt a sudden tingling of expectancy, which could not at all be explained by the discouraging row of empty shelves, and tarnished brass coat-hooks along the white-washed walls. Above him, the cupboard reared like a shaft; it was as high as the bedroom outside, and the shelves continued high above the top of the door. Colin could see at a glance that there was nothing whatsoever in the lower part of the cupboard, so he tipped his head right back, and peered up into the grey-darkness above. It was hard to see properly above the level of the door, but he could tell that the shelves were empty, because each appeared simply as a black, thicker line against the wall. Colin lowered his chin, but he went on standing in the cupboard with his hands on his hips, and the taut, lively feeling did not leave him. He stared intensely at the shelf-wall in front of him, unaware of the wind, and the rain at the window. Yet it was a sound that roused him, one that he had never noticed in this room before. This, he realized, was because the heavy door of the cupboard had always been shut — and perhaps because of the noise of sawing and hammering in the workroom. It was the simple, everyday sound of water gurgling through a pipe, and it was happening very close to his right ear. He turned his head, and saw that in the right-hand corner of the cupboard, in the angle between the door and the side wall, a narrow water-pipe came through the floor, and ran up through the cupboard, about six inches from the wall, to which it was attached at intervals by metal clips. Colin put out his hand and touched it; it was cold, and quiet now. It was, of course, the cold-water pipe which ran through the house, connecting the kitchens and bathrooms downstairs to the tank in the attic. Its brief gurgle had been occasioned by Mrs. Ramsay's turning on the tap to fill the kettle in her kitchen far below. Colin looked at the pipe, then he peered up again into the roof of the cupboard, following its line, expecting to see it disappear straight through the roof as it had entered through the floor. But it did not. By now, his straining eyes had accustomed themselves to the darkness, and he could see that just below the small square of ceiling, the pipe was jointed. It made a right-angled turn outwards, then another one upwards, finally entering the ceiling about eighteen inches from the wall. And in the space thus created, between pipe and wall, an object was wedged, a long box-shaped object, whose details were obscured by the murk that surrounded it. But Colin knew what it was. It was Alan Farquhar's trunk.

Afterwards, he could not even remember going downstairs to Jen's kitchen to fetch her step-ladder, and the torch which Jake kept on top of the refrigerator. It never occurred to him to ask permission, so great were his excitement and his haste. His feet scarcely touched the steps of the stair going down, and coming back he did not even notice the weight of the ladder, which was considerable. Shaking with impatience, he dragged it into the cupboard, set its legs apart, switched on the torch and climbed up. By standing on the top step, he could just reach the box, which was wooden, and covered with cobwebs. It was not what Colin had thought of as a trunk, but then no description of it had been given, so it must be that he and Marion had formed a wrong impression. He needed both hands to dislodge it, and lift it down; it might, for all he knew, be very heavy. So he pushed the torch between the pipe and the wall, a little further down, and forgot about it; it was retrieved by Jake the next evening, with its batteries burnt out. Balancing carefully, Colin put up his hands, and taking hold of the box at either end, tipped it over the pipe so that it fell down narrow end first. He grabbed it in his arms as it came, swaying under the weight, but managed to keep on his feet; carefully he turned round, and descended the steps facing outwards, clutching the precious box to his chest.

When he got it out into the workroom, and had wiped it clean of grime and cobwebs with a duster, Colin's first thought was to open it, but just as he was about to undo the hook fastening which kept down its hinged lid, he thought better of the impulse. This was Marion's treasure, and it must be opened in her presence. He lifted the box, and carried it downstairs to the ground floor.

In the sitting-room, the tea party was evidently in full swing. As he came down the last flight of steps, Colin could hear the chiming of teaspoons against china and the light ripple of women's voices, broken at intervals by Marion's fluting laugh and Jen's wild giggle. They were all enjoying themselves thoroughly. But when he pushed open the door, and walked in with the box in his arms, the silence was as immediate as if a door had been closed, not opened. Colin knew that every eye in the room was turned on him, but he was only looking at Marion, hers was the only face he could see in focus. It was as if this moment was so personal and private to them that the other people gathered round the fire had temporarily ceased to exist; he seemed to withdraw with Marion behind an invisible screen. He put the box down on the rug in front of her.

'Colin, you've found it.'

'Yes.'

'I knew it was there, somewhere.'

'Yes.'

'Yet — it isn't how I imagined it.'

'Nor me. But it doesn't matter.'

'Of course not.'

'If I lift it up, you can open it.'

'No, don't worry about that. It isn't important who opens it. You do it — quickly.'

The fastening was a metal hook-and-eye, a little rusty. It took a long, breath-holding moment for Colin's shaking fingers to undo it, and prise up the lid. Inside, there was one thing only, a kind of parcel, long and narrow, wrapped in dirty sacking, and tied at each end with a length of hairy string. There seemed to be a great deal of empty space besides, and it was not at all what they had expected. Colin and Marion looked at each other questioningly, he with a frown between his eyebrows, she with hers raised.

Then, rather tensely, Marion said, 'Well — we've never really *known* what was in it. Untie the string, love, and we'll see.'

Colin lifted the rough bundle out on to the rug. He could feel sharp and knobbly shapes through the sacking. Sadness washed over him; he knew now what it was not. He untied the strings, and folded back the greasy cloth, revealing — a saw, a crowbar, a large hammer, and a torn paper bag wrapped around a handful of large nails.

'Hell's teeth,' exclaimed Colin in annoyance, and for once Mrs. Ramsay did not reprimand him. Her heart was sore for his disappointment, and for Marion's. Marion looked ill; she was leaning back in her chair, biting her lip, and Mrs. Ramsay knew perfectly well that only the presence of their guests was preventing her from putting her face in the cushion and starting to cry. Colin, who had been squatting on his heels, tipped over backwards, and sat down hard on the floor. The faces above him sharpened into focus, and he saw that Jen and Janet and his mother had gathered round, looking at him with sympathy in their eyes. It was the last thing he wanted, for at the moment he felt more angry than hurt. Jen knelt down beside him, and he watched her thin brown hands begin to turn the dirty tools over on the sacking.

'There are initials burnt into the handle of the hammer,' said Jen. 'Look, Colin — "J. W. D."'

'I'm sick of J. W. D.,' burst out Colin furiously, his face going scarlet.

But by this time, Marion had become aware that they were being very rude. This was Ramsay business, and not, she thought, of interest to anyone but themselves. She was afraid that they were making Janet and Jen uncomfortable. So she made an effort to pull herself together, touched Colin's head, and said, 'Well, never mind. It isn't Alan Farquhar's trunk, but it may be another clue. Put the tools back in the box, Colin, and come and have your tea.'

It was another proof that Marion had grown up that now she could speak with authority, and Colin would obey her. He smiled sheepishly at Jen, and began to wrap up the tools again, securing the bundle with the two pieces of string. He put it back in the box, closed down the lid, and pushed it away out of sight under the table. Then he went to the tea trolley, and helped himself to tea and the remains of the sandwiches. His hands were filthy, but he did not notice, and if his mother did, for once she did not send him to wash them.

What made a bad business worse, Colin thought, as he settled himself at Marion's feet with his cup and plate, was that the guests would not let the subject drop. He had lived with Marion long enough to know when she was exhausted, and he knew that at this moment she too would have preferred anything to a prolonged discussion of the events leading up to the finding of the tool-box. But Jen and Janet were both familiar with the outline of the mystery; Marion had told Jen, and he himself had told Janet all that it was possible to tell. And now, no doubt thinking that they were being helpful, they began to ask him questions, drawing out of him bit by bit the story of his afternoon search, and when they had extracted every detail, they began to speculate about the box of tools, wanting to know all the unanswerable things, such as where Watt Davie had got it, and why he had hidden it in the workroom cupboard, and what he had intended to do with it next. Presently they were the only two left talking in the room; Marion had fallen silent, and Mrs. Ramsay was watching her with an alert, anxious expression in her eyes. Colin ate his sandwiches, fetched himself a couple of cakes, and watched his mother watching Marion. He felt sore and flat inside, and guilty because he wanted it to be time for Jen and Janet to go away. The puzzle of the tools was something he wanted to talk over with Marion later on, when they were alone — for it was their mystery, after all, he thought, with a little twinge of resentment. They could work out the clues without help from outsiders. But no sooner had he allowed himself to think this than he felt ashamed, for Jen was like a sister to him and Marion, and Janet had taken great trouble to help them. Colin had noticed before, at the time when he was so upset over his lost place in the Orchestra, that people are not at their best when they are angry and disappointed. Then they have to blame someone, and tend to blame the wrong person. All the same, for his mother's and Marion's sakes, he wished the girls would stop talking, and go home. Later on, he would be very thankful that they had not guessed what he was thinking, and done as he wished.

Jen and Janet were both chatterboxes; they talked on, not even noticing that the Ramsays were not joining in. Colin soon got to the point where he could not be bothered to listen. The conversation seemed to be passing to and fro somewhere above his head; he was hearing its sound, but not its sense. So it was with a feeling of surprise that he suddenly heard words with meaning dropping down to him, and he strung them together in his mind, understanding them. It was as if some authority outside himself was prodding him, making him take notice.

'What I can't understand,' Jen was saying, 'is why Watt Davie would have a saw and a crowbar in his master's bedroom at all — not to speak of hiding them at the top of his cupboard. What would you use a crowbar for, anyway?'

Then Janet answered her, and as Colin heard her, he knew that now, at the last moment of mystery, J. J. Rickert's great-grand-daughter had taken the broken ends of the thread, and tied them together over the last, spoken clue.

'You would use a crowbar,' she said, 'if you wanted to lift the floor.'

The words acted like an explosive in Colin's memory. For a split second, his mind went completely blank, then in the empti-ness he heard another voice, Jake's voice, repeating words that he had spoken casually on another rainy afternoon months ago, as they crouched together over a crack in the workroom floor, with tweezers and a knife in their hands.

Whoever lifted this floor the last time made a pretty hopeless job of it, and that wasn't yesterday. See where these boards have been sawn across and lifted out? They've just been stuck back and hammered down any old how.

Colin dropped his cup into his saucer with a crash.

'That's it,' he whispered. 'That's it,' he shouted. 'Marion! Wait —'

And before anyone had time to do anything but look aston-ished, he was on his feet and out of the room, and they could hear his voice, high-pitched and childish with excitement, screaming upstairs, 'Jake! Jake, come quickly! You've got to lift the work-room floor. Mother says you may. . . .'

'Oh, dear,' said Mrs. Ramsay helplessly.

For those left in the sitting-room, the next ten minutes seemed interminable. No one spoke, but from the noises above, they tried to figure out what was going on. They heard Jake come out of the sitting-room, and his deep, slow voice in contrast with Colin's piercing tones. Two pairs of feet clattered away upstairs, the distant workroom door opened, and closed, and there was silence for a long time. Marion looked at her mother, while Jen and Janet shifted uneasily on the sofa. It seemed as if the waiting would never end, but at last they heard the door open, and the feet began to descend again, slowly, erratically this time, with stops impossible to explain.

169

'I can't stand it,' muttered Jen, between her teeth.

Marion put her hands over her face.

Jake's voice came within earshot, 'Steady, lad — it's heavy — mind the corner — watch out, Colin, you're going to break your neck.'

Next came several bumps, and Jake laughing, then Colin's voice, squeaking with triumph.

'Marion! The trunk — I've got it! It's coming. . . .'

The door flew open, and Colin and Jake appeared, each holding a handle of a small, brass-bound trunk. It was covered with mildew and cobwebs, and as it was placed on the floor at the side of her chair Marion thought it the most desirable object she had ever seen in her life. Jake took a blue handkerchief out of his pocket, and wiped away the cobwebby dirt from the lid. Brown leather surfaced, and four brass letters, tacked down with small, brass-headed pins, 'A.A.B.F.'

'Colin, open it,' whispered Marion.

Colin dropped on his knees in front of the trunk, found the metal catch, and tried to lever it upwards. Nothing happened.

'Locked,' he said. 'Jake, there's a crowbar —'

But Marion interrupted him, this time in a clear, joyous voice.

'No, Colin! There's no need, I have the key. It's in my lacquered box. Just think — I've been keeping it for Alan all these years, and I didn't know. Please fetch it, Colin — I know it will fit.'

It took Colin only seconds to rush across the hall to Marion's room. He grabbed the red box, and turned it upside down over the bed. The contents showered, he picked up the little gold key, and ran back to the sitting-room. They were all waiting for him. Jake had joined Jen and Janet on the sofa, Mrs. Ramsay had seated herself on the arm of Marion's chair, and everyone was very still. And this time, neither Colin nor Marion felt that they two were alone in a private place. Instead, they knew that gathered in this room with them were all the people who, in one way or another, had helped to make this moment come, and they were glad that they were there to share it. Colin slipped the little key into the lock, and turned it. The catch sprang back as easily as if it had been closed only yesterday. Then he raised the close-fitting lid, and opened Alan Farquhar's trunk.

Everything was as dry and clean as if Alan Farquhar had done his packing only a week ago. The trunk was a strong one, and its thick walls and lid had kept out the damp and dirt which had so defaced its outside during sixty years under the floor. Very slowly, Colin began to lift out the contents, and pass them to Marion. After she had looked at them, she passed them on to her mother and Janet and Jake and Jen. No one broke the spell with words as they took the treasures from another time in their hands, and examined them, turning them over with wonder. First came a set of ivory and ebony chessmen in a box of sandalwood; the sandalwood still smelt as piercingly as ever it had done when the set was placed there long ago. Then there were books, in Latin and Greek as well as English, and a silver paper-knife wrapped in a silk handkerchief. A small oil painting in an ornate, gilded frame appeared next; it was a seascape, with purple mountains away on the horizon. Under that was a pair of skates, rolled up in a striped woollen scarf, in Colin's school colours. There was an envelope, containing a few foreign stamps.

Marion thought that the trunk, which was small, must now be almost empty; she looked over the arm of her chair to see whether there was anything left. Colin had his hands right down in the bottom of the trunk; he had an expression on his face which was compounded of hope and joy, and fear that even at this last moment hope and joy were going to fail. He struggled with himself, then he screwed up his eyes, took a tight breath, and lifted out a long leather case and a large manuscript notebook with a gold treble clef on its shiny black cover. He gave the book to Marion, but kept the leather case for himself. He laid it across his knees, found the gilt fastening, and opened it.

The flute lay bedded in faded green satin, and just as once Marion had been afraid to touch Charles Ramsay's desk in case it vanished, now Colin feared that this wonderful discovery would shimmer away under his hands. He touched the flute first with his eyes, running loving fingers in his imagination over its smooth dark wood and slightly tarnished silver stops. Then his hand followed his eyes, and he knew it was no dream.

Marion, meanwhile, had opened the book. She was not a musician, and the pages patterned with inky notes meant nothing to her, except as proof that her last guess had been the right one. But only the title-page mattered; she understood that, and felt sure that she had been waiting for this moment all her life.

'Come and look at this,' she said to Colin.

Colin got up with the flute in his hands, and looked. Then because they were not alone, Marion read aloud what was written, in Alan Farquhar's familiar hand.

'Eight Themes and Variations for Flute and Piano
The Western Isles
This work is dedicated to Charles John Ramsay
by his friend, Alan Alasdair Balfour Farquhar
20th January, 1914'

'Alasdair Balfour,' said Mrs. Ramsay incredulously, but Colin and Marion did not hear her. They had turned over the first page of the music, and they were staring at the title of the first 'Theme and Variations' in far greater astonishment than they had at the composer's name.

'Colin,' whispered Marion. 'It's called *Jura*.'

Colin took the book from her lap, and laid it on the arm of the sofa. He stood in front of it with the flute, while everybody watched him. He was so excited that for an instant he wondered whether he could control the instrument, but as he curled his lips around the silver mouth-piece, and positioned his fingers over the stops, his agitation left him. He looked at the music, took a deep breath, and blew a pure ripple of music into the silent room. It flew out and filled every corner, as warm as summer, as bright as flowers.

Perhaps only Colin ever really knew that it was not Colin who was playing. The others were astounded that he could play so well, but they could never have understood that he could not play as well as he did, performing faultlessly a work which was far beyond the proficiency of a schoolboy who had taken weekly lessons for two years on a borrowed instrument. But Colin, till the end of his life, would remember that while the music of *Jura* lasted, the hands and brain that made it did not belong to him, but to the man who had last played the flute.

In joy too full for excitement, Marion listened to the beloved music she had thought she would never hear again. High and low, the flute sang on, picking up the old Scottish air and spinning it into new clear melodies, original, yet haunted always by the memory of the first tune. And presently, as on the night when she had slept with Colin in an enchanted room, Marion seemed to be drawn through the music to the deep silence on the other side of sound. The dancing firelight and the faces of her friends faded, and instead of being in her chair in the sitting-room, she was in some other place, which she did not at once recognize, except as a place where she had been longing to be. Her vision cleared, and she realized that she was sitting on a little white stone wall, which enclosed a tiny cornfield behind the cottage in Jura. Further along the wall, there was a green gate into the cottage garden, and briars that had straggled over the stones, so that small pink and white roses were blooming along the margin of the ripening wheat. Marion was facing inland, towards the mountains, which were stained crimson in the fire of the setting sun; sound began to penetrate the silence, and behind her she could hear the gossiping sea, murmuring over and over again the stories it had told thousands of times, and which only the islands could understand. Although she did not look round, she knew that the lamp was lit in the small window of the cottage kitchen, where her mother was busy preparing the last meal of the day, while the baby played on the floor.

Before her, the island gathered itself into the mountains, details of forest and river and habitation obscured as the daylight failed. Nearer and still distinguishable, were the spiky forms and sharp shadows of the pine trees, and the path between. From where she was sitting on the wall, Marion could see the place among the trees where the path forked; there was a little clearing with a pale sandy floor, surrounded by high, eroded banks, where trickling soil had exposed the roots like veins black on red. The path to the right led through the bracken to the beach, but still, Marion thought, she could not remember anything of the path to the left, although she could see the tunnel of its entrance, arched and black between briars and brambles, with thick branches tangling overhead. Further on, she knew, the path turned a corner among the pines. So it seemed that there was a choice before her. She could take the path to the right, and make her way through the bracken, following the track she knew to the sea. Or she could go by the other path, down the tunnel into the wood, and take whatever of the unknown lay beyond. She thought that that was what she would like to do, but it was so long since she had had to take any decision alone that her courage failed her. It would be better, perhaps, to keep to the path she knew. But she went on sitting on the wall.

The sun went down, and the stain on the mountains deepened to violet. The shadows were long, and soon it would be too late to go into the wood at all. Then in that last, hushed moment between day and night, Marion looked again at the path to the left, and all at once she knew, as clearly as if a voice had just spoken the news into her ear, that someone was walking down that path towards her. He was still far back among the trees, but soon he would reach the corner, and make his way through the brambles towards the light. He was coming, and he was the person whom in all the world she most wanted to see. She must go to meet him.

So Marion got up from the wall, and walked towards the pine trees.

16

Ramsays and Farquhars

The loss of the flute, only a week after its discovery, might have been a terrible blow to Colin, if he had not been so happy at the time, on account of Marion. Compared with the knowledge that she was going to recover completely, the news that the trunk and all its treasures were to be handed over to Mrs. Ramsay's lawyer, until the Farquhar family could be contacted, seemed of no importance at all. It was while Marion was away, spending a few days in hospital so that the doctors there could confirm that a miracle had indeed happened, that his mother told Colin what she intended to do with the flute, and the other contents of the trunk.

'We can't keep them, Colin,' she said. 'They don't belong to us, because they didn't belong to Charles Ramsay, but to Alan Farquhar — or Alasdair Balfour, if you like. Whether he is still alive I don't know, but even if he's dead, he must have descendants, and by right his property must pass to them. I'm sorry for your sake — I'd have loved you to have the flute. But the manuscript particularly is of great value and importance, and we must find out whose it is now. You do understand, don't you?'

Colin said that he understood, and that she wasn't to worry, because he didn't care nearly as much as he had thought he would.

'Charles Ramsay would have wanted the trunk to be returned to the Farquhars,' he said, 'and in any case — it doesn't seem to matter, compared with other things.'

So Mrs. Ramsay wrote to her lawyer, Mr. Stewart, and a few days later, a van came, and took the trunk away. No more was heard for a long time.

The doctors at the hospital were delighted with Marion, although disappointingly they would not admit that a miracle had occurred when the flute began to play. They said, rather smugly, that Marion's spine had healed itself in its own time, as they had said it would, and that provided she was sensible, and did not try to push herself too fast, she should make a complete recovery in six months. Marion told Colin all of this one rainy afternoon when he came to visit her in the hospital, adding that

175

to try to convince them that anything out of the ordinary had happened would be a waste of time.

'They're all so sure,' she said, 'that there's a scientific answer to everything, that there's no room in their minds for anything extraordinary. There's no point in trying to tell people what you know they aren't going to believe anyway — it embarrasses them and their disbelief hurts you. It doesn't matter what they think, really.'

'Jen and Jake don't believe it was a miracle,' said Colin. 'They say it was just a coincidence.'

'I'm sure they do,' replied Marion calmly. She looked thoughtfully at Colin, and went on, 'Actually, that's what Mother thinks too, although she hasn't exactly said so. I suppose only you and I will ever know what really happened.'

She said it with such confidence in him that Colin had not the heart to tell her that he was not at all sure that he knew what had really happened. He knew that for a few wild moments he had been possessed by the mind and virtue of another human being; that had been his own experience, his private miracle. But whether the music he had made could actually have had the power to make a lame girl walk, he did not know. He felt that while he believed as firmly as ever in his own miracle, already he was beginning to doubt hers, to drift over to the side of those who spoke so glibly of coincidence. But as he looked around the cold hospital room, with its polished floor and windows full of chimney's and wet black roofs, then back to Marion's positive, happy face, he knew that whatever limitations the passage of time might put upon his believing, he must never let her know.

'Nothing matters, he said, 'except that you're going to get well.'

After Colin had gone, Marion lay watching the raindrops racing one another down the sooty window-panes, and thought about Charles Ramsay and Alan Farquhar. Ever since she had found the first letter, she had known how important they were to her, and after all, she told herself happily, her faith in them had been justified. Whether or not the doctors were right in thinking that nature had cured her, she knew that it had needed the strength of Alan Farquhar's music to stir her feet, and carry her across the hearth rug into Jake's arms, when she thought she was walking up a sandy path on Jura. She still did not know who had been coming down the path towards her; long before she had got to the clearing where the way divided, she had found herself sitting on the sofa with her mother's arms round her, while Colin danced round like a goblin with the flute in his hands, and Jen wept into her handkerchief, saying how happy she was. Perhaps now, she would never meet the stranger of the wood, or know the answers to so many questions she still wanted to ask, but at a time when hope was the air she breathed, she could not stop believing that one day all the hidden things would be revealed.

Weeks passed, and on the day when Marion was first able to walk from the sitting-room to the kitchen without help, a letter came from Mrs. Ramsay's lawyer. It said, in a dry fashion, that contact had now been made with a lawyer in Oban, who represented Mr. Charles Balfour Farquhar, and that the trunk had been despatched forthwith. For a long time, Colin watched for the postman every morning, expecting a letter which would thank them for their trouble, congratulate them on their cleverness, and perhaps clear up some of the mysteries which were still outstanding, But none came, and eventually he wearied of expectancy. He turned down Dr. Fowler's third offer of a place in the School Orchestra, and joined a Swimming Club for the summer holidays. Even Marion stopped talking about Alan Farquhar.

Another October came. And when amber and scarlet leaves dappled the pale sky, and the wind blew from the sea, and Mr. Coombes was saying, 'Now, boys, it is high time that we began to practise for the Concert,' a young man came walking round the corner into Mayferry Street with a parcel under his arm. He paused outside number two to find his bearings, crossed to the side of the uneven numbers, and continued along the pavement, counting as he went. When he got to number seventeen, he went up the steps and rang the bell.

It was two o'clock on a Saturday afternoon, and the Ramsays were not expecting a visitor. They had just finished lunch; Colin was sitting at the table, with the dirty dishes spread out around him, already immersed in his new library book, while Mrs. Ramsay and Marion were having an argument. Mrs. Ramsay was saying that Marion, who had been out shopping with Jen all morning, must rest in the afternoon, and Marion was replying that since she was now as well as everyone else, she had no intention of doing any such thing. She was going to sew up the red jersey she had just finished knitting for Colin, and press it, and after that she was going down to Royal Circus to see Janet for an hour before tea. The conclusion of this disagreement would have depended on Mrs. Ramsay's degree of determination to have her own way; Marion had never yet got the better of her when her mind was really made up. It did not reach a conclusion, however, because the doorbell rang in the middle of it.

For a while, after she had learned to walk again, answering the doorbell had been one of Marion's small delights. The pleasure of being able to get up, go and open the door, and greet Dr. Woolf, or Mrs. MacPherson, or the postman, had lasted for weeks and weeks, until Mrs. Ramsay and Colin got lazy, and for Marion the novelty began to wear off. So now, when the bell rang, catching her with the scarlet pieces of Colin's jersey spread across her knees, and Mrs. Ramsay with her hands full of plates, Marion made a face and said, 'Colin, you go, please. It's probably Thomas or Vincent anyway.'

Since this was true, Colin did not argue, but laid down his book, and went out to the front door. Marion took some pins from a box on the arm of her chair, and began to pin a sleeve to the front of the jersey. Mrs. Ramsay put her plates on a tray, and gathered up the knives and forks.

Often when, in later years, she would live again the events of this day, Marion would wish that some inner voice had whispered to her that the doorbell would never ring more importantly for her in all her life; so warned, she would have gone out to the hall and opened the door, aware in the instant of turning the handle who was standing outside. But then, as soon as she had wished it, she would smile to herself, because she knew that if she had, she would have deprived Colin of the most dramatic opportunity of his life. Not that Colin really made the most of his opportunity, through no fault of his own; at the critical moment his sense of drama was swamped by his agitation, and the words he had intended to deliver in grand, deep tones came rattling out of his mouth in his usual squeak of excitement.

'Marion! *It's Alan Farquhar. . . .*'

Marion remembered afterwards that she felt no surprise, only a little tremor of gladness. She raised her head, and saw the door into the hall as the entrance to a tunnel, surrounded, for just a second, with brambles and branches of pine, and emerging from it a tall young man in a denim jacket, with a parcel under his arm. He had springy fair hair, and grey eyes in a sunburnt face, and he was the man who had been coming to her through the wood.

Marion stood up, letting the pieces of Colin's jersey fall from her knee to the floor. It was the first time for weeks that she had felt her legs unsteady; half-way across the floor she faltered, and was glad when he put out his strong hand to her, and did not let her go till she was back in her chair by the fire.

'I've been waiting for you for such a long time,' she said.

'I'm here now,' said Alan Farquhar.

Mrs. Ramsay, of course, behaved as if a visit from Alan Farquhar was a normal occurrence, which might have been expected any day. She laid down her forks and knives, invited him to sit down, and apologized for the untidiness of the room.

'We always have a late lunch on Saturday,' she said.

Alan said that it didn't matter in the least, and sat down on the sofa with his parcel across his knees. Colin looked long and speculatively at the parcel, then politely looked elsewhere. He and his mother sat down, and they all looked at the visitor, waiting for his story to begin.

'I hope you'll forgive us,' Alan said, 'for not contacting you sooner about the trunk. You must have thought we were terribly rude. The fact is that my father has been in Australia for three months, and the lawyer's letter lay in the house unopened till he came back. We only had the trunk delivered last week, just before I came back to Edinburgh to the University.' He smiled at them, and continued, 'I know you had the fun of unpacking the trunk too — don't you think it's the most exciting thing you've ever done in your life?'

The Ramsays agreed fervently.

'It seems almost unbelievable still,' Alan said, 'that it should have turned up again after all these years. It was one of my grand-father's favourite stories, you know — in fact, its disappearance is part of the folklore of our family. Our only regret is that he didn't live to know that you had found it.'

Marion felt sadness at this answer to an unasked question, even though the answer was not unexpected.

'Your grandfather,' she said. 'It was his trunk?'

'Yes, it was.'

'And now he's dead.'

'Yes,' replied Alan again, and looked at Marion anxiously. In the short time since he had come into the room, he had scarcely stopped looking at her, and not only because he thought she was the most beautiful girl he had ever seen. There was more to it than that, more than the fact that in this shabby room she seemed to him like a clear light in a dark place. When he had put his hand into hers, and she had said, 'I've been waiting for you for such a long time,' he had answered her without thinking, but now, without surprise, he realized that his reply had of course been the right one. She was as natural and inevitable for him as he was for her. Then, and for the rest of his life, he would share her mind, sensing her thinking without the flight of words between them. And so, when she said, 'And now he's dead', Alan knew at once that although she had never set eyes on him, she regarded his grandfather not as a stranger, but as a friend. He hurried on to reassure her. 'He died three years ago, quite suddenly, in his sleep. You mustn't mind too much, Marion — he was eighty-four, and he'd had a marvellous life. He was one of these people who seem to be born lucky — everything always went right for him. I never knew a happier man.'

He watched Marion relax, but not completely.

'He had a lot of troubles,' she said, 'when he was young. We read a letter he left in this house — that was how we first heard about the trunk. He said he was leaving it with Charles Ramsay because he didn't have a home of his own, and he didn't know if he'd ever come back, and that there was someone who was going to decide his future for him. It sounded very serious, didn't it, Colin?'

Colin nodded gravely.

'Oh, when he was young,' said Alan, with a sweep of his long brown hand which put all his grandfather's dramatic statements firmly in their place. 'Lots of people have troubles when they're young. That's the best time to have them, don't you think, when you're strong and optimistic and able to cope with things? Actually, he didn't get on very well with his uncle, who was his guardian, and had control of all the family money. He was a Colonel in the Scots Guards, and he wanted my grandfather to go into the army too. When my grandfather refused, and said he wanted to be a composer, the Colonel cut up very rough indeed. He wasn't used to being disobeyed. He kicked my grandfather out of the house — that was when he was taken in by the Ramsays — and told him that if he didn't do as he was told, he would be cut off with a shilling, or whatever it was they said in those heavy-handed times.' Alan chuckled reminiscently, and Marion knew he was enjoying a private memory of his grandfather. 'I don't know if Grandfather enjoyed it at the time,' he went on, 'but he certainly enjoyed telling the story for the rest of his days. It was second favourite to the story of the trunk.'

'And what happened then?' asked Colin, who was beginning to like this new Alan Farquhar, with his twinkling eyes and wide, laughing mouth.

'What happened then was that the War came along in 1914, and solved the problem, because Grandfather more or less had to join the army anyway. By the end of the War, his uncle was dead, so he was able to leave the army, collect his inheritance, and settle down to write music in comfort. He got married, and went to live in Paris, where his first Piano Concerto was performed in — let me see — 1923, it must have been. After that, he never looked back.'

'Why did he call himself Alasdair Balfour?' Marion wanted to know.

'He said,' Alan replied, 'that he wanted to keep his public life and his private life separate. He used to travel all over the world, you know, playing the piano and conducting his own works, and when he came home, I suppose he just wanted peace and quiet, and a name people wouldn't recognize. He bought a farm in Argyll, overlooking the Sound of Jura — my father farms it now — and he came there whenever he wanted to get away from the hurly-burly of his professional life. It's a part of the country he was very fond of — he and Charles Ramsay used to spend holidays on Jura when they were schoolboys.'

Always Jura, Marion thought, and as always, when the name of that loved island was spoken, she seemed for a moment to feel the salted air of the sea blowing through the room, and hear the desolate voices of the white birds scattered on the sky. Later on, she would tell Alan, but now, to keep the thread of the story for Colin's and her mother's sake, she said, 'Alan, how did your grandfather meet Charles Ramsay?'

'Their fathers were friends — I think they had probably done business with each other, because my great-grandfather was a wine merchant. When my grandfather came to Edinburgh to go to school, he stayed with the Ramsays. He and Charles Ramsay were the same age, and they went to school together — and of course they had music in common. Later on, they had an extra bond of sympathy in the fact that they could neither of them get their own way. Charles Ramsay's father wanted him to work in the shop.'

Marion thought that this was the most fascinating conversation she had ever had with anyone in her life.

'And what did Charles Ramsay want to do?' she asked eagerly.
Alan looked mildly surprised.

'Don't you know?' he asked.

Marion shook her head, and explained to him that until a year
ago, they had never even heard of Charles Ramsay's existence.
'We are the only Ramsays left in Edinburgh,' she explained, 'and
since our father died, there's really no one to tell us the family
history.' But even while she was saying it, she found it difficult to
believe that there had ever been a time when she did not know
about Charles Ramsay.

'I see,' said Alan, rubbing his cheek thoughtfully. 'In that case,
I must know more about your family than you do. Of course,
most of them went to Australia when the business failed in the
nineteen-thirties, didn't they?'

'Yes — Mother knew that,' said Marion, 'but of course that was
long before she was married, so she never met them.'

Mrs. Ramsay spoke for the first time.

'When I was first married,' she said, 'my husband's mother
lived in this house — his father had been dead for many years —
with a Miss Edith Ramsay, who was, I think, a cousin. I knew that
there were other Ramsays in Australia, but I don't think I ever
knew their names. I'm sure my mother-in-law never wrote to
them. I didn't ask about them — I wasn't much interested, to tell
you the truth.'

'Till now,' said Marion, smiling at her.

'Oh, yes, *now*,' agreed Mrs. Ramsay. 'Now is different.'

'So if you can tell us about Charles Ramsay,' went on Marion,
turning to Alan again, 'you'll be solving yet another mystery.
What did he want to do, instead of going into the shop?'

Whatever kind of answer they had expected to this question,
Marion and Colin agreed later that the one they received furnished the greatest surprise of a very surprising afternoon.

'He wanted to be a professional musician,' said Alan. 'He
played the flute — wonderfully, according to my grandfather,
who was able to judge. He always said that Charles Ramsay was
the finest flautist he had ever heard in his life. The first music he
ever wrote was for the flute and piano, so that he and Charles
Ramsay could play together. The manuscript in the trunk was for
him, as you know.'

'We didn't know he was to *play* it,' said Colin, looking at Marion in astonishment. 'We — I thought Alan Farquhar was the
flautist.'

'Yes, I did too,' agreed Marion. 'But it was Charles Ramsay. How strange — especially since Colin plays the flute too. But, Alan —' she looked at him uneasily, remembering all the past tenses in what he had just said, '— What became of Charles Ramsay? He never became a famous musician, did he?'

Alan shook his head.

'No, indeed, poor fellow,' he said soberly. 'It was a shame what happened to him. When the first War broke out, he and Grandfather enlisted in the Scots Guards, because they always did everything together. Grandfather came through the War without a scratch, but Charles Ramsay — well, I suppose he was luckier than some. But for him, what happened was a disaster. He had three fingers blown off his right hand.'

An unhappy silence followed this news, broken at length by Mrs. Ramsay saying, 'Poor man. What a dreadful thing to happen.'

'Yes, it was,' agreed Alan, 'an awful waste. All the same, you know, I don't think you have to worry about him. From all I've heard, I think he must have been the kind of person who always came bouncing back, whatever happened. After the War, he worked for a shipping company for a while, and that must have given him a taste for travel, because during the nineteen-twenties he voyaged all over the world, working in one country till he had saved up enough money to move on to the next. He was a cattle man in South America, and a waiter in Hong Kong, and a teacher in the outback in Australia, and goodness knows what else. He liked Australia so much that he decided to settle there, and when the shop closed, he persuaded his brothers Stephen and Philip, and his sister Alice to go out and join him. There was another brother, but he wouldn't go — I don't know what his name was.'

'Colin,' said Mrs. Ramsay. 'That must have been my father-in-law.'

'Yes. Well, they all lived in Adelaide to begin with, but then Stephen and Philip got married, and moved to Western Australia. Charles and Alice bought a little farm in New South Wales, and prospered greatly — they own a big sheep station now.'

'Own?' repeated Marion, this time startled by the present tense. 'Do you mean they're still alive?'

'Lord, yes,' said Alan easily, 'very much so. He's eighty-seven, and she is eighty-two, and my father says they're the cheeriest, sprightliest old pair you could meet in a month of Sundays.'

'Has your father met them? asked Marion, feeling weak with delight.

'Of course. Didn't I say so? They are the people he's just been visiting in Australia — swopping sheep stories, Mother says. Charles Ramsay is my father's godfather.' Alan laughed, and went on, 'Just wait till he hears that the trunk has been found at last, and who found it! If you've never heard of him, I don't suppose he has ever heard of you either. I shouldn't think he'll even know that there are still Ramsays living in Mayferry Street. I'd like to see his face when he gets Father's letter, telling him all about it. He and Grandfather perhaps lost some bits and pieces when the trunk was stolen, but they certainly got their money's worth of entertainment. It provided them with a lifetime of mystery and speculation.'

'Then it didn't spoil their friendship?' asked Marion, who had often worried about this. 'Your grandfather didn't blame Charles Ramsay, because the trunk was lost?'

'Heavens, no. It was just bad luck — not Charles Ramsay's fault at all. Besides, it was his loss just as much as Grandfather's. The chessmen were part of a present Grandfather was going to give him, to thank him for allowing him to stay at Mayferry Street, while he was under the cloud of his Uncle Colonel's displeasure. The other part —' Alan broke off, turning curiously to Colin, who was sitting on the rug at Mrs. Ramsay's feet. 'Colin,' he said, 'did Marion really say that you play the flute too?'

Colin nodded, scarcely daring to hope. The parcel was the right size and shape but. . . .

'Then you had better get inside this parcel straight away,' said Alan, lifting it and passing it down to him.

Colin knew by the heat in his face that it was going scarlet, and didn't care. He took the parcel and untied the string, carefully folding back the brown paper wrapping. This was not like a Christmas morning parcel, which you tore to pieces in excitement, laughing and shouting thanks at the donor as you pulled out rugby boots or a modelling kit or a tin of toffees. This was the most extravagant, extraordinary gift you would ever receive, coming to you out of the past to make your future wonderful. So you removed the paper quietly, and opened the familiar leather case, and there, lying in the green satin, you saw your heart's desire. Colin gazed at the flute, and the memory of the music of Jura swept over him, with its wind and rain and singing rivers, and a white unicorn swimming in the waves.

'May I really have it?' he said to Alan Farquhar.

'Yes, of course you may. It was my grandfather's, but Charles

Ramsay was the one who played on it most, and Grandfather intended to give it to him as the other part of his present. That's why it was in the bottom of the trunk, beside the manuscript. I don't think you noticed before, did you —' He bent down, and pointed with his finger '— here between the side of the case and the lining, there's a card.'

Colin looked, and for the first time saw the yellowed corner of a small card sticking up above the edge of the satin. He prised it out, and read aloud, '"To Charles, with my thanks for everything. Alan."' He looked at the flute again, then reluctantly, only because he must know for certain, he asked, 'But shouldn't it go to Charles Ramsay now? It was meant for him, after all.'

Alan shook his head.

'No, Colin — I don't think you need worry about that. You see, it wouldn't be of any use to him, and I don't think he'd want it now. We talked it over at home, and we decided that you and Marion must each have a present out of the trunk, to thank you for finding it and returning it to us. Marion is to have the little painting Grandfather did of Jura from the sea, after it has been restored — Father says the canvas is in poor condition, so he's having it put right first. We thought that you should have the flute, and that perhaps you might like to learn to play it, but if you play already — well, then you must have it. I'm sure Charles Ramsay would agree, but anyway, you can settle it with him yourself soon, because he and Alice are coming home for a holiday in the spring of next year. They say they would like to see Scotland again before they die.'

Marion thought she could not bear any more happiness in one afternoon. It was beginning to feel like pain.

'Are they coming to stay with you?' she asked.

'That was the idea,' said Alan. 'However, when they discover that there are still Ramsays in Mayferry Street, I think I know where their first port of call will be.'

Marion thought of her photograph of Charles Ramsay in his soldier's uniform, young and unmarked by time, and in her imagination she tried to add the change of sixty years to his face. But of course she could not, and of course it did not matter. It was not the outside of a person that mattered, but the merry heart within. Such stories he would be able to tell her, about his travels, and life in Edinburgh when he was young — but none more strange and marvellous than the story she would have to tell him. . . . She watched Colin with his flute for a moment, then

185

turned her attention back to Alan, who was having a conversation with Mrs. Ramsay over Colin's head.

'My father apologizes for not coming himself,' he said, 'but you see how it is — he's just back from Australia, and he really can't leave the farm again so soon. He thinks it has gone to rack and ruin as it is. He's going to write to you, though, as soon as he has a minute. He and Mother want you all to come and stay with us next summer — if you'd like to, that is. You will, won't you?'

He looked round them all, as if he were actually afraid they might say, 'No.'

Since she was the only one not completely speechless, Mrs. Ramsay said they would be delighted to come.

'That's settled, then,' said Alan, looking pleased.

'There's only one thing I feel sad about,' said Marion presently. 'It's only a little thing, yet somehow it matters to me. I feel that I know your grandfather so well, yet I've no idea what he looked like. I'd have liked to see him, just once.'

'I could say you have,' said Alan gently. 'If you want to know what he looked like when he was young, you look at me. If you want to know what he looked like when he was fifty, you look at my father. If you want to know what he looked like when he was old, you'll have to wait a while.'

He smiled at Marion, and she smiled back at him, knowing that this was exactly how it should be.

While Colin and his mother shared the flute, gloating over it and touching it with happy hands, Alan and Marion drew together on the other side of the fireplace.

'You know, it's a strange thing,' said Alan, leaning his elbows on the worn knees of his trousers, and looking at Marion quite seriously, 'that all this should have happened just as it has. My father says that all the time he was staying with him in Australia, old Ramsay — sorry, I mean your great-uncle — talked compulsively about that business of the trunk. He went on and on about it — how the servant Watt Davie had stolen it, and hidden it, and how they had searched high and low, and how he had scoured Edinburgh trying to find Davie, and couldn't, because his mother wouldn't tell where he was — and then the War came. I know the past is often clearer to old people than the present, for my grandparents were like that too, but — well, honestly, Marion, Father says he was re-living it all as if it had happened only yesterday.'

Marion thought of Charles Ramsay, who was her past, as she looked at Alan Farquhar, who was her past and her present and her future.

'I often felt,' she said slowly, 'that someone else was thinking about it too.' Then, in a rush, 'Oh Alan, I have so many things to tell you. . . .'

'There's plenty of time,' said Alan. 'There's all the time in the world.'

Hours later, when tea was over and many tales were told, and Alan was sitting in the lamplight with Marion, who was showing him the treasures of her red lacquered box, Colin shot out through the front door, clearing the steps in one exuberant leap. The street lamps were coming on, as he ran in the sharp, smoky twilight along the pavement in Mayferry Street, with the straying autumn leaves whisking at his feet. He was not going anywhere in particular, and he did not much care where he went; he wanted to run because he was happy, and he was happy because he had a flute of his own at last, and Charles Ramsay was coming in the spring, and when summer came he would be going to a farm, where he could run in the sunlight on the grass, with Marion running at his side.